PAST

LIVES

DENIED

A NOVEL

ELLENMORRIS TIEGERMAN, PHD

SCHOLAR DREAMS PUBLISHING

Their ways become part of our world, haunting our minds
with their intrigue.

> — Greg McHugh, author of *The New Regression
> Therapy: Healing the Wounds and Trauma of This Life
> and Past Lives with the Presence and Light of the Divine*

TABLE OF CONTENTS

PREFACE

Today Western culture is increasingly aware of the dynamic influence of prior lives upon current lives. Many have discovered how emotional issues and beliefs acquired in prior incarnations act out in this life. The relationships of earlier lives, with their associated baggage, beauty, trauma, and unfinished soul agenda often replicate in this life. As a Psychotherapist and Past Life Regression Therapist for the past twenty years, I've witnessed several thousand client past-life regressions filled with epiphanies and profound, life-healing realizations facilitated through tools of this modality.

Through the powerful drama of this mystery novel, Dr. Ellenmorris Tiegerman shows us it is time to learn and realize that things in current lives are not always as they appear. Our behavior often reflects unresolved trauma and relationships from prior lives. For example, the real motive in a crime, including murder, is often hidden within the psyche and prior incarnations of the perpetrator. The surmised purpose in a murder case often is insufficient to understand the crime or the evidence. But through the characters' past-life experiences, Dr. Tiegerman shows there is much more to know through hypnosis and past-life regression.

Here is where the author brings the mystery novel through a quantum leap in creativity. Whole worlds in other lifetimes can be investigated. Prior relationships with others in those lives can be revealed and queried. Insights into motive can arise from prior lifetimes. Clues not previously available to the conscious mind can come forward.

Moreover, in *Past Lives Denied*, the characters' self-perceptions and judgments are portrayed with intense intimacy. Their interactions and relationships are explored in graphic detail, bringing them exquisitely to life.

Greg McHugh, author of
*The New Regression Therapy: Healing the
Wounds and Trauma of This Life* and *Past
Lives with the Presence and Light of the Divine*

PROLOGUE

It might help readers to understand important things about *Past Lives Denied* if I provide some insights about myself and my history.

I was a professor at Adelphi University in Garden City, New York, for over twenty-two years in the departments of Communication Disorders and Psychology. The experiences of the main character, Caitlyn Morrys, are based on my own experiences of teaching and working with both undergraduate and graduate students and serving on the university's personnel committee. It was both an exciting and a tumultuous time in the university's history. There were, to say the least, academic and political challenges that could have undermined the core of academic principles cherished and guarded in universities across the country. It is not surprising, therefore, that Caitlyn Morrys faces similar challenges as she battles a growing awareness of her past lives and the realities of a present-day murder.

As I indicate in the Acknowledgments section, my husband, Joseph Farber, is the "brainchild" of the storyline for *Past Lives Denied*. The two of us developed a creative outline, but completion of a manuscript stalled for several years. It was not until I took a course with Dr. Brian Weiss at the Omni Center in Rhinebeck, New York, that the book became a reality and Caitlyn developed into not only a character but a real person. My personal experiences during the training seminar were pivotal in bringing the book and its storyline together. Although the backdrop for *Past Lives Denied* is my academic experience, the theme of the text is Caitlyn's personal discovery and process of investigation and resolution of the homicide.

Dr. Weiss has written extensively about his hypothesis that "souls travel in groups" from one life to the next. The process focuses on an eternal growth experience that contributes to self-enlightenment. The question this book poses is pragmatic: Can investigation of past-life experiences help resolve present-day problems—in this case, a murder? It would present both a tool to therapists and clinicians and an opportunity for law enforcement investigators. To readers who wish to explore or are exploring past-life regression, the question I pose is: How real is the real in past-life inquiry? How can it be used more pragmatically to enhance the lives of today's "travelers"? I would like to hear from readers about their thoughts and experiences on this issue, particularly if you have had relevant past-life experiences.

And finally, for readers who love a good mystery novel, don't think that universities are sleepy, quiet places. American universities are hotbeds of political intrigue, with student activism and out-of-control riots. In my twenty-two years at a university, the most insightful comment a colleague ever made to me was: "There's no sex or money here, only pure power." I would like to hear your thoughts about how in today's climate, universities present intriguing opportunities for murder mysteries. After all, with all those brainy types on campus, the murders can only become more creative.

We are not human beings having a spiritual experience.
We are spiritual beings having a human experience.

— Pierre Teilhard de Chardin

1

ALTERED VISIONS

Past-life regression reveals that your soul progresses through many lifetimes.

In these lifetimes, you could experience your life lesson as a man or a woman. — Ellenmorris Tiegerman

Midnight on the Golan is black as Hell under the shadow of Mount Hermon.

The cockpit of the Centurion tank is slick with blood. Working quickly in the blue glow of a map light, she applies her salve and bandages to stop his bleeding and close his gaping wounds.

Across the Valley of Tears, five hundred Syrian tanks wait for dawn to renew the attack on the Golan Heights that has nearly annihilated Israeli defenders and destroyed half their tanks. And everyone knows, when the sun gives light, the Syrian tanks will sweep the Israelis away.

When the bleeding stops, Captain Avigdor Kahalani is conscious—and in command again.

"It's still night, we can't move," she says. "Their night-vision gunsights control the valley."

"Light!" he says, pushing her hands away. He spits clots of blood through the open hatch, grabs the microphone, and orders all the Israeli tanks, "Turn on all headlights! Attack now! Cross the valley together now! Blind the bastards and fire every damned weapon we've got!"

*   *   *

The soldier in gray drops his rifle as a long Union bayonet penetrates his chest.

She watches silently, unarmed and unable to flee or even to look away.

There is a moment of recognition as their eyes meet. "I'll find you again," he says.

Desperation replaces shock as the Confederate soldier struggles to reach the end of the awful, bloody steel in his body. "I'll kill you," he gasps—and dies.

The field next to the log-built Maid of Orleans church in Shiloh, Tennessee, is covered in dying and dead men in blue or gray. Some moan their pain into the smoke and smoldering grass, while others call to God or their mothers as they bleed out their barely used lives.

The Union soldier in blue jerks his bayonet free of the dead, sucking flesh. Then he looks around the carnage as though searching for other victims, places—or other times.

She calls his name.

He turns slowly, in severe pain from a wound in the side of his neck. He fingers his wound, feels slick, fresh blood, and slowly collapses to the ground. "Help me."

She reaches into her small satchel for healing salve, pulls him closer to her, presses the wound closed, and holds it while she dribbles shiny liquid on both sides of the slash in his neck. Holding the wound together, she slowly, firmly smooths the raw opening closed to a red slit. Blood stops flowing. Color begins to return to his face.

"You will live," she orders.

"Thank you," the man whispers. He leans back and relaxes in her arms. His eyes close, and she holds him close to her warmth in the chaos of smoke and fire and fury.

These were the recurrent nightmares of Caitlyn Morrys.

She awoke in her bed at home. The clock glowed 11:05 p.m. Her Frette Dulcina cashmere nightgown, which kept her warm during the Midwestern winters, was fragrant with salt-sweet body scent and soaked with the perspiration from more of her nightly terror-dreams.

The recurring flashbacks always screamed across her mind: the witch pyres of papal Europe, the ovens of the Nazi Reich, chaos in Israel, and the death fields of brother-against-brother wars in America and Southeast Asia. Each agonizing scene showed her different places, different endings. But the people, although their clothing varied, were always recognizable—they were the faces of her past. What purpose did it all serve? Each phantasm highlighted her other lives and deaths—the Inquisitions in Seville and Rouen, wars and wounding in newer lands across the globe—old apparitions more like wraiths or chimeras, with incomplete messages. She often asked herself if these were messages about her lives and deaths. Maybe the message was one she could never quite understand: that she really did have past lives!

Caitlyn slid out of bed, stripped off her nightgown, and, checking reality in the pale night-light, searched her image in the full-length mirror. She slid reassuring hands down her face, neck, breasts, hips, and thighs. Full and still firm, with long, shapely legs. She smiled at herself, forgetting those awful, otherworldly, firelit visions for a moment.

"You are so beautiful," a voice behind her whispered in the half-light. "What woke you?"

She glanced at the man lying on his side in her bed. He'd been watching her and was aroused by her nudity and self-examination. "My dreams, Ash … You call them nightmares, but the scenes are flashbacks. They're becoming more vivid and persistent. I'm haunted."

Professor Ashford Connor nodded and spoke softly. "Your flashbacks are visions. Those visions are part of you, my dear." He sat up and swung his legs off the bed. "Your bottomless eyes pierce reality with uncanny perception," he droned pedantically. "Professor Caitlyn Morrys, you are sorcery personified. In fact, my dear, in fifteenth-century Europe you'd have been worshipped in castles by royalty or burned at the stake by papal inquisitors."

Smiling at the irony, she moved to him, pushed him back on her bed, kissed and caressed him before carefully straddling his hips. They moved slowly until he gasped and gripped her hips—*too soon*—but she forgave his lack of control and clenched her body on his pleasure. *Too soon, too often.* But she loved him, no matter.

"That was marvelous, my love," Ash said, pulling her down beside his body. "I should stay with you a while . . . do it all over again."

Caitlyn resisted, tried to push away. "Can't lose the sleep. It's almost midnight, you have to go home. I chair my personnel committee tomorrow morning."

"The personnel committee meets tomorrow?" he said. "What the hell for?"

"Peer review—more Blue Book, another tenure try," she said, kissing him.

"Damn, sweetie, that means I've got to be there too . . . damn waste of time."

"Between the Uzinski and Moisescu maneuvers, it's all a waste of time," she said.

Professor Caitlyn Morrys did not look like her *own* idea of a university professor. A "real New Yorker," she dressed office-conservative but was often reminded she didn't "look" like a professor. She was forty, attractive, shapely, with great legs, bright green eyes, and a pouty mouth. Her long, lush russet hair, often tossed back or aside, caught the most attention, but Caitlyn's eyes set her apart as cool, intelligent, and maybe dangerous. It annoyed her beyond all superfluous flattery when colleagues or students drew attention to her glamorous appearance. *Professor* Caitlyn Morrys was oversensitive about her contradictory features, because professors of psychology were supposed to look deep, not delicious.

Always meticulously manicured and usually dressed in figure-friendly, tailored business suits with medium-to-high heels, peekaboo blouses, and Coach accessories, Caitlyn differed from her colleagues, who arrived at meetings and classes dressed down in typical Midwestern style: jeans, sweaters, and loafers. She stood apart. Was she too dressed up? Probably, she told herself. She had once overheard one of her male students describe her as "a smart pain in a great ass." As the years went by, however, faculty and students accepted her appearance as the inbred eccentricity of a re-located New Yorker.

Caitlyn Morrys's real eccentricity, however, was that she recognized the possibility of parallel lives. Long interested in past-life theories, she had come to believe in the limitless options for exploration ... or for retracing the vaguely familiar.

Did she have a rebel mindset, or was it some sort of second sight?

Past Life Regression Therapy was interesting but on the outer fringe of mainstream psychology. "Past Life Regression" allowed the individual to enter into past lives and interpret lessons learned from them to heal present emotional problems. Caitlyn saw how "Future Life Progression Therapy" could, or should, be combined with Regression Therapy—since patients acknowledged they'd had limitless past lives, they should also have limitless future ones.

Caitlyn had her first thorough exposure to past-life regressions in training programs run by Dr. Brian L. Weiss at the Omega Institute in San Antonio, Texas. Since then, however, she had limited discussion of regressions and progressions with her close confidants, Ashford Connor and Carla Breyers. Caitlyn was sure that if she spoke about her flashbacks with colleagues at Coronado University, they would call her a neurotic, a wannabe clairvoyant, or a New Age witch. She would become a laughingstock.

Caitlyn knew she'd had past lives—or so she wanted to believe. But her clinical training as a Freudian psychologist kept her skeptical. Her recurrent flashbacks of other times and places—and the deaths of others—exhausted her, strained her sanity, and made her question her purpose here and now. She was haunted by old secrets, fears, and challenges: unfocused needs, dreams, and desires she could not fulfill or even identify.

Her personal and professional doubts were reopened and recaptured in a stream of questions in emails she received from Weiss's Omega Institute over the years:

> Have you wondered if reincarnation is real? Do you believe you've had past lives? Do you think we come back to Earth again and again to learn lessons? My guess is that you want to answer a confident "Yes" to these questions.... But maybe a part of you is still skeptical.

And there were other invitations:

> Well, you're not alone. So many people just want proof—solid, inarguable proof of their own psychic abilities. If you fall into this category—or if you're interested to know how discovering past lives can help you—I want to invite you to join me for a free four-part healing workshop called "Break Free from Fears, Grief, and Pain with Past-Life Regression."

And then there were the intriguing come-alongs with method magic included:

In this workshop, I've included not only information about past lives, but also techniques that I've used over decades to help people overcome their most debilitating phobias, grief, and pain.

So Caitlyn tried to retrieve her past-life memories through every method recommended in popular self-help books, from waking herself up at two a.m. to record her dreams in a journal to meditating for weeks and months on end with training tapes and CDs from Brian Weiss. This went on for years, but to no avail. Secretly fearing what she might discover about herself in a past life, Caitlyn made no progress in her attempt to "cross over" to the other side. In sheer frustration, she stopped pushing so hard in her waking life to pursue the ever-elusive past-life memory.

Her dreams, on the other hand, were another story. Those simmered every night below the surface until she jolted awake in a shaky sweat, exhausted. Nothing made sense. The images were totally disconnected, visions of burning and death from different periods of war and mayhem. She could not connect names to faces or places to piece together a cohesive story—all she had were fragmented, violent flashes of scenes. Sometimes there were words and phrases in languages she did not recognize. She tried transcribing them, but that led to nothing substantive.

Professor Caitlyn Morrys was not certain who she really was, but she knew down deep she was special, one-of-a-kind. She spent a lot of time thinking about what she *thought* she knew, and liked, about herself. She was, first and foremost, a ruminator's ruminator.

Otherwise, on the outside, Caitlyn was recognized as a talented professor on campus. Students described her classes as creative, challenging, and insightful. They sought her advice and counseling in the Psychology department and even at her home. Primarily based on respect for her intellect and fiery independence, faculty members selected her to chair the influential University Personnel Committee, commonly known on campus as the UPC. The school tasked the committee with judging faculty at important career junctures: firings, promotions, transfers, and other crucially important faculty measures like tenure.

Although fully committed to clinical psychology, Caitlyn was aware of sketchy campus rumors that she was romantically involved with an eccentric "history professor" in Anthropology who supposedly was trying to derail the measured, dated book-world of human anthropology off the main tracks and into the mind-world with his chaos theory of development.

Professor Ashford Connor's perspective on human progress derived primarily from historical disasters, rather than a structured ladder of protohuman enlightenment. He preached that geography had always ruled behavior, gleefully adding, "This repudiates the benevolence of God and the mathematics of genetics."

Caitlyn absorbed the oddity of Ashford Connor, her on-again, off-again love, and mused that his projection of world history reflected his emotional neediness. He had struggled with personal relationships over the years. She had to stop overanalyzing his attractive, very male, dominant personality. She considered Ash a good friend, recalling Byron's calling friendship "love without his wings." Oddly apt, she thought.

Brash, lean, runner-muscled, and darkly British with soulful blue eyes, Ash was a distracted genius with an odd sense of humor, consistently self-effacing while impatient with others, a likable mesh of contradictions stuffed inside a nice-looking man. A world-traveled scholar, Ash published and lectured on issues related to what he called his "Death Harvest Theory." His theory posited that a relatively few unusual instances of vast human calamity over eons had caused equally unusual human endeavors and discoveries, which in turn forced radical new directions, advances, and evolutions in human civilization. Ash knew his excruciatingly dire human-progress theory was shocking and counter to tradition, professionally speaking. But he would insist, with a wry, self-deprecating smile, that his theory was "cutting edge." He was most noted for his caustic Brit wit and a carefully cultivated "unnatural addiction" to chocolate chip cookies.

Caitlyn and Ash's personal relationship was a roller-coaster ride, soaring on tempestuous passion until gravity pulled them low. Sometimes, when on the high side of the ride, "Caitlyn" believed they were hot soulmates consuming each other, but when things slowed down, "Morrys" began her cold, methodical planning again. Ash liked to tell her that "psych professor Caitlyn Morrys was too damned intense for normal mankind."

Talk about self-absorbed . . . and prescient, she thought.

As he dressed, Ash reminded Caitlyn that she'd be "bossing him around" in a few hours in a conference room in the university's Administration building. There, "Professor Morrys" would chair the UPC, comprising a dozen other Coronado professors, which met regularly to change the lives of their colleagues by recommending for or against lifetime tenure. "The boss will change another life tomorrow," he said.

"Merely regulating the flow, Ash. Tenure is the life blood of the modern university," Caitlyn preached, as she often did on the subject. She gestured grandly at the bedroom. "Tenure grants scholars lifetime security, as it has for you and me, so we can concentrate on our academic pursuits and achievements. Then we don't have to play kiss-ass-or-kill office politics with authoritarians like Uzinski and Moisescu."

Ash peered at her over his sunglasses. "If you had an MRI, you'd find a brain ruptured from too many twists in psychic winds," he said. He shook his head, grinned, and squinted quizzically at her.

As she often did, she silently weighed his words, waiting for the punch line—he always craved the last word.

Then it came: "You ever notice you never get a headache *after* sex?"

Caitlyn's persistent headaches *were* getting progressively worse. The "migraines" began behind her right eye and traveled to the top of her head until she had to take Imitrex and lie down. Bad, as migraines go, the headaches habitually preceded her nightmare visions of the past. The death and carnage were so horrific and graphic, she'd often awake tasting and smelling blood. Night terrors and sweats left her tired and shaky the next morning, and the occasionally present Ash could do nothing to comfort her.

Caitlyn never let him know how bad it was. The dreams repeated over and over in different times and places. Ashford Connor appeared in those dreams, along with others she almost recognized.

Around five a.m. each day, Caitlyn visited the university gym behind the Admin building. The scene that greeted her rarely changed and was etched in her brain. Usually, she'd find the same sweaty, familiar men and women there: Ash, Maryann Mathews, Ted Carlisle, and Neil Braxton, as well as a cluster of other compulsive and motivated university professors who exercised zealously before showering and heading to work next door.

University President Richard Uzinski was punishing his rather soft, upper-middle-aged body by bench-pressing too much weight for his average-sized arms and shoulders. He'd sometimes glance at her as if wanting to chitchat, as if they had something in common, were part of the same world. She'd always avert her eyes, and he never dared speak casually to her.

The too-devoted, too-muscular Professor Neil Braxton of the Bioscience department stood next to him, urging, flattering, and serving as spotter. Braxton didn't work hard at concealing his obsequiousness.

In a far corner as usual, isolated, Theodore Carlisle huffed as he did endless sixty-pound barbell curls behind the row of multiple-exercise machines.

The slim, sinewy Maryann Mathews finished her pull-ups and dropped her body with a grunt to the mat for push-ups. Mathews's sweat-soaked shorts and sleeveless shirt covered but didn't conceal her runner's body, all muscle, long tendons, and but a few softer curves under lightly tan skin.

Ash Connor smiled at Caitlyn from the endless treadmill as though he wasn't doing anything difficult. He was out of breath.

As usual, all the academics were pushing themselves as though in reparation for the sloth of the academe. Caitlyn knew the group well; weight and physical fitness were critical to their self-esteem. Unable to ignore professional routine, she had categorized them from a copy of the *Diagnostic and Statistical Manual of Mental Disorders*, her DSM-5, which she kept on her office worktable. Her busy mind had concluded that the same passage applied to each one of them:

> Compulsions are repetitive behaviors or mental acts a person feels driven to perform in response to an obsession or according to rules that must be applied rigidly. The behaviors or mental acts are aimed at reducing stress or preventing some dreaded event or situation.

She greeted Maryann with a big smile and leaned down to hug her. They shared news and plans and promised to get together at lunch.

Caitlyn's daily routine included at least six mornings in the gym, more for loosening up and retaining her wind than gaining muscle—her physique was due more to genetics than sweat. She worked out for an hour, stretching, pushing, pulling, and exercising on the elliptical machine. She wore a Lululemon exercise outfit, sports bra, and shorts with a loose, sleeveless white shirt, which got in the way but made her feel comfortable under all the eyes. Caitlyn was proud of her body, but she was particular about who enjoyed her display. The give and take with the other professors was the price she paid for the health benefits.

Men watched her, trying not to be obvious and invariably failing badly—she could see them maneuvering for a better view. She pitied most of them, all except Braxton, who decided to exercise next to her and explain a barbell mistake he'd made. He enjoyed showing off and boasting about his weightlifting out of the tough-guy corner of his mouth. His persona repulsed her for reasons she could not explain, even to herself. She ignored him but felt uneasy doing so.

2

MALLEUS MALEFICARUM

If Christians are all going to experience being Jewish in a life,
what are we? How can any one of us be antisemitic?
— Ellenmorris Tiegerman

Professor Caitlyn Morrys lived alone, in a split-level ranch house in an older neighborhood blocks from campus, with her Jane Austen books and professional texts. The house had been empty for several months after prior owners defaulted on their loan, making it a classic fixer-upper with a good mortgage—an attractive deal for a single woman with imagination. Caitlyn put her heart and soul into renovating her "orphan" and giving her favorite authors, Weiss, Yeats, Freud, Huxley, Brontë, Dyer, Redfield, and Dickinson, a new place to live all over again. A devotee of Chip and Joanna Gaines on HGTV, she hired a local contractor to gut and redo everything from kitchen to bathrooms and study. She loved watching renovation shows in the morning while running on the treadmill. Time-consuming as it was, she enjoyed trips to Home Depot, *Architectural Digest* in hand, picking out tiles, appliances, fabrics, and furniture. She even made a special trip, while visiting friends in New York, to the Americana Manhasset shopping center on Long Island to visit Mitchell Gold + Bob Williams to pick out new furniture, room by room, for her latest "new" home.

Books and furniture tend to define people: Caitlyn disliked most contemporary poetry but loved most contemporary furniture and design. She planned certain rooms to "customize" sofas and chairs, a literal no-brain logic she enjoyed immensely. With plenty of creative choices in fabrics to satisfy her taste, she indulged all her dutifully hidden and carefully unconscious needs for individualization. Caitlyn, who mockingly called herself a typical Easterner or a haughty New Yorker, perpetrated her delusions with home design choices that infused her intimate surroundings with the taste and feel of a modern, monochromatic palette.

She had always secretly wanted to teach in a large East Coast metropolitan school, but she stayed at Coronado University due to her early receipt of tenure during a prior administration. And also, probably, because Ashford Connor was there. Besides, the intensity of what she called her "second world," and her morbidly mesmerizing nighttime oppressions, seemed less depressing when she was surrounded by fallow Midwestern plains with mild, soothing foothills. Caitlyn feared her dreams involved her in *one* past life, as well as possibly others. Would her past become her destiny—or her doom? Was this inevitable, or merely random chance?

Her restlessness was restrained, however, by the offered position of Associate Professor with early tenure when she'd first interviewed at Coronado University many years ago. Then tenure had emerged as an urgent talisman, a Holy Grail, as it had nowhere else. Now, Caitlyn didn't intend to leave her Coronado U life. Unless her "migraines" had other plans, she was set to stay until called away.

Caitlyn and Ash had seen each other off and on for five years. It was one of those intense periods when they occasionally dated "with no particular intentions." She enjoyed him. And, in spite of his sweeping cultural anthropologic theories of massive dislocations many years ago, Ash aspired to be a traditional, middle-class man-about-town. He said—no, he *confessed*—that he wanted to marry her and have a family together.

Caitlyn never thought about family and did not consider her lack of nesting instinct unusual. She favored independent ideas. She wanted to live, write, teach, and publish grand psychic milestones, with no permanent set-asides for a family. She loved her career and was extremely ambitious. She tried to set goals and benchmarks, spiritual and temporal, and brooked no compromise with anyone. And she had a deep, lonely-but-urgent need to prepare, to get ready for *something else*—just what, she wasn't exactly sure, but she knew it would be unlike anything else she'd experienced. A traditional relationship would tie her down, she knew—or so she thought.

That was the point of departure: Ash would pressure her, shake his head, and narrow his eyes. "So how much could you love me if I'm always competing with your career plans?"

"I'm beginning to change," she'd admit carefully ... very carefully, so as not to offend.

Both bore the scars of romantic massacres, but she had not learned her lesson, and he had, all too well.

"I've insulted you over the years with my own reluctance to make a commitment to our future life together," she told him.

Both usually aborted conversations about a traditional future. But when push came to shove, she'd glare an icy warning, grit her perfect teeth, hold her shoulders back, and then, with an alluring smile, say something like "Ash, you are strangely irresistible," instantly disarming him.

Caitlyn frightened Ash in a specific way. She'd become deadly serious, pursuing him with an intensity that chilled his bones and made the Midwestern air shiver with church bells . . . or perhaps they were funeral bells, tolling the death of his inquisitive soul.

Ash kept the rest from her. He feared she was too intense for him, too driven. She was a thought scientist, he a life scientist or maybe a death scientist. Whatever it was, he dreaded she'd consume him with her past-life theories and flashbacks and relentless drive into places unknown.

Ashford Connor was ex-everything: ex-writer, ex-lover, ex-paleoanthropologist, and ex-drunk. He was a dabbler, good at things until the novelty wore off or reality kicked him in the stomach. Facing reality was discouraging to a forty-five-year-old who still wondered what would be left of the world when he grew up. Ash was a tall, solid, lean-muscled 165 pounds with slightly graying black hair, boundless curiosity, chiseled features, and a short fuse. A longtime militant president of the university's Faculty Union, Ash's nearsighted blue eyes peered through life with an impossible mixture of irritation, dry cynicism, and undaunted optimism. He was wounded and wary, but invariably yearned for a rainbow despite his "advanced" knowledge.

To Ash, knowledge was answers and reasons. The theorem he'd posited for years traced the passage of earth-peoples through millions of years, through deaths and half-measured cataclysms, from ice to flood to eruption to plague to bloodbath—all brutally harvesting humans, civilizations, and cultures. They'd grown ever more complex civilizations and recovered again, always better than before. He called it his "Genetic Bottleneck Theory," his "Death Harvest."

Ash's research was less bookish than field-based, a point of contention between him and Caitlyn. She found his cynical views of history and religion a projection of his family history and negative childhood experiences. He did have a dark history, having endured physical abuse from an alcoholic father with a strap and a long reach. Ash grew up on a dairy farm in Devonshire, England, that produced cheese and butter products. His mother died when he was a teenager, leaving a father with five children ranging from three to twelve years old. Ash was the oldest and had clear memories of his mother. But he retained especially vivid memories of his father, who had raged at the children, life, and the unfair world.

Dairy farming is an intense, around-the-clock siege with an abiding commitment to the lives of animals. Ash's father milked cows each day from the crack of dawn until after sundown. For their part, the children silently witnessed a bipolar, unconsciously suicidal father working all day and drinking himself into a stupor at night. The oldest daughter, Victoria, functioned as a second parent and caretaker and defender of her younger siblings.

Ash's memories of his father were of dirty hands and a scowling face spattered in cow milk. The family cow herd numbered a few dozen, and the business required that milk be on supermarket shelves in seventy-two hours. The cows were kept in pasture during the warm season and indoors in cubicles during the winter—small, straw-filled cells full of demand, acceptance, constant expectation, piles of manure, and heavy movement. Trusting cows were born, kept clean, milked, fed, nurtured, gentled, and eventually parceled out to slaughter by their guardians. Everything was mundane and inevitably horrible—milk, manure, and blood, with no allowance for feelings. The dairy farm tolerated no vacations from its all-consuming life. But the siblings stayed, except Ash, who could not get away soon enough.

According to Caitlyn, Ash's grim theorem was inevitable given his perceived destiny traced to his awful past. Significant, she thought. And Ash's early childhood life, brimming with impossible dreams, was parched with the grind of climbing to an education that freed his body to wander away from the mundane world and find somewhere, anywhere, to explore his mind. Ash worked his way toward books through a circuitous route that took him from farm to village through London nightlife, straying into drugs, gangs, and petty crime. He found himself at last on an academic treasure hunt in a boarding school for homeless boys who "showed promise." Nothing curbed his abstract sensibilities. The grimiest of crime encounters barely shocked him, since he'd absorbed repeatedly the dire cycle of life and death on the farm.

As a smothering scholar, Ash faced a contemporary and festering crisis: stillborn hope in the face of each human relationship. He couldn't handle the tenuous fragility of loving and allowing himself to be loved. He shuttered his vulnerability and, even worse, he knew Caitlyn saw through him. She was an aphrodisiac, an addiction he could not get enough of. She laughed at him and his ponderous theories about the end of days and their beginnings. On a fundamental level, he retreated from her, from an overwhelming terror she would eventually consume him. The problem was, he couldn't escape her, not even in dreams. The mere possibility that they shared not just nightmares but past lives mesmerized him.

"I've repeatedly offered to work with you on your dreams and what appear to be your past-life memories," Caitlyn said quietly to Ash's rejection of guided hypnosis, which she had been trained to do.

Caitlyn had introduced Ash to Dr. Brian Weiss's seminal book *Many Lives, Many Masters.* Ash summarized the book in two words: hocus-pocus. He adamantly refused to have Caitlyn tinker with his thoughts and memories.

"Ash, you've absolutely rejected my attempts to help you understand the significance of your dreams. You keep telling me to go deal with my own flashbacks, but I'm not avoiding my issues. I've scheduled my own meditative sessions to get at the source of my nightmares. You need help dealing with yours, either from me or someone else. We're coming back to the belief I've shared with you. Your Death Harvest Theory reflects your unresolved childhood issues, which in turn are a rerun of our past lives together."

"Caitlyn, we've been over this ad nauseam. I don't believe in past lives, dream therapy, soulmates, or the eternal soul."

"You ask me all the time, 'How do I know if you're my soulmate?' And my answer is: It was a 'click' in my head when I first met you and looked into your eyes. I just *knew* that I knew you. Haven't you heard colleagues and friends share similar experiences, and wondered if it will ever happen to you?"

"Truthfully? No, I have not. I don't wonder about anything to do with your past-life mysteries, my buttercup!"

"There are relationships and then there are *relationships*. We've all experienced a huge range and intensity of feelings in our different relationships. But what you need to keep in mind is all the lessons you've learned from having them. Every relationship teaches us something about ourselves and another human being. Our partner mirrors our emotional concerns and issues so that we learn valuable lessons about love, kindness, and grace," she pressed.

"I hear you, Caitlyn, but I don't believe in what you're referring to as the power of love, or even the eternity of the soul," he stated firmly.

"Ash, you learn from other souls about your ability to give and receive love during moments of joy and anguish. You push your patience to the utmost extremes during challenging life events, crises, and disasters. You can only learn about yourself in relation to someone else. Don't run away and hide. Even when relationships end badly, when you're disappointed and hurt, you've learned something about your persistence, or your stamina, or your ability to commit. Look inside yourself and expand your emotional knowledge," she continued, leaning toward him.

"I'm not running away, I just don't believe in past lives as you do," he said, in a tone meant to end the exchange.

"Please, Ash! Think of our relationship as a classroom: It will teach you something important about love. Each of us is a teacher for the other. We should treasure what we've learned in our relationship. Think outside the box for once. Focus on how you've changed and grown since we've been together. What have you learned about yourself?"

"I've learned how much I love chocolate chip cookies, Caitlyn," he said grabbing her around the waist.

Caitlyn continued needling Ash, trying to convince him of her fundamental conclusions about creativity: that no matter what form it took—literature, art, research—it mirrored eternal souls and reflected past-life experiences, influencing how they saw the world. Each life added to a collective perspective, and by nature, each life seldom subtracted anything but time.

"You can't escape childhood experiences. Past lives shape you like sculpture. I'll work with you on a regression to see how your theorem is connected to a past life," she offered again, in their eternal dance of approach-avoidance.

But Ash's response never changed. "Stay out of my head, woman!" And off he'd stomp.

In an unguarded moment, after a loving encounter with Caitlyn, Ash confessed that he appreciated any divine explanation and unburdened himself of suspicions involving humanity's naivete and its various fraudulent, codependent, and copycat religions. "Will organized religion survive?" he said. "Wouldn't all human beings be better off worshiping divinities in their own personal, intellectual, and conceptual cathedrals?"

That didn't surprise Caitlyn. She had thoroughly explored such thoughts since her introduction to Past Life Regression Therapy. "Your question echoes my own apprehensions since my flashbacks began torturing me," she said. "Prepare yourself, Ash. When open-minded people dig up religion, they almost always excavate the same unwelcome, but very basic, conclusions. You *do* know some people will believe almost anything to avoid blaming themselves for evil."

As usual, Caitlyn's hidden depths fascinated Ash. "Do tell, sweetie. Just what conclusions have seeped into that amazing mind of yours?"

Caitlyn sat up in bed and ran both hands through her hair, combing it back over her shoulders, seemingly unconscious of the sensual sweep of careless copper hair on ivory skin.

He reached for her. "Or maybe we can talk later," he muttered.

She pushed his hand away and began to explain. "No, this is important to me, Ash. First, I've noticed people—students and professors too—who don't believe in God and are eager to believe in something else, anything else. The evidence is everywhere: It's delivered into all our living rooms by a careless, reckless media that celebrates woke differences, normalizes oddities, and pushes cancel culture with religious fervor. Both modern media and ancient religion encourage the unconscious toxicity of narcissism. That's where human insight and psychology have made all the difference in human development and historical evolution. We don't agree, Ash. History is not about war and disaster, it's about motivation and aspiration," she said patiently and emphatically.

"My God, you should lecture more often," Ash said, smoothing her disheveled hair. "Salvation, my pet, is a personal mission—the most personal—and depends on no one but you and your particular vision of God." He pointed at the ceiling. "The notion of a collective salvation is where *me* becomes *we,* and we designate a savior or an avatar to rescue *us* from *it.*" Ash had gradually forgotten about Caitlyn's smooth body and was concentrating on persuasion. "Religion is a means of controlling people by assigning guilt to a few," he said, turning to face her directly.

Caitlyn paused to study his intensely focused expression. She nodded at him and continued the disagreement. "Yes, my dear, we always assume the guilt of the past. In the human quest for meaning in our lives, gods have been an excuse. Religion, we're all into it in one form or another." Caitlyn spread her hands. "We're all doing it. We're all trying to prevent future despair with an organized force to control human events—unanticipated and unspeakable human events—like the Holocaust, Ash. Like the Holocaust."

"Go ahead, Caitlyn," Ash encouraged sarcastically. "There's a therapeutic point in there somewhere."

"That quest for meaning in humans isn't necessarily squeezed into our present lives," she said. Her green eyes flared in the semigloom. "But that same quest fits much better into our deep, sorrowful memories of a narrow past and our boundless visions of an eternal future."

Ash leaned back to again admire his half-naked paramour. "Curbing past despair and controlling the future? Caitlyn, my sweet, your dangerous mind threatens all those big, modern religious organizations and invites a deadly, defensive response—their modern version of the *Malleus Maleficarum*."

"The *Malleus Mal*—What do you mean?" Caitlyn said.

"*Malleus Maleficarum*, the 'Hammer of Witches,' was a book written in Latin in 1487 by Dominican monks Heinrich Kramer and Jacob Sprenger to foment the Inquisition for Pope Innocent VIII. It pointed the finger at supposedly evil people and tested their devotion to God." Ash pointed a finger at his hauntingly beautiful companion. "*You* would probably have been a target of Pope Innocent's 'hammer.'"

"Why me, and what does this hammer have to do with religion?" she said.

He focused again. "*Malleus Maleficarum* deformed organized religion for at least three hundred years and had tremendous influence on our so-called European culture. There were witch hunts and witch trials in England, the European continent, and the New World. Thousands of poor people, mostly female, were put to death for supposedly being witches."

Caitlyn pulled the sheet around her shoulders. "How could this happen? How could civilized people believe in witches . . . and why haven't I ever heard of this awful book?"

Professor Connor, Caitlyn's body completely forgotten, resumed his lecture. "You've been too sheltered for your own good, Caitlyn. The *Malleus* was used by the Roman Papacy as a judicial casebook for the detection and persecution of witches, specifying rules of evidence and the so-called canonical procedures by which suspected witches were tortured and put to death."

"Canonical procedures, you say? What kind of religion is that?"

"Yes, my dear, thousands of people, almost all of them women, judicially murdered as a result of the procedures described in this book. And for no other reason than because they had a strange birthmark, or lived alone, or had a purported mental illness, or cultivated and administered medicinal herbs. Or these poor, unfortunate women were accused simply for financial gain. Although largely ignored in modern literature and history, *Malleus Maleficarum* serves as a horrible warning about what happens when intolerance takes over a society. The 'Hammer' is manifestly a document that provoked and displayed the cruelty, barbarism, and ignorance of the medieval Inquisition."

Caitlyn felt the haze melt away. She could nearly recall the burning. "Horrible things done to women in the name of medieval men. You should be ashamed, Ash." She scowled at him with a gut-deep, primeval distaste.

"You're the one who needs regression, not me," Ash said, feeling the need to defend himself and quickly changing the subject. "You need to figure out what your Inquisition nightmares mean and why you're having them more often and with such painful force."

3

TENUOUS TENURE

In clear contrast with the requirements of participation in the major religions, Past Life Theory is universal and all-inclusive: one life and one religion.   — Ellenmorris Tiegerman

Caitlyn Morrys's life changed focus radically when Uzinski, the newly appointed Coronado President, joined longtime Coronado Provost "Doctor Death" Moisescu in a union-breaking, tenure-testing academic repression at Coronado University. She wondered if university presidents could be dually possessed.

Coronado University was a contentious throwback to the post–World War II 1950s and 1960s, when student bodies were "democratized" through the revolutionary GI Bill, which made college possible for millions of working-class Americans. The pre-war CU had been a stuffy, almost private, Midwest university, inhabited by traditional hierarchies of upper-middle-class students. Gradually the GI student body and ascendant draftees and veterans became more senior, more radical, and things changed. After the 1950s passed, anyone who cared remembered how the CU Faculty Union had voted to strike in nearly every contract negotiation. Needless to say, the university's power structure was chronically upset, and in those same years Coronado's nouveau-riche notoriety had been serially resisted by a persistent turnover of hard-charging university administrators. They, in turn, were aided and eventually crippled by provosts who tried to limit and harness all those brash new ideas, like tenure and teacher unions.

Caitlyn realized she could never—*would* never—surrender to tyrannical demagoguery. But she was learning how the postwar, quasimodern drones of academe were fighting a grimy, secret war. Were professors *supposed* to join teachers unions? And who was really the enemy?

The enemy was apparently a multifaceted, two-headed monster called the Administration. The ivory tower was an organized religion of the socialized academic faithful, led by an Administration as ruthless as the Inquisition. This was the beginning of Caitlyn's descent into woke reality. A crisis of faith, initiated by flashbacks of past lives.

The Coronado President administered all university planning and performance from a third-floor suite in the Administration building. The Provost, from a more obscure office in the back of the Administration's ground floor, filled in when the President was absent and dealt with the more specific performance of individuals and programs. Presidents therefore were largely above it all, while provosts were on the ground on the front lines. Coronado presidents tried for many years to control teachers and unions by advocating for funding limitations or economic class restrictions. This led eventually to Coronado provosts resorting to ritually misapplying and manipulating the process of hiring, firing, and awarding or denying teacher tenure. The dirty work was dished out by a committee of professors who investigated and interrogated faculty and students on a candidate's publishing history and record.

Caitlyn rewound what she knew generally about tenure, a status granted teachers after a specifically designated and regulated academic trial. She was relatively ignorant about tenure before the 1950s and what she considered effective "academic democratization" as student numbers rose due to the GI Bill. Most institutions of learning allowed a limited time for a teacher, professor, preceptor, or mentor to establish a good record. At Coronado University, an employee could remain a nontenured instructor or professor for no more than seven years. This choose-or-lose regimen compelled institutions to eventually grant tenure, or possibly terminate an employee at the end of a clearly specified period.

The question then became, who chooses the time or acceptable record? Some institutions even required a promotion to Associate Professor as a condition of tenure. Over the years, some schools and universities offered non-time-limited academic positions, with titles such as Lecturer, Adjunct Professor, or Research Professor, that were not tenure track. Typically, these positions carried higher teaching loads and offered less compensation, little influence, few benefits, and no job protection.

Caitlyn had learned that the original purpose of academic tenure was to guarantee the right of a teacher to dissent from prevailing opinions. Supposedly, academic tenure was like federal judicial tenure, which protects judges from political pressure. Without job security, teachers could, in theory, be pressured to favor the most proper or currently observed academic interpretations. Tenure aimed to allow original ideas to flourish by giving scholars the freedom to investigate and report their honest questions and conclusions. It protected teachers from summary dismissal.

Caitlyn had also discovered, after many years at Coronado University, that tenure could be a tool of lethal force. A professor's career could live or die based on whether they received tenure.

The heart of the Coronado University campus—aside from the athletic fields, a gym, and the dorms clustered around the Student Union behind the Admin building—was a rectangle as long as two football fields, surrounded by eight imposing, turn-of-the-nineteenth-century, colonial brick buildings. The buildings dedicated to Arts, Computer Science, Ecology, Engineering, Architecture, Agriculture, and Social Sciences were situated along either side, with Administration at one end and Humanities with its Psychology offices at the other end. The classical-looking pillars and heavy concrete casement windows were built to last, but they always needed sandblasting, cleaning, or repair, despite a multimillion-dollar endowment from the famous Midwestern Stutts Foundation for campus renovations. Money flowed for furniture, computers, lab equipment, dormitories, and slightly plush offices for professors. Through all the years, however, with the darkened brick, moss-edged concrete, and overly mature trees, Coronado University had always managed to look outdated and slightly worn, like an elderly madam.

The buildings were connected by walkways across grassy fields dotted with oak and evergreen trees and strategically placed concrete benches. At the west end of campus, the Administration building, housing the President, Provost, campus police, and all meeting rooms, was about a ten-minute walk from Caitlyn's Humanities building at the east end.

Several years ago, faculty and students from Environmental Sciences had developed innovative landscaping designs in front of each academic building lining the main walkway between Admin and Humanities. Coronado was beautiful but not special, with second-tier scholastics and only average football and basketball teams.

But Coronado had a secret few other colleges shared, and even fewer talked about.

Caitlyn's office was on the second floor of the Cartwright Humanities Building, mildly embarrassing due to its namesake. To her occasional irritation, few mentioned the building, except as an amusing aside familiar only to older faculty.

Former President Harry Cartwright *had* been an embarrassment. While President of Coronado University, he'd divorced his wife of thirty years to marry a young master's student in the Psychology program who was proudly carrying his child. Because of his fundraising prowess—he'd raised millions for the school—the powers that be swept the messy, mortifying scandal away as long as Cartwright managed to remain on an extended honeymoon somewhere near Palma de Mallorca in the Balearic Islands. In his stead, a brand-new, hired-for-purpose Provost from back east named Timur Moisescu ably performed Cartwright's duties.

The President administered departments and programs; the Provost levied authority on people. Provost Moisescu, a bent-over, cadaverous-looking man with poor eyesight, sparse hair, and scaly, lesioned skin, controlled both jobs for many months. Working long, solitary hours, he instilled strict fiscal control while keeping his death's head out of sight.

Moisescu was not a people person. Discipline tightened, and tenure became tenuous. Certain professors left hastily, under dubious circumstances. Unruly employees and erratic students got removed with minimum paperwork. And Moisescu became the "Doctor Death" of a grim regime bearing a gruesome visage.

Eventually his rule at Coronado became too absolute. Those with the money on the Board of Trustees decided Coronado needed a President with a charismatic personality and vision for the academic future that could build a university endowment. Following years of interminable meetings, muted publicity, and many whispered arrangements, and with hardly any fuss, the school appointed Richard Uzinski, who hailed from the East Coast, thus mysteriously but efficiently recreating the full administration of the university.

Every morning at nine a.m., Caitlyn climbed the stairs to the second floor of the Humanities building, entered the Psychology offices, and nodded to Carla Breyers, who'd been her Psych department assistant and friend for many years. Carla was of middle height and matronly, a graying widow who supported herself, had no close family, and was tight-lipped about her past. The Psych faculty had become her family, and she ran the office competently and with an iron fist. Exacting of the office, faculty, and students, she often bragged about working for the US Internal Revenue Service before "finding real purpose at the university." She was an integral part of an openly secret, underground network of campus secretaries who had spies everywhere and always seemed to know all the gossip and everything worth knowing on campus. She lived across the street from the campus gymnasium and walked to and from work at the same times each day.

Carla's major idiosyncrasy was a silver monocle either placed on her right eye or strung from around her neck on a black cord that bounced off her ample chest. When she was particularly interested in something or generally wished to appear authoritative, she'd carefully fit the curved glass circle between cheekbone and eyebrow. She also enjoyed shocking newcomers by using her "burning glass" to casually reheat her morning coffee in the bright sunbeams that shone through her west-facing office window, high above the long campus quadrangle, while watching students loll on the lawn between classes.

Carla Breyers reserved a soft spot for Professor Caitlyn Morrys, treating her like a daughter or a younger cousin, periodically warning her that Professor Ashford Connor was not the right guy in her life. She did not approve of Ashford Connor, who was seen by many older women on campus as an unfit magnet for younger women. Carla felt he couldn't or wouldn't commit to Caitlyn. But Caitlyn knew Carla could not even guess the truth—that Ash was hesitant, and he was definitely *not* the problem.

Carla met Caitlyn in the hall outside her office. "Professor Morrys, the paperwork for your tenure review meeting on Professors Brown, Mathews, and Tierney is on your desk." She smiled tightly and added, "They seem well qualified, don't they ... for all the good that'll do them."

"Thank you, Carla," Caitlyn said, ignoring the unsolicited opinion. Despite her earlier conversation with Ash, Caitlyn had temporarily forgotten she was chairing her University Personnel Committee that day. "We will make do, as we always do."

Carla smiled, aware that Caitlyn had forgotten. "Yes, Professor Morrys, we always do," she said, then turned back toward her small hallway office.

The exchange reminded Caitlyn for the hundredth time how much she depended on Carla in performing her multitiered, many-faceted duties as Psych director, Psych professor, and chair of the all-important Personnel Committee, not to mention in her tangled life journey. Carla knew as much or more about Caitlyn's duties than Caitlyn did, a fact they both acknowledged.

The storyline on campus about Carla Breyers was a clear warning concerning her "good side." Word was, if Carla didn't like you, your classes could well end up at the extreme ends of the day or the far ends of campus. Rushing across campus during the busiest times of the day was a challenge. She was also greatly skilled at retrieving—or not retrieving—important and needed department files and documents. Most Psych department denizens knew it was unwise to annoy Carla Breyers. Very few did . . . twice.

Caitlyn's double-beveled corner office windows gave her a panoramic view of distant Midwest mountains and countless prairie sunsets. Anne Geddes pictures graced her walls, but most notable was a Swiss cuckoo clock, a gift from her mother, that hung askew over the door. Ash had learned about the clock from scornful students. On visits he often turned, scoffed, and saluted what he called the "bird machine," announcing, "A cuckoo clock along with all your psychobabble in the air is all too perfect, just perfect."

The eighteen-square-foot office was organized around Caitlyn's larger-than-life, antique carved-wood desk with plenty of cubbyholes, which faced two brass-buttoned, red-leather armchairs, all situated on a Persian rug. A long, rectangular mahogany worktable stood against the hallway wall next to the door, piled high with papers and psychology journals. Her swivel chair centered on the window and, when turned slightly, provided a breathtaking view to the northeast. On top of a three-drawer cabinet in a corner sat a redheaded, pigtailed Cabbage Patch doll, a gift from a fellow professor with a unique sense of humor. Caitlyn often took the doll to her undergraduate Developmental Psych classes as a mascot.

Each time she looked at her redheaded doll, she recalled a true love in her *current* life.

Caitlyn loved her child development courses with undergraduate students from a diverse range of disciplines: psychology, nursing, social work, education, speech language pathology, and even undecided majors. Over the years, she had developed a syllabus that involved a baby-doll project.

Caitlyn's teaching ideas were different and initially seemed quirky for college students, but she was appealing to the child in all of them—the lost, frustrated, and dissatisfied child. That persona was always there, although it took some soul-searching to find that angry inner child. Caitlyn made them look inside themselves, and that introspection launched a search for the eternal soul, leading to past-life awareness. Caitlyn's thinking was, it begins with and in the child—and in this case, the doll.

Students had to bring a baby doll to class twice a week. There were specific weekly writing assignments that required an analysis of child-related issues that mirrored the material discussed in each chapter of the textbook. Caitlyn regularly provided students with provocative assignments, urging them to write about some problem related to the baby's health and development. The students named and carried their babies all over campus. They received a demerit if they failed to bring their babies to class, and after fifteen weeks of writing assignments about "little Michael" or "little Alice," most students became significantly attached to them. It was amazing to see the growth in their ideas and attitudes as they engaged in what they at first thought was silly but became highly personal by the end of the semester. After she reviewed and graded their journals, Caitlyn told the students they had been talking about themselves: their own feelings, their own problems, and their own unresolved childhood issues.

That fulfilled one leg of the tenure process: student engagement. Using comprehensive templates prepared by the computer processing center, students evaluated junior and nontenured faculty at the end of every semester. The classroom became a fishbowl, increasingly pressurized as students became more actively involved in judging faculty teaching, grading, and performance. The classroom became the "nursery" for student rioting and work activism. Professors with unpopular political and social ideas were aggressively challenged by organizations on campus, sometimes even getting screamed at until they apologized or left the classroom. Because they were members of the University Personnel Committee, Caitlyn and Ash were acutely aware of the role students played, particularly as they aggressed against conservative faculty and Jewish students. They both tried to intervene on several occasions and barely managed to control the ensuing altercations, in classrooms, lecture halls, lunchrooms, and dormitories. Banners, posters, and political signs sprouted all over campus: FREE OCCUPIED PALESTINE and GET THE JEWS OUT NOW. Caitlyn wondered what it would be like to be Jewish in such a hateful environment, with people threatening you all the time. She would soon find out for herself.

Relationships in every lifetime provided the vehicle to learn the lessons of love and tenderness. Learn those lessons or repeat those experiences until you learn to cope, Caitlyn warned Ash. Simple, right?

Considering all this, Caitlyn concluded that from a religious perspective, it was much easier as a Christian to wade through the pain and grief of *one* lifetime and then directly head to heaven, as in Monopoly, where you pass GO and collect $200. Dr. Brian Weiss's model and Jewish beliefs about reincarnation presented exactly that double-edged sword. She was comforted by the thought of future lives—and love affairs—with Ash, but the thought of Ash as her father or son set her back on her heels.

Additionally, there was the unfinished business of Caitlyn's toxic relationship with her mother—a torturous task, to say the least. If there was one person she did not want to ever see again, it was that frightfully abusive parent. It wasn't that she didn't understand or accept her mother's mental illness. A professional and clinical psychologist, she *did* understand her mother better than most people. She just never wanted to repeat a horrible childhood, victimized by an unloving woman who had nothing to offer a little child. A parent like that negatively impacted the entire family, and any effort at reconciliation would be akin to taking a pebble, throwing it into a pond, and watching the ripples spread wider and wider, invading ever larger areas of the water. When there was pathology in the family, the children often bore the burden for years unless there was extensive therapeutic intervention.

Caitlyn had also had a strained relationship with a younger sibling. They had not talked in years, and then he died in a strange swimming accident, with no apparent witnesses and no specific cause. Caitlyn suspected her clinically depressed brother, who subsisted on multiple medications, had died by suicide, succumbed to the temptation not to breathe anymore. Nothing was ever proven, and there was no one to converse with in her totally dysfunctional family. So the ripple stopped and faded, leaving Caitlyn with suspicions and unresolved regrets.

4

PERSONNEL COMMITTEE

Past Life Theory proposes that we are all connected on a journey across lifetimes to learn lessons that ultimately bring us closer to God. In that process, we will experience every religion and gender to learn our lessons about love and kindness. Where are you along the continuum of faith from religious to spiritual, and how hard is Past Life Theory for you to accept at this point in your life?

— Ellenmorris Tiegerman

That morning, as usual, Chairwoman Caitlyn Morrys seated herself at the head of the table. Ten other university professors, eight men and two women wearing casual office attire, occupied their favorite seats around both sides of the highly polished, twenty-foot-long wooden table worthy of a state dinner. When Caitlyn cleared her throat, they dutifully wrapped up their group conversations, consultations, and gossip.

Caitlyn passed out the weekly agenda and said, "Hello, everyone, let's begin."

The committee was academics personified: Everyone at the table had settled into a life of inquiry, immersed in academic routine. Ranging in age from late thirties to early eighties, most were egotistical, anxious, and only mildly interested.

The two other women, Louise Ladner and Jane Quigley, were close friends and highly intelligent full professors and senior academicians who shared their thoughts sparingly and resented Caitlyn's authority. They sat at either side of the farthest end of the table and shared little of their sparse conversations or their traditional points of view with others unless specifically asked.

And the men: Some were more familiar to her than others, and those few who tended to participate more sat closest to her at every meeting. Ash sat to her immediate left. Ted Carlisle sat to her immediate right for strategic purposes, to help Caitlyn with paperwork and secretarial committee responsibilities. Carlisle was unusual for a university professor, a big but sensitive mathematician with no airs who wore work clothes to class and was often stingy with opinions. He generally tried to steer conversations with smoothly intelligent discourse while squinting through tiny, wire-rimmed spectacles. Like Ash, Carlisle was quite enamored of Caitlyn and had an annoying habit, intensified by a naturally aggressive nature, shared by many men: staring incessantly at women's bodies, thinking the leering went unnoticed.

Next to Ash sat the absolutely brilliant Michael Conklin. He was Ash's male opposite: fiftyish and short, with a petulant mouth, his wispy blond hair receded from a domed forehead, and his shy, almost frightened blue eyes peered out from under ridiculously bushy eyebrows. Conklin was deeply intellectual. He boasted a vast vocabulary that completely overmatched his rather timid personality and gave him an air of puckish wisdom. His nonthreatening, calm, cool intellect brought rationality to the temperamental University Personnel Committee, no matter what the provocation. He provided needed respite from many often-emotional crises—a comfort to Caitlyn in her role as chairperson.

She called them her three Cs, and they fashioned consensus through verbal combat. The rest of the committee followed closely and threw in tentative encouragement or criticism as warranted—altogether a productive committee, as far as Caitlyn was concerned.

"Does everyone have an agenda?" Caitlyn said.

Voices murmured assent and ten heads lowered to read the title page.

"Where're the cookies?" Ash said, and then complained about the "healthy" snacks.

A little boy in a man's body, Caitlyn mused, and then laughed out loud.

"Caitlyn, are you laughing at me?" Ash frowned at her.

"No, I'm not," she said, thinking again of the morning, blushing, and quickly peering down the table at the expectant faces. And, of course, everyone was looking at her expectantly. She laughed nervously and lifted the first page of the ten-page committee agenda.

The first names listed were Brown and Tierney:

University Personnel Committee Meeting Agenda
1. Professor Jeremy Brown   Tenure Review
2. Professor Axelrod Tierney   Tenure Review

"Colleagues, there are two peer review items to begin our committee agenda: Professor Jeremy Brown's tenure report and also a report for the coming Outside Review Committee meeting involving Professor Axelrod Tierney's Administrative Action Reconsideration," Caitlyn explained.

The group looked over their agendas and shuffled paper for a few minutes.

Professor Carlisle leaned forward, holding up his agenda and pointing. "Professor Morrys, why is Professor Axelrod Tierney second on this list? He should be first. Tierney has been a disruptive lightning rod on campus the last few years. And how did he come to an Outside Review Committee? Isn't he primarily responsible for most of the violent political activism on campus? What's his backstory?"

Caitlyn yanked out a file containing her papers that reviewed Professor Tierney's personal background. "Axel Tierney has been an Adjunct Lecturer and Assistant Professor in the Physics department. His research has focused on chaos theory. He has published extensively in peer-reviewed journals and presented work at major scientific conferences. As you will see, in my opinion, the tension in this specific tenure case is not about professional scholarship requirements, but because the school views him as a political embarrassment."

She nodded at Ash. "Why don't you explain the participation of the Outside Review Committee in Professor Tierney's case?"

Ash leaned back in his chair, suddenly in his element of political intrigue. He glanced at the ceiling lights, then recited the facts from memory. "Axel was a friend and devotee of Ben Shapiro, an American conservative political commentator, writer, radio and TV personality, and host of *The Ben Shapiro Show* who was also involved with Breitbart News. Shapiro has published many books, the first being titled

Brainwashed: How Universities Indoctrinate America's Youth. What do we do now?"

Sensing a lack of understanding among his half-attentive audience, he glanced carefully at each in turn before gesturing broadly at the room and continuing, "You see, Axel has become academic advisor to the Conservative Students Club on campus. It was his idea to invite Ben Shapiro to a campus event two years ago, which was not in and of itself an issue until a group called Antifa threatened to protest Shapiro's appearance. Antifa, as you all know, is a militant antifascist organization that is oddly controversial given its penchant *for* fascism—for physically challenging the rights of conservative groups to be heard."

He looked around to confirm he had the attention of his audience. "Antifa is a mixture of left-wing antisemitic, antifascist militant groups who have been aggressively active on college campuses across America. They have been violent and destructive, from wild, insensate property destruction to throwing eggs at conservative students and police. What did they want with Coronado U and the Uzinski Administration? Well, the evening before Ben Shapiro was scheduled to speak, President Uzinski's office was notified Antifa was prepared to protest violently if Shapiro showed up."

Ash shrugged at his own words and smiled like a soothsayer. "What was the Administration's response? Uzinski directed his Provost to cancel the Shapiro lecture. He could have had police ensure safety on campus while Shapiro was speaking and protected free speech rights. But no, Uzinski not only cancelled the lecture but also issued a campus-wide memo castigating Professor Axelrod Tierney for inciting protests and chaos on campus. Uzinski actually blamed Tierney."

Ash shook his head in exasperation at his own words. "And you can be damn sure Tierney was not shy in his response to our University President. He argued back, and not just in a memo. He appeared on local and national news shows, ramping up the tension on campus. The only break came when the academic semester ended and most students were gone. By then, the damage was done and Tierney's burgeoning career at CU in severe jeopardy."

Ash paused for effect and lowered his voice conspiratorially to a near whisper. "Axel enjoyed extensive student and colleague support, but not from our Provost. The guy has an excellent academic record, so his only possible punishment, denial of tenure by the Provost, had to be based on something other than academics, on something else that—"

"So why is this any different from all the other cases?" Professor Conklin interjected.

The disruption visibly annoyed Ash, and he growled his answer. "On its surface, Conklin, I guess it's not any different. But it's my contention, as our union president, that President Uzinski is misusing the CU tenure process and undermining the entire system.

"Let me remind everyone about our tenure review process. We collect data and interview each prospective tenure candidate. We meet directly with students, faculty, and administrators to evaluate a junior faculty member's academic performance record, teaching effectiveness, and scholarship and decide if they have achieved a level of excellence. We discuss each candidate and vote by secret ballot whether to recommend tenure, a lifelong contract. Our recommendation goes up the chain of authority, from department chair to dean to Provost and, finally, to the President for the final determination. If we all agree on tenure but the President disagrees with us, an Outside Review Committee of professors from other universities is constituted to make the final decision.

"The tenure review process is a long and arduous journey for junior faculty, emotionally draining and taking weeks, often months, to complete. We are duty bound to operate in good faith, with the vision of excellence in teaching and scholarship as our *only* standard. But here at Coronado, our President has a political agenda. To him, no one is good enough to receive tenure, and each of our recommendations for tenure has been denied! As far as I'm concerned, that's a fight for the union. Think about the time and work that goes into each candidate for tenure, hours and weeks of interviews and reports. And for what?"

Ash stood up abruptly, grabbed his coffee cup, and walked away from the table. "I need a break. I need a chocolate chip cookie—and I need it now."

Caitlyn raised her hand like a traffic cop. "Okay, we don't have time to discuss the political implications of the Tierney case in committee at this time. We'll take up the preparation for Tierney's outside review at our next personnel meeting."

Ash stood at the coffee table in the back of the room.

Caitlyn continued, "We need to move on." She shook her head. "Suffice to say, I will represent the personnel committee at Axel Tierney's Outside Review Committee meeting next month. I will make it clear that this case against his tenure is about political issues and not about scholarship in our next UPC meeting this week."

Silence and scattered nods signaled acceptance and relief that the buck had been passed.

Caitlyn picked up another page from her file. "Now, I'd like Professors Connor, Carlisle, and Conklin to present the preliminary report on Professor Jeremy Brown," she announced as she distributed the relevant copies of Brown's peer evaluations, student evaluations, and letters from the CU Administration and four outside academic reviewers. "Jeremy Brown is from Communication Sciences. Professor Connor, since you have common research interests with Professor Brown, would you mind being one of his reporters?"

She looked at Ash's smiling face, and their eyes met. When she looked into those eyes, she felt herself falling into a well. *If I could only make the relationship work.*

"Well, what about you, Conklin?" said Ash. "You and I should be able to wade through some of Brown's clinical writings in speech language pathology."

"Frankly, Ash, you're a snob," retorted Conklin, fumbling with his oversized reading glasses. With his bushy eyebrows protruding over the thick-lensed black frames, he looked like a quizzical owl. Conklin was a frail, nervous little man who was usually afraid to challenge authority and rules. "I know of Brown's work over the years, and I find his material quite interesting, thank you very much."

"Thank you, Professor," Caitlyn said, recalling how buttons were often, as now, missing from Conklin's neatly creased shirts. Did he twist them off when he got overanxious?

Conklin started on cue, his voice pitched lower than normal in a classroom-lecture monotone. He remained seated, as customary. "Professor Brown received a master's degree in 2000 in communication disorders from Emory University and a PhD in 2006 in speech language pathology from the University of Kansas. He taught as an Assistant Professor at Northwestern University from 2006 to 2010. In 2012 he started teaching at CU in the department of Communication Sciences. He holds a Certificate of Clinical Competence from the American Speech-Language-Hearing Association. His area of specialization is in child language disorders, specifically in autism and intellectual disability. He teaches masters and doctoral level courses in language development and disorders, and specific courses on autism and intellectual disability. He is the department's field supervisor for undergraduate and graduate students who require clinical field placements in hospitals and schools affiliated with the University."

Ash returned to his seat with a coffee cup, which he placed on his agenda.

Conklin paused to wipe his glasses and clumsily slurp his cup of tea. "In terms of teaching, Professor Brown indicates he has a practical teaching philosophy within his discipline area. It is of utmost importance that students be able to connect the theoretical material discussed within the classroom to the practical experiences of children and adults with developmental disabilities. He describes the extensive research on childhood autism completed over the years, as well as how he uses the classroom as a mechanism to introduce as much practical information about the profession as he possibly can. Professional lecturers, media presentations, and parents of children with disabilities are all invited into his classrooms to discuss the impact of a communication disorder on various aspects of our society: home, school, and community."

Conklin stopped again, wiped his nose, and adjusted his glasses. "Next, Professor Brown received outstanding commendations on all his student surveys. Connor and I called students from his classes for the last three years. We completed thirty face-to-face and telephone interviews. Students were extremely positive about Professor Brown's teaching style and his relationship with them. They described him as easy to talk to, available before and after classes, fair about grading, and stimulating in class. They described his ability to make complicated scientific material comprehensible and interesting and explain and interpret with illustrative clinical experiences the driest of statistical data. Professor Brown also presents real world analogies, stories, and articles to explain theoretical material found in textbooks.

"Students were aware of his teaching philosophy. Students with grades from A to F were complimentary and recommended tenure for Professor Brown. The following student statement is representative of how all interviewed students felt: 'I decided to become a speech language pathologist because of my courses and experiences with Professor Brown. His understanding of the material, and the profession, attracted me to Communication Sciences. Although I did well in Professor Brown's courses, the grades were never as important as what I learned from him,'" Conklin finally finished, ready to solicit comments and corrections.

Carlisle began, "Your report is unnecessarily loquacious, too wordy. It needs to be concise and *precise.*" He squinted sternly through his pince-nez style glasses. "We don't need all your side comments in the report, just the facts."

"Absolutely not, Professor Carlisle," Ash said, tapping his pen on the table. "Detail is vital to the report. You know Brown's not getting early tenure, damn it. The union is going to grievance at some point over these cases. They are all based on Uzinski's plan to bring in and tenure only professors *he* selects for Coronado."

Carlisle waved the agenda report across the table in Ash's face. "Ash, as usual, you're getting way too far ahead of yourself," he said, smirking at his version of his own private joke.

"Carlisle, get those papers out of my face," Ash snapped. "Whatever do you mean?"

"You know very well what I mean, Professor Connor." Carlisle smiled insinuatingly.

Silence filled the room. Even Ladner and Quigley were quietly amused. Connor and Carlisle always fought. Everyone on the committee knew that both vied for Caitlyn's favor and had competed for her attention, publicly and privately, for at least a year.

The situation both embarrassed and pleased Caitlyn. A year ago, Ash had avoided her for weeks because he thought she'd reciprocated Carlisle's clumsy affection. Understanding dawned for both of them when Ash finally broke down, dramatically declaring his love and "discovering" that Caitlyn was not in love with Carlisle after all. She had then realized that Ash was much like his theory, both overwhelming and overbalanced at the same tumultuous time. She could never read him accurately, let alone understand his carefully cultivated, stoically controlled British persona. But she knew he was so overwhelmed and confused by his conflicting feelings—alternating between hot passion and cold fear of some surreal intimacy—that after they argued, he often tried to ignore her for days . . . and always failed.

Conklin rose from the table and interjected his cool annoyance into the hush. "Carlisle, let's try and remember we have a process to follow. When our chair, Professor Morrys, goes before an Outside Review Committee to defend our recommendation on Professor Brown, she needs a detailed report in hand."

Ash nodded and said in a louder voice than normal, "Hear, hear."

Conklin turned toward Ash and nodded. "And we all understand Professor Connor's union can only get involved in the Coronado University tenure process after every single detail of every administrative procedure is thoroughly exhausted."

"Okay, details are important, but we all know Professor Brown is going down in defeat like everyone else," Ash said angrily. "I hate doing all this work, knowing we're just spinning our wheels. Meanwhile, during this so-called peer review, Professor Brown and the rest of the tenure candidates are nervous wrecks." He folded his arms and sat back, signaling that for him the discussion was over.

Conklin took his cue and turned to Carlisle. "Give me all of your corrections; you're the expert on grammar and committee reports. Let's see if I can move this along. I'm tired of hearing the two of you bicker all the time. You're like two bitchy old—uh … sorry, Caitlyn." He cleared his throat and continued, "The most important area, of course, is scholarship. Ash and I reviewed Brown's résumé. He's published extensively in the past several years. His doctoral dissertation on children with autism yielded two significant research articles in the prominent *Journal of Autism and Developmental Disabilities* in 2007 and 2010. In 2012, he published an article in *Topics in Language Disorders* about families of children with autistic tendencies. In 2013, he published a textbook entitled *Language, Autism, and Developmental Disabilities*, which has gone into several printings and revisions. He's now completing a textbook entitled *Autism: A Changing Theoretical Model in Science and Education.*"

He took a breath and turned to Ash. "It's your turn to discuss the letters you received from other universities."

Ash began without preamble, as though he'd been interrupted. He sounded tired and annoyed. "The letters I received from the four external reviewers were all highly complimentary of Professor Brown's research and publications. Recommendations were received from Dr. Bret Smith from the University of Southern California, Dr. Jack Green from Hofstra University, Dr. Susan London from Columbia University, and Dr. Lauren Morton from Northeastern University. The letters all describe a consistent but developing progression in Professor Brown's scholarly activities that substantiates his ability to maintain an active research record. Each Outside Reviewer recommended tenure, and there is no reason—"

He stopped abruptly, then turned back to Professor Conklin. "I've had enough; this whole thing makes me sick. You finish the report, I need another cookie." Ash stood and tossed the packet of letters aside in front of Conklin. "Caitlyn, there are no chocolate chip cookies. I hate oatmeal raisin, tastes like cat litter." Ash's sarcasm broke the tension in the room, and everyone got up for a cookie break.

Thirty minutes later, finally settling back down, Ash returned to reading the report. "The department chair's letter is positive. He describes Brown as an important asset to the department: 'Brown has made a significant contribution to the affairs, growth, and development of the department by being involved in various committees, student advisement, and curriculum development. Professor Brown plays an important role in teaching, advising, and providing research support for all students,' yada yada yada. The department chair strongly supports Brown's early tenure determination at the university. And now for the administrative claptrap. Conklin, old man, take it away." Ash stood up, did a couple of tap dance steps, and plopped back in his seat.

"Ash, are you on something?" Carlisle said. "You're acting stranger than usual."

"Carlisle, just ignore him, otherwise we'll never get finished," Caitlyn snapped.

Carlisle seemed hurt by the rebuke but smiled at the chair to make amends.

"Conklin, what about the Uzinski letter?" Caitlyn said while trying to find the damned thing in her folder. She suddenly couldn't find or remember anything.

Conklin began to respond but sat back when Ash spoke over everyone. "As expected, President Uzinski wrote a peculiar letter," he said sarcastically. "It is politically correct, but thoroughly idiotic. Uzinski described Brown as an excellent teacher who was broadly involved with university affairs. He noted Brown's extensive publications but expressed concerns about his ability to *maintain* his present level of research commitment. He went on to express his concern that Brown would burn out, so the university would be taking a risk in granting tenure. What an idiotic comment! He also tried to connect Brown to the incident on campus with Antifa.

"So, although Uzinski acknowledged Brown's potential, he did not recommend tenure. He ended his letter reiterating his purported concern about Brown's long-term level of research performance." Ash tore up his copy of Uzinski's letter into little pieces. "Of all the asinine reasoning," he grumbled. "Hey, Caitlyn, give me your copy so I can tear that up too."

"Ash, you're losing it," Carlisle said dryly out of the side of his mouth. "Have Caitlyn recommend a therapist for you, will you, please?"

"Stop it, both of you," Caitlyn said, turning to Ash, who shrugged and stared at the pile of torn paper in front of him. She gestured vaguely at Carlisle. "What does this mean? What should we do here?"

"Well, first," Conklin interjected, trying to take command again, "I feel strongly about this committee's recommendation for tenure. The criteria are very clear in the peer review document: excellence in teaching, research potential, and university service. Brown satisfies all criteria in an exemplary fashion. Uzinski's comment that Brown can't keep up with his research is ridiculous, clearly—twisted reasoning. Brown is an outstanding candidate and Uzinski can't find anything to criticize about him, so he describes Brown's research strength as a negative risk factor. The President is a coward. I pray for the day he is gone.

"The reality is, the university has benefited from Jeremy Brown's teaching and research for years. Otherwise, why would Provost Moisescu renew his annual contracts? The President is apparently using the tenure process to keep or terminate certain Coronado University faculty so he can staff it with academicians from the Stutts Foundation." The Stutts Foundation was an ultraliberal international think tank headed by Mical Bazyli, a Holocaust survivor who had started the One Global Society, or OGS group, which funded foundations and progressive organizations. "The Foundation is specifically interested in liberalizing American universities by replacing tenure-based academicians with 1960s radical Marxist activists, BLM, and antisemitic, anti-Zionist professors. You can see what's happening, not only here but at Columbia University and universities throughout the United States—diversity, equity, and inclusion officers and curriculum programs, curricula, and classes."

Caitlyn surveyed the room. *Every candidate will be a victim ... abused and then humiliated by a broken tenure system.* She had no idea what was coming, what would hit her and her UPC full force next. She pictured him: Jeremy Brown, a young family man who had the look of a bearded rabbi, tall, dark, and driven. Was he Jewish? He had three young children and a devoted wife. They'd left Florida to come to CU. His wife had given up a longtime position teaching French and Spanish in a public school to give her husband his chance. There was friction between them about "pulling up stakes," taking such a risk, leaving the entire family behind—and for what? Even if Brown were granted tenure as an Assistant Professor, he'd only make a measly annual salary of seventy-five grand! *Uzinski's publish-or-perish rat race keeps everyone hungry and busy.*

"Does anyone have any questions?" Caitlyn said. Other than the shuffle of papers, silence greeted her question. Turning to Ash, she said, "Pass out the slips of paper and let's take a vote."

The committee members filled out the slips, checking either "tenure" or "no tenure," and returned them to Ash, who, after reading them, announced, "The vote is unanimous—eleven in favor of tenure. I'm relieved. Brown deserves early tenure, and I mean to get the union involved. I've had enough of this crap. Here, Conklin, you can tear up my copy of the report, it'll make me feel better watching you." He laughed. Everyone else laughed, too, as Conklin ripped the report into shreds.

Caitlyn's thoughts overrode the laughter. *Andrews, Tierney, and now Brown will never get tenure with Uzinski as President, UPC approval notwithstanding. Conklin is right. Uzinski has to go . . . and none too soon. He's a menace, a threat to the lives of hardworking, devoted teachers—and the sanctity of the profession and learning. When you think about it—the pain he has caused already, and will continue to cause—he's flat-out evil and has no place in an educational institution. But how to get rid of him? Is that remotely possible?*

Caitlyn led the committee through the rest of the schedule: calling on all the members, reciting reviews, presiding over debate, and taking votes. After almost another hour, she adjourned the meeting, and everyone began to get their things together to leave.

"You know, Caitlyn," Ash said sarcastically, "you should try tearing something up too. It's cathartic, you'd feel a lot better. Maybe it would loosen you up a bit."

Caitlyn ignored the remarks and banged on the table to get everyone's attention before they left. "I'd like Conklin and Connor to provide us the final report on Brown for submission to the Provost's office. In addition, I think Professor Brown should be called about our decision. Ash, would you call him? Make sure you tell him that his report is to be submitted to the Provost. I don't want him feeling anxious longer than necessary—although he probably knows not to be too optimistic, no matter how we vote. You'll get the opportunity to ask Brown about his research since it's the most critical criterion for tenure determination."

Ash nodded.

"Finally, before we all leave," Caitlyn added, "I want to remind all of you that after our report is submitted to Provost Moisescu, we will be meeting with him to discuss his recommendation to the Board of Trustees. We will be essentially covering the same ground with the same man—please be prepared."

Conklin began, "When do we begin the process—"

"Which we know will be negative," Ash interjected, "but we can always hope that Doctor Death finds redemption and President Uzinski grows some balls."

"Ash, cut it out," Caitlyn said, annoyed.

Ash began waving his arms in the air. "Brothers and sisters, let us put our hands together and call out to Jesus to save the soul of Provost Moisescu." He wiggled his hands over his head.

"Ash, will you be quiet?" Caitlyn said, trying to sound serious. She grabbed her appointment diary and threw it at Ash, hitting him on the shoulder.

Ash spun on his heel and moved toward her with outstretched hands. "A sinner, you are a sinner. I will lay my hands on you and shake the devil from your soul. Help me, Jesus."

"Ash, if you take another step, I'll brain you with my DSM-5," Caitlyn said, reaching for the textbook with a grin on her face.

"No, no, not the book! Please, not the book! Hit me, strike me with anything else. Don't use that book on me," Ash whined dramatically, putting his hands to his chest as if he were having a heart attack.

"Caitlyn, do you remember whether there were any cases in which the Provost agreed with us on tenure?" Carlisle said, placing his hand on her shoulder.

"In the past year, only once," Ash said abruptly, staring at the offending hand.

Carlisle, noting Connor's annoyance, asked, "And do you remember who that was?" He did not wait for any response. "That happened with Uzinski's pet, Professor Neil Braxton." Carlisle continued to rest his hand on Caitlyn's shoulder, aware of how much it was irritating Ash.

Caitlyn was flattered but embarrassed by the inter-male interlude. She straightened, arched her back, and tossed her hair.

Ash stared at Carlisle and asked, "Are you being judicially probative or psychologically analytical? Do you think I could forget that romantic Shakespearean drama with Braxton and our University Provost Moisescu?"

Carlisle, distracted by Caitlyn, was caught off guard. He blinked and smiled.

Ash continued, "The scuttlebutt at the time stressed our sudden, unexpected, and wholly unholy alliance with the Provost of Doom. At first, I was disgusted . . . nauseous . . . revolted! I've never wanted to be on the same side of anything with Doctor Death. But, when *he* agreed with us and the President disagreed with *him*, the tables were turned, and Professor Neil Braxton was denied an Outside Review Committee! How delicious an interlude in such an unpromising career! Justice, as rare as it is, can be so satisfying sometimes. I believe there comes a time when only violence can make a difference—"

He stopped suddenly and glared. "Don't look at me like that, Caitlyn, you know your eyes glow when you wrinkle your forehead. You must've been a witch in one of your past lives," he said in an off-key, near-falsetto pitch.

"Past lives," Caitlyn repeated in a whispery tone, more to herself than to Ash. She moved away from Carlisle's hand

and sat down at the table again, staring at Ash without realizing it.

"What the hell is the matter with you?" he demanded. "You're a nervous Nellie. I can't tease you. I can't needle you. I can't make you laugh. Are you sick? Are you having a nervous breakdown or something? This isn't a convenient time, dear, next week you have to report to Axel Tierney's Outside Review Committee as his primary advocate, his Joan of Arc."

Caitlyn didn't move. She kept staring at Ash, her expression distracted.

Ash shrugged his shoulders. He turned, grabbed a cookie, and sidled sideways out of the committee room as the door began to close, nearly catching his fingers.

5

"HE'S DEAD"

In each life your soul takes on a "shell" or a lifetime of lessons that will advance your progression to God. Each lifetime the trials and tribulations take you closer to divine knowledge and oneness with that Divine Spirit. — Ellenmorris Tiegerman

Approaching her corner office, Caitlyn heard her telephone ringing. She passed Carla's office, slipped the card in her lock, and grumbled to herself about how her damned headache made her nauseous.

Carla called out stridently, "I need to speak to you, Professor Morrys, wait!"

"In a moment, Carla, let me get my phone." The phone continued to ring insistently as if nagging her. She tossed her hair aside and lifted the phone while imagining revenge for someone, somewhere.

Ash's deep voice blared, his words interspersed with laughter. "He's dead! That contrarian son of a bitch is dead!"

Her silence echoed on the line. "Caitlyn, do you hear me?"

"Who's dead?" Caitlyn gasped and hurriedly sat behind her desk.

"Didn't you see the police cars on campus?" Ash demanded. Before she could answer, he continued, "I just came out of a computer science meeting and went over to the Admin building. The place is crawling with police. Where've you been since that damned personnel committee meeting? I've been calling you constantly for an hour. President Uzinski is dead."

"What? He killed himself?" she sputtered. *What did I just say?* "That slipped out."

"What the hell are you talking about? Are you having one of your headaches?"

"I don't mean anything. I mean … I don't know what I mean." Caitlyn's throat tightened. She felt dazed and disoriented, an all too familiar feeling.

Carla walked in and stood in front of Caitlyn's desk, pointing at her phone. "I have a lot of the details," she said quietly.

Ash was still laughing. Caitlyn absentmindedly placed the laughing phone on its cradle.

"You obviously know," Carla began, as if they were already in the middle of a long conversation. "Donna from President Uzinski's office called me when she first found his body, before she called the police."

Caitlyn tried to recover. "You mean, his death was not, uh … natural?"

"What? No … um … I mean, I don't know," Carla replied unsteadily. "Donna said she found Uzinski sprawled across his desk and didn't know what to do. I told her to call campus police. I had to give her the number. After calling them, she called me back. Poor Donna was hysterical, crying about the body and the blood." Carla laughed nervously. "She even used President Uzinski's office phone to call me.

She wound up with gobs of blood smearing her hands and blouse."

"When did this happen? I was in our committee and down in Records today in that same Admin building." Caitlyn was trying to think clearly and avoid awkward mistakes.

"She found him a good while ago," Carla said. "You must have seen *something* in the lobby as you were leaving, like the police or an ambulance."

Caitlyn quickly rewound recent events and realized her reaction was all wrong. "No, Carla, I ... um ... didn't see anything at all like that. I was buried in Maryann Mathews's personnel files. You remember her confrontation with Uzinski over tenure, don't you?"

"Yes, and you and Mathews share a heart-vocation in children's education, I remember."

"Carla, your memory is astounding." Caitlyn nervously laughed. "We also have a casual friendship and share gossip about men and women and education over endless cups of coffee. But it's what we *didn't* share about Mathews's past that amazed me."

Carla sensed something titillating, something possibly connected to the death of their University President. She leaned forward. "And what, pray tell, is that, Professor?"

"Maryann Mathews apparently works for a secretive part of the US government."

"What part of the government is that?"

Caitlyn frowned. "Not sure, but she corresponds with people in Langley, Virginia."

"Ooooh, top secret stuff, huh, Professor?" Carla scoffed. She could not hide her resentment that, as secretarial staff, she was prohibited from using the central source of all university information, the official Records room underneath the Admin building.

"Yeah, Mathews is a real big deal." Caitlyn understood Carla's annoyance. Unlike her, she often worked in that hidden room full of records, a medieval dungeon behind password-protected doors and rows and rows of head-high metal filing cabinets, at a seldom-used work desk.

"Anything to do with our dead President, do you think?" Carla asked.

"Anything's possible, Carla."

The Mathews files comprised two large folders. Caitlyn had taken them from the filing cabinet marked "M" to a work desk in the back of the Records room, where she had stayed immersed in personal and professional data, shielded from the scuttlebutt about the campus tragedy. Since starting her research, Caitlyn had been disturbed by the eerily familiar coincidences in Mathews's struggle with the school's bureaucracy. She didn't think the troubling incidents could *all* be coincidental.

Maryann Matthews was articulate and aggressive and had missed her calling in choosing education as a primary goal. Girl-handsome, with a dark sense of humor and assertive intellect, she *should* have been a tall, sleek-muscled college athlete with short black hair. Mathews's pale tan complexion and blue eyes suggested interesting ethnic mixes. She played "fast forward" on a traveling women's soccer league, smoked thin cigars, and typically dressed in slacks and T-shirts or sweaters. She and Caitlyn shared an interest in education, and particularly of children with disabilities. They did not travel in similar circles but met often for lunches in the Student Union building or for coffee before classes. They enjoyed each other's company, their conversations spiced with applied psychology and the cruel sense of humor that went with street psychoanalyses. Caitlyn had fun observing other people with Maryann. Maryann had even given her the Cabbage Patch doll that sat in her office as an icon to "strive after," red hair and all.

When Caitlyn had exited through the front door of the Admin building that morning, she hadn't noticed the marked campus police cars or any other parked vehicles nearby. Because the President's office suite was on the third floor of the four-story building and her committee met on the second floor, she'd had no reason to notice anything when she'd entered or left the committee meeting, gone down to the basement, or climbed back upstairs to the lobby. Focused on "secret" administration tragedies, reckless romances, and a tenure denial or two, her mind had wandered far from campus as she went down the front steps, past parked cars, and down the Coronado Promenade—the wide main street of the campus—and toward her Humanities/Psych building at the other end of the quadrangle.

"You didn't see the police asking questions or anything?" Carla repeated her question.

"Good lord, no," Caitlyn answered, a little too decisively. "My mind was on something else, and I didn't notice anything unusual up there." Her eyes darted about the room with no destination. She realized now that the campus police were a seemingly hidden, but apparently constant, background in her university life, seldom seen and rarely heard except in parking disputes and lost property recoveries.

Carla inserted her monocle between her right brow and cheekbone, glaring at Caitlyn. "You say you walked right through an active murder investigation, Professor, and you didn't even know it?"

Caitlyn jerked her head back. "It was murder? A murder investigation, you say? How do you or Donna—How does *anyone* know the President was *murdered*?"

"Donna said he had a knife sticking in his back," Carla answered. "She also said he was half naked and blood was all over and under him."

"What else did she tell you, Carla? Where was the blood coming from?"

"Evidently everywhere," Carla said. "He had a knife *and* a white, trumpet-shaped flower like a lily sticking out of him."

Caitlyn again pulled her head back and crunched her eyes. "A white lily? What do you mean?"

The crime questions made Carla nervous. She inched toward Caitlyn and lowered her voice. "We need to be careful what we say here, Professor, don't we?"

"Careful?" Caitlyn repeated. "What for? Was Uzinski murdered or not?"

"The lily was in his butt and the knife in his back," Carla said quietly.

The phone rang again. Caitlyn grabbed it. "What?" She held up the receiver and mouthed to Carla, *What now?*

Carla nodded and whispered, "Put the speaker on. Let's all find out what he knows."

"Ash, I'm tired," Caitlyn said into the receiver, and pushed a button. "Don't include me in one of your little-boy tantrums. You're not exactly what I'd refer to as—Never mind, just tell me what happened to Uzinski, tell me all you've heard," she said, nervously twirling a strand of hair. "What do the police know?"

He began quietly and slowly, "Campus police wouldn't let me stay in Uzinski's office, but I got a good look before they made me leave. Our illustrious President Uzinski was face down across his desk, hugging himself in a pool of blood, a knife in his back, pants pulled down, and a white star-petaled flower sticking out of his rear end. Poetic justice, and I couldn't have staged his demise any better."

"Poetic justice? What're you saying?" she interrupted.

"The funeral flower says a lot about motive and attitude. How humiliating this is for him, our University President. How delicious—pants pulled down." Ash laughed. "This was a set-piece stabbing, an obvious combination of ceremony, scorn, and anger. Somebody bent him over the desk and really stuck it to him." Sarcasm dripped from his words.

"Why the sarcasm, Ash?" Caitlyn asked, leaning forward on the desk.

"Talk about love and hate, Caitlyn. I despised him for how he browbeat this faculty and hurt the lives of colleagues. Look at our UPC. Look at how he's been trying to destroy the whole tenure system by circumventing everything we do. Just deny tenure to everyone and appoint professors from the Stutts Foundation! Who was Uzinski involved with emotionally and sexually? Who did he trust enough to get naked with? Who hated him so much?"

Caitlyn raised her eyebrows at Carla, who shrugged and shook her head. "Ash, dammit, tell me what you know. Who could've been up there? Have the police questioned anyone?"

"Anybody could've been on the third floor of Admin on an early morning, including anyone who attended the personnel committee meeting." He laughed again. "Hell, they don't know when he was stabbed, whether it was late last night, this morning, or sometime yesterday."

"How could they *not* know?" she said. "Weren't any people in there earlier today?"

"Nobody's there at night in Admin," he responded. "Provost's offices and campus police are on the ground floor, committee rooms on the second. The President's way up on the third floor—he lives up there, nobody would go inside his private office suite, anyway. His secretary said she didn't even look in there for an hour or more after she arrived this morning, didn't even know he was there. Campus police are examining everything and looking for witnesses. They haven't figured out when it happened, said the body was cool and the blood congealed. They called other police departments, trying to contact some outside homicide detectives, and word is they found somebody who knows what he's doing. After talking with this *somebody*, they quickly asked me to leave the area and stopped everybody trampling all over the murder scene—a bunch of crass amateurs."

"Right, Ash, and you're a professional detective."

"Caitlyn, I do have an associate of science degree in criminal justice. I know my shit."

"Yeah, that and all my psych degrees don't amount to anything in a *real* murder."

"Well, now that you mention it, you'll have a field day analyzing this whodunit. This is a murder method for psychologists, no doubt about it. Ya know, my love, this would be a terrific opening for a murder mystery. This is better than chocolate—although not better than sex with you—but definitely better than chocolate. What a pip." He hung up.

Carla removed her glasses, dropped them on her chest, and leaned forward. "So, he evidently doesn't know much more than we do."

Caitlyn leaned back against her chair, her mind tracing her movements over the past twenty-four hours: who she'd spoken with, who'd seen her, what she'd done. She tried to visualize the murder scene, with Richard Uzinski lying across his desk. Her mental vision of the crime scene was intermingled with a real-death nightmare of blood—*and a body she knew.* "Professor Connor knows more than he thinks he knows, Carla."

"Right, he knows lots of things, but doesn't know he knows them," Carla repeated, and smiled. "Just like you and me, right, Professor Morrys?" She looked at Caitlyn suspiciously.

Caitlyn ignored the look and didn't answer. They were referring to different issues, Carla to the President's murder and Caitlyn to the past-life flashbacks and images of death and mayhem that she and Ash shared. She shook her head to clear the images and focused on the present situation. She wanted to *be* there; she searched her mind for a solid academic reason to get past the police and back into the President's office suite. She craved the details of what was there, as well as the finality and clinical silence of a murder scene in *real* time. She felt an urge to compare—to what, she didn't know yet. As her mind spun rapidly, she began to fear she might be implicated. The police would find out for sure that she had visited the President's office late last night and might have—no, definitely *had*—left evidence.

Uzinski, pathetic Uzinski, President of Coronado University—medium height, medium weight, graying hair with midlife muscle flab from too-occasional workouts, with a petulant, indulgent narcissistic personality, even to some degree criminal. Somewhere deep in her mind a dark cloud gathered, growing in size and strength as she considered *this* murder. She knew without doubt that this chaotic murder reeked of a threat to *her*, and to all she held dear in her life—

it complicated the groves of her academic world. *He could no longer vote against tenure.* That thought thrilled her.

"Suddenly, your life has gotten more complex and your job has gotten easier," Carla remarked.

Would Uzinski's death make her committee work easier? Or would the police focus on her as a possible suspect, thus complicating her *real* life?

Caitlyn forgot Carla and concentrated on the personal and psychic implications. First of all, why Richard Uzinski? Second, all the tenure denials would highlight the rejected candidates—and draw attention away from her.

As to the first, her mind browsed the DSM-5:

> The essential feature of a narcissistic personality disorder is a pervasive pattern of an acute need for adulation coupled with a lack of empathy. Individuals with this disorder have a grandiose sense of self-importance. They routinely overestimate their abilities and inflate their accomplishments, often appearing boastful and pretentious. Often implicit in the inflated judgments of their own accomplishments is devaluation of the contributions of others. Individuals with this disorder believe their needs are special. Individuals with this disorder generally require excessive admiration. Their self-esteem is almost invariably very fragile. This often takes the form of a need for constant attention and admiration. Individuals with narcissistic personality disorder have difficulties recognizing the desires, subjective experiences and feelings of others. Arrogant, haughty behavior characterizes these individuals. They often display snobbish,

disdainful, or patronizing attitudes toward their peers.

A clinical, but near-perfect, description of President Richard Uzinski, she thought. She tried to see the situation as law enforcement would.

Why was he dead? Who would want to kill him like that, in his office, of all places?

Who? According to most reliable campus rumors, President Uzinski had problems with verbally combative women in particular. She thought of herself, tossed her hair, and frowned. One would think that the last place for him to work was a university swarming with intellectually successful women.

She looked up at one of those women, who had a monocle screwed into her face. "What was he doing at *this* particular university, Carla? What if he had particular problems with particular people?" She nodded sharply. "For instance, he and Neil Braxton have been nearly inseparable." She summoned up a recent gym incident, a cosmic moment that transformed the gym visit into something she would regret remembering for the rest of her life.

Caitlyn had been about to start her workout one morning and, en route to a workout machine, passed close to Uzinski. Out of respect, she'd called a half-formal greeting to the University President. As she did, Neil Braxton had taken his eyes off Uzinski's heavy bar and leered at her, a general habit of his, and missed a signal, allowing the barbell to slip sideways, away from the rest stand. Uzinski's shoulder shifted, and he screamed as the weight concentrated on his thumb. Braxton grabbed the falling barbell-end in time and set it back on the stand.

"Goddamn!" Uzinski shouted, and slid off the bench, squeezing his twisted left hand. "Braxton, you clumsy fool, you missed the bar. Now my thumb's broken all to hell!"

Caitlyn saw that his left thumb had bent back toward the side of his wrist, the bone end bulging at the base. She reacted instinctively and grabbed his left wrist. "Hold still, sir, it's just dislocated," she said, with a solicitous tone she'd never used with him before.

Uzinski groaned at the sharp, grating anguish from the dislocated bone and gristle. Caitlyn turned his left wrist in her left hand, clamping his upper left arm into her right armpit and yanking his dislocated thumb as hard as she could, out and up and back into the gristle where it belonged. The bone popped back into its socket.

"Damn!" Uzinski yelled in shocked surprise more than pain. He grabbed his left hand from her and squeezed the reset thumb into its palm, the prior acute pain now a dull ache. "That was amazing, Morrys," he said in relief, looking at her with admiring eyes.

Caitlyn walked him to the first aid locker, taped around the wrist, and cross-taped his thumb to the hand to keep it immobile. She advised him to take aspirin and keep it still for a few weeks. She added, with a bright, confident smile, "It'll ache in wet weather but will soon work good as new."

"Where did you learn to do all this?" Uzinski said in a seriously inquisitive tone.

She merely shrugged and smiled.

"Professor Morrys, we've had our differences, but I've underestimated you. You have my gratitude. When there's anything I can do for you, you have but to ask." He smiled and shook her hand. "Thanks for handling my little emergency," he said stiffly, nodding at her and walking out the rear door toward his third-floor office, fifty feet away in the Administration building.

Looking back on that episode, now under the shadow of the man's evident homicidal demise, she wondered what it meant. She didn't know but told herself it was not an idle happening. It contained important information.

Jumping way ahead of her personal analysis, Caitlyn turned to her assistant. "Carla, get on the phone and see what you can find out. And just for the hell of it, I'm going to take a walk over there and see how the police react to me."

"Right, Professor Morrys." Carla nodded her complicity before returning to her office and deciding who to call first among her long list of campus police who owed her a favor.

Caitlyn walked back down the quad to the Administration building to see if she could observe the police, get a look at the crime scene, and maybe ask questions. She entered the building as though she belonged there. Uniformed city and campus police clustered in the entrance and parking lot, talking to each other and to official-looking men in suits who thought they were in charge. They were all polite but refused her entry and rebuffed all her questions with courteous smiles.

Oddly, a thought burst into her mind like a divine voice from up above: *At the very least, I'm not an immediate suspect.* At least, not that she knew of—yet!

As she went back down the promenade to her own building, a few students, professors, and school personnel stopped her to ask questions about the police presence. Some knew about the murder and who the victim was. They carefully approached Caitlyn as if she was important and knew something the rest of them didn't.

Of course, she did not know anything—at least, nothing she could talk about.

An annoying voice in her head reminded her about those persistent nightmares of bloody battles from different times in history. Caitlyn thought she'd seen a dream sequence in which Uzinski was killed over and over again, or in some other military context. How many times had she seen herself and Ash—and Uzinski—at other times and in other places? She didn't know, and the mere idea shook her to the core.

If she focused on one flashback at a time, she might be able to figure out who the characters were. Maybe if she meditated and hypnotized herself, she could work through the horror scenes. Maybe if she concentrated on their eyes— the eyes always revealed the real warriors and the real victims. But she was afraid to see their faces. She feared taking that path, the path of the unknown and potentially ominous. Her suffocating inertia and fear of self-exposure gnawed at her.

What would her peers think if they knew about her past-life musings? How could the dreams be anything but fantasies? They could not depict *real* events, could they? Were they just wild projections of her fears or other nightmares? And what specifically did the murder portend for her? Did she have something specific to fear?

Caitlyn realized she did not have time for all this speculation now. Coronado University's President was dead, but its psychology professor had a class to teach in less than an hour.

6

THE INSPECTOR

There are many paths to God's divine presence; can you at least accept that as a first step? Or do you still think that there is only one true religion and everyone else "burns in hellfire and damnation"?

— Ellenmorris Tiegerman

Next day, the air burst with suspense, rumors, questions, and countless impossible scenarios among students and faculty, while the black-and-whites gradually disappeared. The powers that be had cautioned the few who had meaningful information to discretion.

The crowded campus information highway that Carla Breyers frequented buzzed with suppositions and loose talk, but virtually no useful information. Carla admitted her frustration to Caitlyn but remained working the phones. "Professor Morrys, I hate to say it, but everyone on campus is talking about several names as being connected with President Uzinski's murder—and yours is one."

"*My name?*" Caitlyn exclaimed, too loudly. "Why me?" she bellowed. Realizing that she sounded more defensive than she wanted to, she added quickly, "And who are the others?"

Carla smiled and lowered her voice. "Well, the teachers who didn't get tenure keep coming up, and—check this out—Doctor Death and Neil Braxton, too, since they were the two people closest to President Uzinski," she said, nodding her head with confidence. "There's a very aggressive rumor mill on this campus." She shook her head. "I don't know where *your* name came from."

Caitlyn said nothing, indicating to Carla she needed to complete some work. About an hour later, her head buried in discussion papers she was grading at her worktable, she was interrupted by a confident double knock on the frame of her open office door.

"Come on in," she called, slowly lifting her head and expecting to see Carla with a murder update.

But the person standing there was *not* Carla Breyers. She gazed with mixed feelings of curiosity and unease at a large, bald stranger in tinted aviator glasses who resembled the fictional detective Kojak from the 1970s TV series. The Kojak in front of her was wearing a white shirt, blue bow tie, and sport jacket over sharply pressed slacks.

When their eyes met, he smiled broadly like a salesman. "I asked your secretary not to bother announcing me," he said, maintaining the wide smile. "She's evidently upset with me."

The fit-looking older man removed the aviator glasses and, with a too-casual air of authority, stepped into her office, looked quickly around, and nodded at her again in a friendly way. Too friendly, too familiar. *Is this a cop?* Probably—he bore all the markings of a stereotypical TV city detective—but he looked to be about sixty, too old for a cop.

I've seen this guy before. The busiest blue eyes Caitlyn had ever seen twinkled with amusement at her inspection as he thoroughly examined her and her office, doubtless making note of the careless disarray.

Carla stood behind him in the hall, frowning at the intrusion, aviator glasses firmly in place. "Professor Morrys, he wanted to surprise you and he was too quick for me. Sorry about that."

"It's okay, Carla." She carefully swept back her hair with both hands, arms akimbo, and watched his eyes scan her body. "Can I help you?" she said.

"Of course you can." He didn't blink or look away. He readjusted his gaze and met her direct look with an amused expression.

He certainly acts like a cop, authoritative and full of himself.

"Professor Caitlyn Morrys, I am Acting Chief Inspector Cormac Robertson of the state police," he announced with practiced formality, and offered his hand.

Caitlyn reciprocated and they shook hands. "*State* police, you say? That's unusual, no?"

He handed her a sheet on the state governor's stationery with his photo and a short introduction, below which was the governor's signature. "Pardon the seeming informality, but I was rather suddenly appointed by the governor as a special investigator for Coronado University, due to the rather unusual and sensitive aspects of President Richard Uzinski's death." His smile reappeared as his eyes wandered again. "It's nice to meet you in the flesh, so to speak. I must say, you certainly don't look like any professor I studied under in college."

"But you definitely resemble a policeman," Caitlyn said, smiling back. She returned the sheet of paper, turned, and walked over to sit behind her desk. She motioned broadly for him to sit in one of the two big leather chairs. "So, Inspector Robertson, how can I help you?"

He sat, reconfigured his glasses on his nose, and thought a moment. Then he began, "So, if the killer was not you—and I offer no opinion on that intriguing question— who do *you* think stabbed President Uzinski in the back?"

Her vocal cords froze. She stared at him. *Does he really suspect I am the killer?* The answer might be lurking in those nebulous dreams that scared the hell out of her. She frowned and answered sharply and a bit self-righteously, "What a ridiculous question, Inspector. How could I possibly know anything about the killing of our University President?"

"Rumor is, you had a contentious relationship with the school administration, Professor Morrys."

"I chair the personnel committee, and that makes my relationship contentious."

He nodded knowingly at her. "Professor Morrys, I understand that you and your assistant, Miss Breyers, are chock-full of information about the workings of the university. In fact, virtually every faculty member I've interviewed volunteered that you are paid to know everything about them all as Chair of the University Personnel Committee." He stroked his chin, nodded again, and added, "Also, it is common knowledge around campus that President Uzinski hated most of the faculty, particularly the women, and the feeling was reciprocated. Some of your colleagues say that Uzinski harbored particular feelings against women like you. Some might say you hated him as well."

"Might?"

Robertson shrugged and let that last exchange simmer for several seconds, studying Caitlyn's body language.

Caitlyn filled the void. "I'm not aware your statement is correct, nor am I aware there's such common knowledge." She shook her head and tossed her hair back again. "Though I can only speak for myself, I wouldn't describe the faculty's feelings for the President as *hatred*."

"Well, how *would* you describe their feelings?"

"I've not had any deliberate therapy sessions with the faculty, Inspector," Caitlyn shot back sarcastically. "That said, there is a natural tension between President Uzinski and many of my faculty colleagues because of the tenure process."

"Tension, Professor?" he repeated, and added, "Seems pretty typical in most American universities. I've heard that's because of low salaries and the tenure process."

Caitlyn smiled at his impudent assertion of inside knowledge.

Inspector Robertson returned the smile. "Really, Professor, I've been at this for about twenty-eight hours. I've read the files of specific faculty members and researched their testimony about a number of Uzinski's often-insulting letters to the Coronado faculty. You academics are not the only ones who do research."

"Testimony, you say? Okay, so you've done some research." She carefully controlled her voice. "Those letters may have given an inaccurate impression." Sparring with this confident, articulate man, she felt strangely amused.

"I've also heard about that sultry voice of yours and your ability to pitch it," he said.

She was oddly flattered. "Who told you that? Really, Inspector, where have you heard about me and my voice? And exactly what information are you ... probing me for?"

"I'm simply analyzing your responses," he said slowly in a solemn voice.

"You seem to have a well-studied manner of pitching your own voice, Inspector," she said, slyly covering a fake, nervous laugh with a hand.

"Now, now, Professor Morrys. I've already undergone some quick federal government vetting and amateur analysis in the governor's office and Department of Public Safety to prep me for this job. I don't need a therapist, and I'm being paid to ask *you* questions."

She looked steadily at him across her desk. "Okay, what else do you want to ask me?"

"Tell me about Professor Neil Braxton."

She dropped her pen. Caitlyn wanted to pinch herself for appearing off guard. *Why now with Braxton? Wait … slow down … breathe. Use your weapons to distract.* She wet her lips, arched her back, pushed farther away from the desk, and crossed her legs.

Inspector Robertson's gaze remained fixed on her face.

Undeterred, Caitlyn placed her fist under her chin and tucked her arm between the armrest and the side of her chest, emphasizing her cleavage, while she pretended to concentrate. "If you're asking me about Professor Braxton's tenure case, then you must know I was chairperson of the University Personnel Committee during his recent review. You must also know the UPC, the personnel committee, did *not* recommend Professor Braxton for tenure."

"Yes, Professor, I read the file."

Caitlyn nodded. "Then you also know that our negative recommendation displeased President Uzinski greatly. Even more surprising was that the Provost agreed with us. That had never happened before, so why now with Braxton?"

She raised her voice. "It was the first time the President and Provost disagreed on a tenure review, to my knowledge."

"Provost Moisescu did *not* approve Professor Neil Braxton?" Robertson repeated rhetorically. "Do you know why not? And don't some of you call Moisescu Doctor Death?"

"That would be unprofessional, Inspector," she said, tapping her pen on her lower lip. She knew full well that the Inspector did not believe her denial for a moment. "And, since I can't discuss the particulars of the Braxton case, I'm not sure how I can help you," she said dismissively.

The Inspector watched her performance carefully but struggled to conceal his impatience. His hands gripped the arms of his chair as if preparing for a fist fight. "As I've already said, I've read some files—*all* files relevant to this murder case."

Caitlyn tracked his eyes as they moved up and down her face and body, stopping and resetting as though taking snapshots. Was he distracted at all? She would not allow the long silence to intimidate her.

As she studied his face, a long scar on his neck caught her attention. Images flashed in her mind: He was lying among a thousand dead and near-dead in the 1429 siege of Orleans. Or he was a Union soldier in 1862, bleeding badly, along with thousands of others, in a Shiloh field next to Maid of Orleans church. Or he was a wounded Marine in Hue City during the Tet Offensive in 1968, in a death field of civilians executed next to Joan of Arc School. Or he was a tank commander in the Golan Heights in 1973, shot in the face and head in the Valley of Tears. In each case, he had the same face and neck injuries, inflicted while fighting for Holy Causes. And each time, he had received the blessings of Caitlyn's healing salve and skilled fingers.

"I see you've *remembered* my scar, Professor Morrys," he said softly.

She snapped back to reality, annoyed at herself for daydreaming and missing his emphasis on the word. "I'm terribly sorry," she fumbled. "That was rude of me. Something about your scar? You have a wound, do you?"

"Yes, indeed," he said slowly, peering over his glasses. "How do you think I got it?"

"Well, I don't know."

"Yes, you do. Look," he ordered, and pointed to his neck. "You believe you can read psychic knowledge by observing certain people. Where do you think I got this scar?"

She was shocked. Could he read *her* mind? What did this police officer know about her?

"It was at Hue City in '68 next to the Joan of Arc School for children, Professor. They found the bodies of twenty-eight hundred civilians buried in mass graves around the school, all shot in the head."

Caitlyn was near panic but forced out a few strangled words. "Inspector, I have no clue what you are talking about. Besides, my mind and my work have nothing to do with you—or, for that matter, with Professor Braxton. You are here about President Uzinski's murder, are you not? Why do you keep changing the subject?"

"Or when we routed five hundred Syrian tanks with a hundred men that desperate night near Ahmadiyeh in the Valley of Tears and saved the Holy Land from certain Syrian recapture."

"No, no," Caitlyn pleaded, "that has nothing to do with President Uzinski's murder."

"Oh, but all this history *does* have to do with his murder—and with you, your mind, and your visions—and, I dare say, your flashbacks." He paused. "And with me also, Caitlyn. You must remember, and realize, that I'm not here with you by accident."

What does that mean? Does he know more about me than I know about myself?

She must be one of his last interviews, Caitlyn thought, and many of her colleagues had probably talked about her and, unconsciously or deliberately, revealed too much … including some of her darkest, most cherished secrets.

Did someone throw me under the bus? Has he interviewed Ash? Did Ash say something flip, as he is wont to do, about my dreams? Did he unwittingly undermine me, make me—how do they say it—"a person of interest?"

"Have you spoken with Professor Connor yet, Inspector?"

As if reading her mind, he nodded and smiled reassuringly. "I've talked with your closest colleagues and with Professor Connor in particular. And I have read some of your research articles. You believe there can be palliative results from past-life regression. You believe therapists achieve revolutionary results working with patients' dreams. Don't you think flashbacks, or memories about the past, can convey intentions, meanings, and messages about people's present and future lives?"

"Really, Inspector Robertson, what does all this have to do with murder?"

"Everything, Professor Morrys, everything to do with your rejected tenure candidates. And your dreams, visions, and nightmares will probably help me discover who Uzinski's murderer is."

Caitlyn sat up straight. "My visions—or bad dreams—make little *real* sense, even to me."

"Don't look surprised, Professor Morrys. Investigative clues come from strange places. I am suggesting to you that your flashbacks and visions are the key to solving this murder case. Murders, like so many other patterns of behavior, are based on dysfunctional relationships that repeat themselves over multiple lifetimes. Uzinski's murderer has committed other crimes with you, in other lifetimes that you've shared. You can regress yourself, or I can help you access your past lives, to identify who the murderer is. You should also know that the murderer knows all about you and me in this lifetime. He knows that I am here to help you find him, flush him out, and stop him from killing again. You need to go back to move forward. You need to find him in one of your past lives to solve the Uzinski murder and prevent any future murders on campus—including your own," he ended quietly.

"That's fine with me." But Caitlyn knew he was right. She squirmed in her seat. Her nightmares and dreams had power, and she was suppressing it, afraid of what she might learn about herself. She was especially frightened by the possibility that she had been a murderer or terrorist. *Is it possible I went to see Uzinski in his office in a hypnotic state? What am I missing here? Does this have something to do with Ash?* There was a certain mystery about Caitlyn and Ash, but it was better not to know. The problem was, now a mystery lurked on campus too. *Are they related to one another in some way? Oh my God, this is getting out of control.* Her stomach tightened.

"Let's leave this for now and return to the issue of tenure." He heaved himself out of the armchair and walked past her desk to one side of the beveled bay windows facing the distant mountains. "Nice view you have here, Professor," he observed. "Coronado U is such an idyllic place to attend school. Which prompts the question, why did an American aristocrat like Richard Uzinski agree to take over a school located in the backwoods of America? Why did he care so much?"

Caitlyn was confused and resentful. As he faced the window, his back partially turned, she could see his eyes reflected in the glass, bearing down on her. She decided to play along and be honest with him. "Odd as that question is, I'll admit I've asked that same question over the past few years."

Robertson continued to stare out the window. "Do you think maybe President Uzinski just disapproved of all of you countrified, Midwestern professors and did not share your provincial obsession with tenure?"

Her eyes met his reflected in the window, and she raised a hand in protest. "Wait a minute, Inspector, you're all over the place. Why do you think tenure is important in President Uzinski's murder case?"

"There are few, if any, other scholastic issues here at Coronado, are there?"

"Most people don't know, and couldn't care less, about the issue," Caitlyn insisted. "Let's face it, the only time tenure becomes newsworthy is when a disciplinarian tries to fire some poor teacher because she's supposedly incompetent, when she's just insubordinate—and *subordinate* is the point!" Her voice rose steadily as her unfiltered passion gushed.

Robertson smiled at her fervor, his eyes fixed on her reflection in the window glass. "We'll assume you are referring to Neil Braxton's rejection, and Jeremy Brown's. Hallelujah! Sinners be damned," he teased as he turned from the window, nodded, and smiled down at her conspicuously. For a quiet moment, they looked into each other's eyes with a familiar warmth that belied the awkwardness of a new relationship.

"You used the feminine gender there, Professor," he remarked. "Is there a female professor we should be discussing? Maryann Mathews, perhaps?"

Caitlyn cleared her throat, stood, and turned around to rearrange the pens and papers on her desk. She felt his eyes on her. Suddenly, the black pantsuit she'd recently altered felt way too snug. Why were her clothes so tight? *First it's your boobs, now it's your butt!* She had purchased the pantsuit at Woodbury Commons with Ash, during a shopping trip to New York. Caitlyn smiled, recalling how irritating Ash could be about how she chose her clothes. How would he be on a shopping trip to buy new clothes if they were a permanent couple? Over time, he would probably go through her closets and throw things out because he was tired of seeing them.

She became aware that she was smiling to herself and, realizing the detective had moved, hastily searched to find him.

"Over here, Professor," Inspector Robertson said, now seated and cleaning his brass-rimmed glasses on a handkerchief as he waited for Caitlyn to return to the present. "You went far away after I mentioned Maryann Mathews. You were preaching tenure and insubordination, and then Professor Mathews threw you off."

"Sorry for drifting off like that, Inspector. It's a bad habit I have."

"Yes, I know, Professor. I know about your lapses into dreaming," he said cryptically.

"You know? How could you possibly know, Inspector? We've just met!" she said, surprised and quite confused.

"No, we haven't. We've known each other across life-times, Professor . . . lifetimes," he insisted.

"What in heaven's name are you talking about?" she asked, leaning forward against the back of her chair.

"Never mind, Professor, that's for another conversation. Let's move this along."

She sat down again and flung her hair up and down. "What did I want to say? Yes, okay, why are you trying to connect our tenure issue, a female professor, and President Uzinski's murder?"

"The tenure candidates are key to solving the case. There are five or six cases of denied tenure. It's a good starting point from an investigative perspective. President Uzinski despised his faculty, and for their part, they challenged his Administration every step of the way. Certain recommendations and addendum letters from you and your committee, for example, are scathing, to put it mildly. For instance, the one you wrote—"

"So what? It doesn't mean a faculty member murdered him. Inspector, you can't really think that some professor hated Uzinski enough to kill him. Hated him for what, school events?" she said sarcastically, arching an eyebrow and pursing her lips.

"Tenure!" he fired back, eyeing her over the top of his glasses with some frustration.

"Tenure? That's ridiculous. No one could have done such a thing." Her voice trailed off. The implications of his theories shocked Caitlyn so much, she could barely string sentences together.

A prolonged silence ensued. Robertson was the first to fill it. "No one could have? No one, you say? Why are you so sure? Tenure means money, position, and security, important things that everyone craves. Tell me about how tenure works here at Coronado, and *exactly* what it means to you, Professor . . . Caitlyn . . . Morrys."

Caitlyn took a long, deep breath, arched her back from long practice, and began, "Tenure has protected freedom of academic expression in American universities for decades. Acquiring tenure is a mark of distinction every professor seeks. To be acknowledged as a significant contributor to an academic discipline by one's colleagues is a high level of achievement and enduring distinction. The entire process involves extended interviews, voluminous reports, secret ballots, and recommendations, all confidential. There is obviously a financial component, but tenure is a prized and long-cherished honor.

"A denial of tenure constitutes a negative statement about your teaching, research, and lack of potential as a professor. Professors often leave universities when denied tenure. After all, the university—in theory, at least—wants only the best and the brightest on the faculty. It's painful, complicated, and difficult."

"My dear Professor Morrys, your idealism verges on fanaticism. There's a fine line between the two. History bears witness to the madness of demagoguery and its deadly results."

"Inspector, surely an underlying pathology provides motive for this murder." She nervously tapped her pen on her desk.

"I'm sorry to disagree with you, Professor Morrys, but there's more to this case than murder and campus politics. Was Professor Braxton reviewed by an Outside Review Committee as required by Coronado University's complex tenure process?" He put this question smoothly, almost by rote.

Caitlyn could tell the Inspector was more knowledgeable about the peer review process than he had let on, or he'd not know to ask that specific question. She was becoming increasingly upset by the direction of this interview. Still, she felt compelled to answer. "Professor Braxton again ... Braxton," she repeated slowly, a little confused. "Why are you focused on Neil Braxton? He was just another tenure case that came up before my committee."

Robertson leaned forward. "Why don't *you* tell *me* how Neil Braxton might apply here."

"So you think he's connected to the President's murder in some way?" she asked softly, her head beginning to throb.

"I don't think anything—*yet*," he responded. "Tell me what you think of him."

"Well, Inspector, if you're asking about Braxton's outside review, I can only assume you've read our peer review document—we call it the Blue Book—and are well informed about the review procedures. Professor Braxton, given the peculiarities of his particular case, was *not* vetted by an Outside Review Committee for the simple reason he wasn't entitled to one."

"Not entitled to one?" Robertson repeated. "Why not?"

Caitlyn shrugged. "That only happens when the personnel committee disagrees with the Administration on a tenure candidate. In Braxton's case, the committee did not support Braxton's application for tenure. Nor did the Provost. Uzinski disagreed, which led to a public disagreement between the two senior officials, who traditionally presented a united front. Their embarrassing display shocked us all. Braxton is finished professionally at the university. His tenure case is moot for our purposes, except Braxton takes issue with the practice of professors leaving universities that deny them tenure."

Inspector Robertson processed this for a moment, then asked, "How many people have been denied tenure at Coronado over the past three or four years?"

"I'm not sure—six, maybe seven."

"Let's turn the question around. Has *anyone at all* been granted tenure during the past five years, Professor Morrys?" he said, pointing at the ceiling.

"No," she responded, turning her head again and resting her chin on her hand.

"You said yourself, people's lives and reputations are at stake, right?" he asked softly, leaning forward. "Anyone—particularly a prideful professor—would hate being refused tenure."

"Hate, you say?" Caitlyn looked at him with a pained expression. "Inspector, you're the policeman. Since when is hatred *not* a common motivation for murder?"

"Hatred," Robertson responded, "is a reaction to real or imagined injury. Pride—or self-esteem, or conceit, or vanity—is what makes reality subjective. Few men and women are immune to pride, but in my long experience, only a few proud people indulge in what you are calling murderous hatred."

Caitlyn nodded. "This school is a petri dish for pride and hatred, but the key word is *few*—few people indulge in murderous hatred."

"You're right. Sorry if I upset you back there." He switched to another area of inquiry. "What do you know about the Stutts Foundation and its relationship to the university?"

She shrugged. "From all I've heard, we have received many substantial grants from Stutts to facilitate the President's vision for reform."

"Did you see Uzinski as a visionary?" he said, leaning forward again in his chair.

She looked at him a long moment. "I saw him as a charismatic narcissist—in a purely psychological incarnation, of course."

"That's certainly a cautious description of a President who had become an extremely controversial figure on this campus."

Caitlyn pursed her lips, tossed her hair, and remained silent.

"Professor Morrys, do you care to make any personal comments at this time?"

"My personal feelings about President Uzinski have nothing to do with the academic changes he imposed on this university."

"Personal feelings have everything to do with this case," he asserted. "Particularly since the coroner's preliminary autopsy report is in." He gave Caitlyn a piercing look. "You *do* know the report notes a potent muscle relaxant in the victim's blood, don't you?"

"I heard a rumor about the muscle relaxant," Caitlyn said, startled by her own words.

"Of course, you know about the relaxant," he retorted quickly.

"I-I mean . . . I don't know how I know," she stammered, now squirming in her chair and tapping her pen again nervously on the desk. "And what do you mean, *of course*, I know?"

Robertson laughed but evaded her question, waving his hand as he spoke. "The pathology report indicates that a benzodiazepine like Ativan was mixed with his brandy. He was probably immobilized at the time he was stabbed, and until he died from blood loss. The murderer apparently had access to President Uzinski's evening liquid intake and his glass, which had been put away, and knew about drug compounds and their effects."

"Like any hypochondriac or pillhead would," she added.

"And, of course, a chemist would have such knowledge," he casually remarked.

"*Chemist*? What chemist?"

Robertson smiled as if he welcomed the question. "Provost Moisescu has a degree in biochemistry, for instance, and President Uzinski has written critically about professors in the Chemistry department. Has anyone else been denied tenure in the past several years?"

"Oh my God, now it's someone in the Chemistry department who was denied tenure? Tell me, Inspector, are you suggesting that each professor denied tenure is a suspect?" Caitlyn tried embellished mockery but didn't get a rise out of the too-calm detective.

"Now, that's a good question, Professor Morrys," he said, chuckling. "You tell me."

"How would I know, Inspector?" Caitlyn paused. *Everything paused as she tried to parse what was real. Something is familiar here. How could I know Uzinski would be murdered in his office, drugged and stabbed? How the hell is that possible? There must be a rational explanation. Well, it makes sense that anyone as controversial as Uzinski would have enemies—deadly enemies—but Uzinski seems to have set himself up for murder. What is the matter with my thinking? What would have made him even contemplate something so suicidal? Hell, what would have made him stop? What deep despair could prompt self-destruction? Normal people don't act out hate. What psychopathology are we confronting?*

"Professor Morrys, are you going to answer me?"

And how could Inspector Robertson think I know what happened—that I'm the superglue?

"How would I know?"

"Right." He nodded. "Most things in President Uzinski's office were fingered only by him. No furniture was moved around. Everything was apparently in its place and in order, except he was lying face down on his desk, half naked with a knife in his back."

"I know, Inspector. I know all about that." Her voice lowered to a monotone.

Robertson paused. "Yes, you *do* know a lot about it. Maybe we're finally getting somewhere. Anyway, the scene was unusual because Uzinski's pants were down—and a white, trumpet-shaped flower was placed between his buttocks." He stared at her. "Now, what could *those* two things mean?" He shot the question toward her.

She remained silent, eyes down, her silence defiant.

"From a psychological viewpoint, wouldn't a posed flower predicate sexual motives?" He sat back and continued, without waiting for an answer, "And *that* white flower is very strange—maybe even significant." Robertson pointed toward the Administration building. "According to the coroner, the flower in Uzinski's buttocks was a *Datura stramonium*, known as Witches' Weed, one of the most poisonous plants on Earth."

"*Datura stra*—what weed?" she stammered. "I've never heard those names before."

Robertson nodded. "Right, most people haven't. In fact, the coroner said he had to look it up, said he was fascinated by the odd-looking star-shaped-trumpet flower that looked a lot like a lily. He actually researched it while I waited on the phone. He told me *Datura* is apparently a Hindi word for a white or purple plant originally from the Himalayan foothills in the Punjab area of northern India." Robertson studied Caitlyn for her reaction. "He said *Datura* is a killer *and* a healer. It's in the same family as nightshade, henbane, and mandrake. Professor Morrys, did you know the leaves and seeds of *Datura* plants are poisonous, but the seeds, when ground into a paste, are used as medicine for many skin diseases or lesions, as has been the case in India for centuries?" Robertson searched Caitlyn's face for any recognition.

Her silence held only a moment more. "Inspector, so now you think a flower killed President Uzinski?" She shook her head. "I thought you said he was stabbed in the back."

Robertson nodded. "You're correct, the lab said he died of blood loss. That nasty flower didn't kill Uzinski, but it was certainly there to send a message—or maybe point a finger."

Caitlyn frowned as she tried to analyze all the strange new information.

"Well, Professor Morrys, since you're not answering my questions about Uzinski, let's change topics."

"Was there evidence of semen?" she asked suddenly.

"So you're considering an actively sexual angle? Who's your suspect?"

"Inspector, you're not answering my question!" she insisted in a louder voice.

"No, no evidence of semen," he said. "But it *does* look like an inside job. The President knew his assailant, no sign of struggle. Time of death was three to four a.m. Who had access to his office at that hour of the morning? Who could possibly be in Uzinski's office before dawn? Wouldn't a bleeding bastard screaming bloody murder alert security at that hour? Does a University President normally conduct *any* business at four a.m.?"

Caitlyn did not respond. She was focused on Uzinski's visitor that night.

The peculiarities of the murder circulated in her mind. She decided to list them. "Inspector Robertson, Professor Uzinski obviously must have seen his murderer and known what was happening." Caitlyn nodded. "The murderer *wanted* him to know, wanted to watch each excruciating detail. For any victim, even Uzinski, those last agonizing moments must have been terrifying. Unable to defend himself, he watched his murderer gloat while he bled and suffered. He probably knew he was going to die."

"Professor, I think that's enough of that for now. Let's talk about the University Personnel Committee," Robertson said, trying to redirect her intuitive acrobatics.

"I can't, Inspector, I have a class soon," she lied, needing time to gather her thoughts.

"Professor ... Professor, perhaps you can explain other things to me, like the tenure review processes, at your next personnel committee meeting?" His sharp look and tone indicated this was not a request, but a demand.

She nodded, suddenly acutely aware of how familiar his voice and verbal nuances were.

"And then if I have any questions, the entire committee will be present," he added. "It'll be more friendly—collegial, you'd say, Professor." He stared into her eyes until she dropped hers.

After a long silence, he rose and walked to the door. Without turning he said, "We'll speak again later, Professor Morrys, particularly about any past or current faculty members who were denied tenure. You might want to think about those tenure cases, since each one has a life-changing motive for murder."

Inspector Cormac Robertson left her office and walked down the hall to the stairs without speaking or even waving to Carla Breyers.

Caitlyn knew Robertson was right. He didn't sound like the traditional police detective. She realized that the flawed stereotype of a police officer in her head was going to be a problem in dealing with *this* member of law enforcement.

Then she remembered. *Someone who looks like Robertson is in my nightmares, along with Ash. Could it be?* What could she unearth about him? She had over an hour to get to her Developmental Psychology class which, thanks to Carla, was in the lecture hall downstairs in the Humanities basement.

She swiveled to her computer, jumped on the internet, and searched newspapers, the library, and other public information documents for anything connected with his name. Surprisingly, she found a great deal on him, a montage of avocational activities that portrayed an almost surreal Renaissance character. The gentleman Inspector was referred to as a Marine, a cop, a mercenary, an author, a political writer, an activist in conservative politics, and a member of the Fraternal Order of Police. The bald, well-connected investigator was the subject of literally dozens of newspaper articles and was responsible for, or instrumental in, the exposure and ruin of many otherwise respectable politicians and notables for their secret sins and public sector corruptions.

Although relatively well-known from a Google perspec-tive, Inspector Cormac Robertson had managed to avoid becoming too famous.

7

THE PSYCHIC RABBI

In truth, we are immortal beings who never die and are never separated from those we love. We have eternal soulmates and soul families. We are never alone. — Brian Weiss

Later, in her office after an early-ending class, Caitlyn descended into deep introspection. The opportunity to sit and privately explore one's past was delicious. She pulled out a desk drawer, kicked off her heels and put her feet up, and leaned way back, arms overhead, turning her office chair into a chaise lounge so she could gaze out her wonderful, many-paned bay window as though on a cruise. The skyline shimmered red and orange with low, black mountains chewing at the color, like memories trying to eat time—*and maybe restore the past.* She thought back to Inspector Robertson's reminder about her psychic past and her therapeutic training at the Omega Institute in San Antonio, Texas.

The Omega Institute for Holistic Studies was an innovative educational training center that prided itself on its social change mission. The Institute offered workshops, conferences, and retreats, and its Omega Wellness Center for Sustainable Living was situated among woodland trails and prairie gardens. The brochure read: "Omega is a travel and tourism destination known best for its health and wellness programs and commitment to lifelong learning."

She had loved her visit there.

The accommodations were not the Ritz-Carlton, rustic but manageable. Her single room had a double bed and private bathroom, more like a cabin than anything else. There were three buffet-style meals a day in Omega's large and airy dining hall, which was certified by the Green Restaurant Association and easily accommodated several hundred people. No meat was served. Caitlyn was not a vegetarian by any means, and the change in diet had been radical for her.

During her visit to the Omega Institute, the program had been "Healing through Regression Therapy," the special mission and beloved project of doctor and therapist Brian Weiss. Dr. Brian Weiss was a clinically trained psychiatrist who, through cosmically arranged circumstance, hypnotized a patient named "Catherine" during what started out as a fairly traditional therapeutic session. While in a hypnotic state, Catherine had emoted at length about past-life experiences—what she called her "current past life"—creating a dramatic meeting of their psychic minds. This paved the way for Regression Therapy to evolve into a therapeutically healing methodology. Dr. Weiss detailed his experiences with Catherine and her multiple past lives in his 1988 book *Many Lives, Many Masters: The True Story of a Prominent Psychiatrist, His Young Patient, and the Past Life Therapy That Changed Both Their Lives.*

Caitlyn had wanted to attend one of the training seminars, both because of his book and an experience she'd had twenty years earlier on a flight home from Los Angeles. Traveling alone on a plane en route from college to home, she'd found a copy of *Time* that someone had left behind. While leafing through the magazine, a thought had mysteriously popped into her head—from where, she had no idea— about a psychiatrist interested in past lives. She searched for the article and there it was: "Yale Psychiatrist Writes about Past Life Experiences." After perusing it three times, a voice in her head said, *Changing the future by changing the past? You're going to meet him one day.* She chuckled to herself. Her rational voice, the voice of reality, said, *How silly.*

Fast forward twenty years, and there on her desk was the brochure for a training course for therapists. And, of course, her decision had only been hardened by the latest email from the Omega Institute:

> If you want proof that past lives exist, that we reunite lifetime after lifetime with the people we love, and that there's no such thing as "death"—have I got a story for you.
>
> Back in 1980, my world turned upside down when one of my patients, Catherine, began recalling vivid past-life memories under deep hypnosis. I was astounded—because as Catherine unearthed each memory, she inexplicably began to heal.
>
> Years of recurring nightmares, phobias, and anxiety attacks subsided and disappeared.
>
> At the time this was happening, I was a skeptic. I just couldn't believe what I was seeing, and I figured there must be some other reason for her transformation. But soon enough, my thinking changed. Because not only was Catherine healing herself of long-held anxieties, but she was also bringing through remarkable messages from the spiritual realm—information about people from my own life that she couldn't have known.

From that moment forward, I embarked on a new journey in my career, investigating the truth about reincarnation and healing thousands of people from physical and emotional pain through the power of past-life regression.

And now it's your turn.

Was she being ridiculous? This was outside the realm of everything she had believed in at the time. Past lives were not exactly scientific. More like science fiction?

Then again, that gnawing voice in her head had become more persistent and demanding over time. It was consuming her—and had taken over her dreams, she feared.

When she had made plans to fly into JFK and attend the week-long conference, she had not told Ash. She'd waited until the last moment to break the news.

Of course, he'd laughed. "You're kidding, right? You're going to a conference on past-life regression? Would you like to share that with the Administration and put it on your résumé? You're going to be in a room with a bunch of wackos," he declared, "and you'll be called a wacko for going!"

"Coronado's Administration won't care what I do. I'm already on their hit list," she said.

"But these people think they can actually *see* what happened in the past, and that knowledge of what happened in the past can radically change their future?" he pressed.

Caitlyn was becoming exasperated as he edged closer to the truth. "Ash, just let it go."

"How can I let it go when you try to analyze your 'flashbacks'"—he raised his hands to flash visual quotation signs—"with some hocus-pocus therapy?"

At the end of the conversation, he asked her to call him every night because he "wanted to know about all the wacky works that occurred during the day."

Dr. Weiss had pioneered Regression Therapy, guiding people through the use of past lives. When she visited, Caitlyn found Dr. Weiss used the same paths but went beyond Regression Therapy into "mirror image" Progression Therapy: a scientific, responsible, and healing way to use an assumed knowledge of people's pasts to help them project their future lives.

Caitlyn distilled this information in her head: *One before the other, all of it depending on inducing self-hypnosis.*

One regression Caitlyn witnessed was of a thin young woman named Sarah. Hypnotized on stage, she related a past-life memory that was extremely moving and powerful. She had been a young girl of fifteen living in Bukovina, Romania, in 1941 with her parents, older brother, and younger sister. In describing her house, neighborhood, and local synagogue in great detail, Sarah spoke in a calm, controlled voice, like she would to her family and friends. Her voice lowered, however, and became more forced when she described the day the Nazis came to her house, beat her father, raped her mother, and crammed her into a cattle car with thousands of other Jews from the neighborhood. She had watched as flames swallowed the local synagogue and children screamed and mothers cried, petrified for their lives. Sarah clenched her fists against her face and protested Romania's occupation by Germany in 1941 and the vast numbers of Romanian Jews killed by Romanian soldiers. After she'd recounted gruesome details about the brutal selection process, Sarah became distant, eased away from her own story. Like a spectator, she slowly described the way she had died in the Dachau concentration camp.

She spoke as if she had been a witness to her own death.

Sarah shared that her mystical experience had changed her perception. "When I died, my soul floated above my body. As Dr. Weiss has explained, when you leave your physical body, you bring the life experiences you've acquired to the other side. You can review your thoughts and actions and determine the lessons you've learned about kindness, giving, and loving—all lessons you must return to Earth to learn while you are *among other people*."

The emphasis Sarah placed on the last three words had stayed with Caitlyn.

Sarah's story easily could have been considered the main attraction at the Weiss Regression Conference, but others had an equally profound effect. The most searing takeaways for Caitlyn were a fellow class member's comments during a regression exercise: "Humans are spiritual beings. We all keep returning until we learn all our lessons. We never die." Dr. Weiss had similarly commented during one of his lectures: "These past-life memory fragments may emerge in dreams as actual memories, not Freudian symbols. Through Regression Therapy we can actually perceive outcomes and use this process to bring more joy and healing to our present lives."

Caitlyn purchased all his books and CDs, but she couldn't relax and meditate effectively to achieve self-hypnosis as a doorway to her past lives. She didn't doubt what people were sharing; she just couldn't accept the underlying premise unless she'd experienced it herself. And an underlying fear nibbled at her.

What if I succeed in self-hypnosis and hate the truth about myself?

It wasn't that she hadn't tried. She had on multiple occasions. She knew the therapeutic steps like a drill, could detail it all in her head. She had even made a relaxation training tape for herself to follow. Of course, she did not have a quiet, distinctive voice like Dr. Weiss's. She'd used his CD to see if she could achieve a more meditative state. She followed the taped instructions to lie down, close her eyes, relax each part of her body, starting from her head and moving down to her toes; to travel down a staircase, go deeper, imagine a beautiful garden; to imagine a door, open it, walk into the light. But there was always a distraction, or she'd fall sound asleep.

But she hadn't given up. She'd kept practicing, but after all this time, she was not getting better at meditating and her nightmares had become more graphic and frightening. She was frustrated with the whole thing. There were therapists who utilized regression techniques, but she could not bring herself to call for help. Some therapist she was! She couldn't get herself to do what she advised her students to do. She couldn't come to terms with the fact that she needed help—some advice and counseling. Caitlyn imagined asking Dr. Weiss but fell back on self-defeating excuses like *He's out of town, He isn't seeing new patients,* or *He'll scorn my failure.* She never tested the possibility by seeking an appointment.

Her persistent flashbacks had begun to interfere with everything in her life. Now the voice in her head was pushing her to evaluate her past lives.

You are resisting. I can feel your energy. You know there is something here for you and you are actively rejecting it, resisting what your subconscious is telling you.

She'd had her doubts at the Omega seminar. Were these people part of a cult, feeding off each other? Then Dr. Weiss had conducted a group exercise that had shaken her traditional belief system.

He'd had everyone in class, about one hundred fifty in attendance, pair off and share an object. The assemblage included psychologists, social workers, therapists, and psychics from all over the world, virtually everyone an energized, enthusiastic follower of Dr. Brian Weiss and his theories.

There was one scientist in the room, a true skeptic who could not be readily or easily challenged, and that skeptic was Professor Caitlyn Morrys. What could she possibly share?

Caitlyn held desperately to the physical world and clinical training she'd received. But during that exercise, all the twenty years of scholarship, all her accumulated collection of knowledge and her reading regimen, became skewed and then shattered by her paired partner. Miriam Yeller was a spiritual practitioner from New York City, a female rabbi who was also a marriage and family therapist. The two of them, from divergent backgrounds, began discussing reincarnation, the Kabbalah, and clinical practice.

Rabbi Yeller was a tall, imposing figure. A Reform rabbi at Beth Shalom Synagogue in midtown Manhattan, she was sharp and articulate, with a dry sense of humor. Her short, curly hair bounced girlishly as she spoke. She was animated and gestured expressively. The topic of Kabbalah had been brought up during the morning seminar, along with its application as a therapeutic methodology. As the only theologian in the room, Rabbi Yeller had answered many questions, and Caitlyn was not only intrigued by the topic but impressed by the extensive knowledge the rabbi had at her fingertips.

"Miriam, give me some history here, so I have a context for what Kabbalah means in Judaism. I mean, I'm trying to understand it as an evangelical Christian."

"Kabbalah represents a mystical tradition in Judaism," Rabbi Yeller responded.

"Mystical, Rabbi?" Caitlyn said, smiling. "What does mystical even mean?"

"Mysticism is an attempt to encounter God in the world. The mystical movement has existed as a component of Judaism for generations. In the late eighteenth century, a synergy developed with the Chasidic movement. The founder of the movement, Israel Baal Shem Tov, created a new Jewish religious culture in which joyful prayer became part of ritual Talmudic study. Jewish mystics teach that the soul cannot completely fulfill its entire mission in a single lifetime, which is why reincarnation is discussed at length in Kabbalah. Through various reincarnations, the soul is elevated across lifetimes. Kabbalah represents that one soul spiritually travels through different bodies. Like the title of one of Brian Weiss's books, *Same Soul, Many Bodies*," she added, laughing.

While Rabbi Yeller chuckled, Caitlyn wandered a little, filled with an odd but vague sensation of familiarity and a disconcerting calling to some place outside her body, where turmoil loomed. It jolted her. She shook it off and returned her attention to the rabbi.

The women discussed how to put reincarnation theory into practice to address the therapeutic needs of their respective clients. Caitlyn finally asked the question that had been torturing her. "Okay, how can I apply this to myself?

I've always had this feeling about being Jewish. I've always had this strange connection or interest, pulling me toward Judaism."

"Well, if we accept what Brian's been saying about past lives for the last week, I'd suggest that your feeling or affinity derives from a past life. You were Jewish in a past life. Remember, in this theoretical model, people travel in soul groups. They have different relationships with each other in past lives. You could be a man or woman, your soulmate's mother, son, daughter, or brother. You could be a Christian, a Muslim, or a Jew. You may have cycled through these roles and relationships to learn different lessons."

Caitlyn called up the nightmares: fighting for King Charles and her subsequent burning; death in a concentration camp in Europe; fields of fire and death in the United States, Asia, the Middle East—and her eventual Jewishness.

How could she explain this to Ash? She wanted desperately to talk to someone about her thoughts and fears about past lives. The haunting nightmares suggested she'd had past lives of her own, if only she could face them.

There just was no explanation for the entire day. She had seen two dramatic regressions and participated in a group activity that resulted in a very personal experience—all unexplainable.

After each daily session, Caitlyn was sorely tempted to speak to Dr. Weiss. Her chest tightened with tension and her breathing became shallow and strained. She could not get up the nerve to approach him. Dr. Weiss wasn't the problem. He spoke to everyone and anyone at the end of every training day. But Professor Caitlyn Morrys never convinced herself to face him—never.

Caitlyn knew in her heart that she was erecting blocks to achieving a relaxed, self-induced hypnotic state. The voice in her head kept asking a frightening question: What if she found out she had been a mass murderer, a terrorist, a pedophile in a past life? What if she had been a Nazi guard in Auschwitz? Could she handle *that* truth? She didn't want to know, and certainly didn't want to discover the mystery of her own past while meditating alone! The class ended and she meandered to her room.

She burned to call Ash with a report but thought better of it. She needed to think. She wanted to be alone.

But then the phone in the room rang noisily, shattering her introspection. It was Ash.

"Hello."

"Do you know your cell phone isn't working up there?"

"No, Ash, and I've not been on the phone," she said with some disdain. "Nice to hear you too."

"Well, I had to make five different calls to connect with this room. These Omega people of yours don't like outsiders distracting guests. Well, no matter, buttercup. What happened today in la-la land? I'm all ears!"

Like a punctured dam, she poured out in torrents the day's collection of unexplainable material, which she desperately wanted to process and understand. Dr. Weiss's theories, the power of the past, how healing could be achieved through past-life regressions, the past-life regressions she had witnessed, and, of course, her personal experience with the psychic. It all came out.

And then she stopped talking, a hard stop, as if she had lost her voice. She took a deep breath, hoping for words of wisdom and deep connection.

"Wackos, Caitlyn," he said. "They're all a bunch of wackos. And by the way, you've been camped out in a cabin in the woods for a week. I understand they gave you sheets for your bed when you registered and you had to make your own bed, which you never do. True or not true?"

She burst out laughing and nearly dropped the phone. "Oh my, you really are so annoying." Ash had dragged her back into reality as only he could. "That's why I love you so much."

"You know, you haven't laughed like that with me in a long time," he said. "You need to do more of it. How about coming home early? I miss you, my buttercup. Besides, how much of that stuff can you tolerate?"

It was a good question.

8

CHECKING THE PAST

In the Library between Lifetimes, there is a fluidity to lifetimes and choices that allows for the growth that each religion offers and teaches. Humankind created religions, but God created faith for humankind. This religious paradox can be viewed in two distinct ways: You could have a soul religion, like Christianity, from lifetime to lifetime; or you could have a soul faith that varies religiously from lifetime to lifetime. — Ellenmorris Tiegerman

Caitlyn printed several newspaper stories, marking with a yellow highlighter provocative aspects of Robertson's personality and life, which allowed her to form a profile of him.

While a detective by profession, Robertson specialized as a maverick hired by police departments for high-profile political felony cases. A hard man in the present, but with a soft heart in the past, Robertson had married his childhood sweetheart, now deceased. They'd met when they were twelve years old, and he told an interviewer it was love at first sight. Five years after that first meeting, they eloped. They'd had one child, a girl, who died as a preschooler from a genetic disease he never spoke about, the same disease that took his wife's life.

The psychic in Caitlyn knew the hyper-tough Robertson was passionate and loyal but had an Achilles' heel ... *the child*. Was there ever a child in her dreams?

She thought about their interview. The more she knew about him, the better her ability to predict and affect his behavior and defend her position. Robertson had researched *her* background and references and conscientiously devoured her research articles and perhaps even her textbooks.

Robertson talked as though he was open to psychic regression and even sounded like he welcomed the potential of inducing visions and dreams. Could he be actively probing her, pushing her to regress *herself* for some reason? It was not so easy to do that. Caitlyn had tried meditation on multiple occasions, but all she'd achieved was a deep state of relaxation. How annoying it would be to discover someone who thought—and imagined—like she did. Caitlyn would have to outthink herself in a game of mental chess if she wanted to outplay this experienced man with the energetic eyes.

Queasiness bubbled in the pit of her stomach. Ash ... where was he anyway? She called him and left a voicemail scolding him for sharing her secrets with a police officer and asking him to find out everything he could about Inspector Robertson before coming to her house for dinner that night.

She had old secrets and recent ones, particularly about President Richard Uzinski. Uzinski had recently become a sub-rosa part of her life, complicating her already complex existence in ways she'd never thought possible on a staid Midwestern collegiate campus. First, the President lived in suite 303 of his Admin building, for privacy and—not surprisingly now—for security reasons. Second, he'd confessed to her once that his life had gone off a cliff. Third, the University President had apparently tired of his life, no longer feeling comfortable in the seat of power and terrified about how his life might end.

So, Caitlyn reflexively backed into self-defense mode. She was determined to dive back into the personnel files of faculty who had unsuccessfully sought tenure at the university the past few years. Those case histories doubtless contained investigative clues.

Neil Braxton was a case in point. He presented a complicated situation on a few levels—socially, politically, and who knew what else. His tenure case had been contentious, the worst ever. Caitlyn had opposed his application mainly because he lacked any meaningful body of academic research.

Braxton had been on campus for several years, but academically he was all show and no substance. He was politically active and routinely wrote opinion pieces for state and local newspapers and magazines, while other professors filled time correcting papers, doing clinical and basic research, writing textbooks, and seeking major foundation grants.

Caitlyn had long pondered the bizarre relationship between Uzinski and Moisescu, but when Braxton got added to the mix, the bizarre had turned ridiculous. In fact, as time passed and her duties as personnel committee chair gave her access to a bevy of personnel secrets, Caitlyn could see that Neil Braxton had a special place at Coronado University. He leveraged the gaps in his academic schedule by spending a great deal of time on and off campus with President Uzinski, meeting and greeting local personalities and business movers and shakers and entertaining various out-of-town donors to the university, particularly promoters and fund executives from the Stutts Foundation.

Many months before her committee considered his tenure application, Caitlyn realized that Coronado had probably hired Braxton to be the cheerleader and money-man connection to the wealthy Stutts Foundation. Liberal-leaning woke professors for hire. The campus teemed with political activism, banners, and signs hanging from windows and doors. Cancel culture and antisemitism thrived at campus rallies, where conservative-leaning speakers were screamed at and hounded off campus. BLM advocates and Arab groups like Peace and Justice in Palestine harassed Jewish students while the Administration remained silent.

The Stutts Foundation had directed Braxton's tenure application. And so, the refusal of the personnel committee to recommend tenure had possibly infuriated some important people.

Caitlyn shook her head as she emerged from her thoughts. She had upheld the decision of her UPC. She had spoken for the good of Coronado University and against Braxton's tenure. But while that was all true, she had to admit it didn't imply he might have committed murder, no matter how much she despised him. She needed to learn more about the backgrounds and possible motives of *all* the tenure candidates, for sure.

$$9$$

TYRANNY IN ACADEME

In past-life regression, souls progress through many lifetimes. In these lifetimes, you could experience your life as a man or a woman.

— Ellenmorris Tiegerman

The crime notwithstanding, school administration matters continued in their normal course. In the wake of Uzinski's murder, Caitlyn was not savoring the next committee meeting. The rules laid out in the all-powerful Blue Book required that at each meeting, Caitlyn, as the chair, review tenure procedures to refamiliarize everyone with the peer review process.

The UPC meetings invariably included a debate about campus politics. Now, a new and rather large distraction would be added into Caitlyn's much-practiced routine, as Inspector Robertson was slated to appear as an "invited" guest. Rest assured, she thought, his official presence, unpleasant mission, and intrusive questioning would not be an insignificant disruptive force. But Caitlyn was determined to control the Inspector like she did everyone else.

The UPC met on the second floor of the Administration building, in meeting room 202, which sat right beneath the now-deceased President's office suite and scene of the crime. Room 202 sat above room 102, Provost Moisescu's office suite on the ground floor. The synergies were eerie. As she climbed up the central staircase to the second floor, Caitlyn bumped into several colleagues engrossed in the recent awful but scintillating news. Not wishing to be delayed, she stepped around the talkative ones, nodded and smiled, and continued to the meeting room. The sign in the slot mounted on the door read UNIVERSITY PERSONNEL COMMITTEE. On the doorknob a cardboard sign, hanging slightly askew, read MEETING IN PROGRESS—DO NOT ENTER.

She entered through the small, square office attached to the larger meeting room, at the center of which was a conference table long enough to seat at least twenty people.

Committee secretary Angela Rivers occupied the small anteroom. Angela had been an undergraduate student in the English department at CU. While in school, she'd supported herself as a secretary in the History department and loved it so much she never left the secretarial pool. Carla Breyers had taken Angela under her wing. Six years earlier, Angela had been promoted to administrative assistant to the UPC, and she continued taking academic courses for personal enrichment. Angela was a 1960s throwback to psychedelic "flower children" and wore combinations of loose-fitting clothes to cover an overweight frame that never saw the inside of a gym. Attractive in a dramatic sort of way, with lots of makeup and hair spray, above all she was a phenomenal secretary who could type as fast as anyone could talk. She also recorded each UPC meeting with precision. When

Caitlyn was preparing to dictate letters to the Administration, Angela always told her, "Professor Morrys, all I need right now is a large red lollipop!" Today they limited their interaction to a smile and a perfunctory hello.

As committee members shuffled here and there around the conference table, the buzz of conversation was focused on President Uzinski's murder and their individual experiences navigating Robertson's intrusive interviews. And while most seemed fascinated by the emerging details of the now days-long murder investigation, no one exhibited any sadness about the tragedy. The truth was that virtually none of them had known Uzinski well.

Caitlyn assumed the head of the table, banged her gavel, and called the meeting to order. "Colleagues, we have a great deal to cover since this is our first meeting of the academic year. Please open the folder bearing your name on the front and get the meeting agenda. Before we begin, we each are aware of recent events on campus and have received by registered mail, as required by law, notice that Inspector Robertson from the governor's office will join us later."

"What's this all about, Caitlyn?" Ash asked sharply, speaking over everyone else's questions. "Questions by policemen should be handled in private." He glared around the table. "Everyone should be upset," he snapped, and then stared fixedly at Caitlyn.

"We'll talk about the Inspector shortly," she said to the whole group, quietly pitching her voice down. "Let's just get through our regular business, Ash, okay?"

"No, it's not okay. I got that officious message from the governor's office too. What's the Inspector doing here questioning us?" he asked, leaning forward with his eyebrows arched and his teeth clenched. "He's already talked to me at some length. Does he need to air *all* our private business in front of everyone?"

Caitlyn smiled ingratiatingly, knowing he hated these polite little mind games. He often told her how administrative politeness made him puke. "Ashford Connor, you're getting upset about nothing. The Inspector paid me a visit and basically invited himself to our meeting." She nodded at him. "And you are surely aware the police can gain access to *all* our records if they wish. I'd like to avoid unnecessary talks with the police, but we certainly don't want to appear as if we have anything to hide here, except our old, yellowing files." She looked directly into his eyes as she emphasized each word.

"Oh, just *protected* personnel file questions, then," Ash responded, leaning back and feeling foolish, a little boy who'd lost his temper over something silly.

"Yes, Professor Connor, most UPC meetings are about reviewing UPC files. He's saving time. Old files, that's all we have, nothing of interest to anyone. You know that." She spoke slowly, emphasizing the last few words.

Ash rubbed his nose and shook his head. "Okay, Caitlyn, Professor Conklin and I were curious. We got information on the guy in a computer search. He's from Arizona, was a decorated Tucson cop and later ran an investigative agency that uncovered various scandals involving a state senator, a state House speaker, a US senator, and even a governor. He also busted an *Arizona Republic* editor named Pat Murphy for killing an elderly woman in a hit-and-run. He's a devotee of Korean karate and a guest on talk shows because he knows where bodies are buried.

"The *Arizona Republic*, which evidently hates Robertson for a successful libel suit against them in 1988, listed his decorations in the US Marine Corps. During the Tet Offensive, he earned a Purple Heart and Bronze Star when his Fifth Marine Regiment retook Hue City and discovered almost three thousand civilians in unmarked graves, shot in the head by the retreating North Vietnamese Army.

"He was recruited from Quantico Marine base into Operation Mongoose and worked out of the CIA's Miami Field Office, training anti-Castro Cubans in the Everglades, raiding into Cuba and smuggling refugees out. Florida police records reveal that Robertson spent two months in the Dade County jail with other CIA special ops members for conspiracy to break the Neutrality Act and conspiracy to smuggle weapons of war. After Operation Mongoose officially ended, all American CIA members of Alpha 66 were released, and all those set-piece political charges were dropped by suddenly disinterested US Justice Department prosecutors."

"A Purple Heart means he was wounded, right?" Caitlyn asked, vaguely visualizing prior dreams.

Ash nodded and grimaced. "Robertson was wounded at Hue. Supposedly his Marine Corps specialties were rifleman and demolitions instructor—an explosives expert *and* expert rifle shot. Now he's semi-retired, and the governor appointed him as his Chief Inspector in the Inspector General's office. According to a friend of mine in our Criminal Justice School, he also purports to be a literary agent and is quite the courtroom witness showman." Ash turned to the small, balding man in wrinkled corduroy hunched at the table to his right. "Professor Conklin, what've you got?"

Conklin put on his outsized reading glasses and pulled out a large file of newspaper and magazine stories, which he began methodically to lay out side by side across the table.

Caitlyn thrust her right arm forward to halt Conklin. "No, no, no, Professor Conklin, dear, we don't have time for an academic lecture here. We can agree you've done a thorough search on the Inspector's life. That is wonderful, but this is not the time and place for a debriefing. Just highlights, please," she said, smiling.

Conklin reinserted everything into the folder and pushed it down the table to Caitlyn. "Well, you and Ashford can look at it later," he said. "The Inspector is a man of contrasts. Ashford, did you find the anti-Castro American mercenary story in any of Robertson's four books?"

"I remember, you said something about his CIA mercenary days, right?" Ash said.

Conklin nodded. "The first one, yes, but others are about actual investigations in Arizona and Mexico. He investigated some famous people and wrote about them using fake names, but you can tell who they are by his descriptions. One Robertson book features Goldwater, the Giancanas, and a famous scandal about a young, martyred newspaper reporter named Don Bolles whose car was blown up. The guy who ordered him killed was Kemper Marley, a bigtime, well-connected Scottsdale landowner and permanent member of the so-called Phoenix 40. He had connections to Pete Licavoli of Detroit and Sam Giancana of Chicago and through both families to Arizona senator John McCain's father-in-law, Jim Hensley." Conklin paused in thought. "I didn't even know there *were* such books around, and I've lived and worked in Arizona often over the last forty years. Did anyone else?" He removed his reading glasses and looked around the room at all the shaking heads.

"I would've remembered his bald head," Ash said, patting the top of his head and pursing his lips tightly for effect, which drew chuckles around the table.

"Let's move this along," Ted Carlisle snapped angrily from his seat on Caitlyn's immediate right, next to Conklin.

Carlisle was the typical absent-minded professor who wore plaid shirts and worn jeans. Caitlyn had worked with this near-sighted bear of a man for years. A depressive personality with a sour sense of the world, he was constantly late to classes. But he was a brilliant mathematician, a quiet but effective researcher. Caitlyn enjoyed his underlying sweetness but couldn't help feeling uncomfortable with his awkward attempts to express his obvious attraction to her.

"And this guy sounds like a weak sister in spite of all his service," Carlisle continued. "This Robertson has grown old bouncing from job to job and writing books criticizing people instead of doing something himself, something worthy of a *real* full-time career."

"He fought in Vietnam and has been in law enforcement and the CIA most of his life," Caitlyn objected.

"But law enforcement and the CIA are damn near the same thing," Carlisle answered.

"Don't underestimate him," Ash groused. "There's something unusual in all the articles and stories. The Inspector is not your typical brain-dead bureaucrat. He's a no-nonsense iconoclast. He's no easy pushover, and we won't be able to outtalk him—or outthink him, for that matter." Ash shook his head. "We certainly won't be able to intimidate him. He's reputed to be incorruptible. There's nothing more daunting than an honest man with a sense of moral justice. Nor does he seem to care what people think politically, either."

"Robertson is obviously a nightmare for his superiors," Carlisle said, "but they use him when they need a club, a political wit who can handle the press as needed. When there's a messy case, and that's what we have here, the state sends Robertson. The campus police admire his work, but they apparently don't like him much."

Ash pointed at Caitlyn. "He's dangerously independent, just like our Caitlyn here."

This last remark drew amused smiles and sideways glances.

"And what's that supposed to mean?" Caitlyn said, faking annoyance but welcoming the silence. "Let's complete today's work before the notorious Inspector gets here. We'll work in small groups. I want to remind all of you that we are on a tight schedule. And although the Inspector aims to extract as much information as he can about our personnel files and tenure candidates, we will, if necessary, seek court intervention to keep the files sealed. Our attorneys can request that the judge review files on camera. Our personnel files are private and protected.

"All of our reports for new tenure candidates must be completed and submitted to the Provost's office by the end of the semester. You have student interviews, peer interviews, administrative interviews, and, of course, interviews with outside faculty reviewers. This must all be completed confidentially, and then each candidate's application must be reviewed by us.

"We will vote by secret ballot on whether to support or deny tenure, or promote. I will write the final report on each candidate for submission to the Provost. We must adhere to the timeline or we will jeopardize the candidates' reviews. Once we've started, I want to strategize on how to best present each case. The fact that no one has received tenure here for the past several years is disconcerting. Maybe I'm paranoid, but we have a clear pattern, and this secretive Stutts Foundation seems to be the organizing force behind it."

Silence fell around the table.

"Well, enough said! I've given all of you assignments, but let's go over the list to make sure everyone agrees. Let's start with the first page."

Caitlyn distributed a multipage agenda. Papers riffled and glasses were adjusted as everyone began to review the various assignments.

She started with the first three on the title page:

Tenure Review 2017–18

1. Professor Axelrod Tierney	Outside Review	Professor Morrys (Psychology)
2. Professor Eric Andrews	Early Tenure Review	Professor Prentice (Chemistry)
3. Professor Maryann Mathews	Tenure Review	Professor Morrys (Psychology)
		Professor Connor (Anthropology)

"The first candidate is Axelrod Tierney, whose outside review is set for later this month. As I mentioned at our last meeting, I'll handle the Tierney tenure matter. I'll prepare our recent report from the last meeting and represent our tenure recommendation to the ORC.

"Second, Eric Andrews of the Biology department is up for early tenure review. Professor Prentice will report our request to the now-deceased President's office, which will be taken to Provost Moisescu. I'll accompany Professor

Prentice unofficially, for obvious reasons. Does that assignment sound okay?"

Caitlyn stopped reading and scanned the table. "Yes? Good. As I've noted, Eric is requesting an early tenure review against my advice. I cautioned him against it because the school's standard for early tenure review is higher than what is required for a normal tenure review. I didn't get into Professor Maryann Matthews's early tenure review, but he's aware of it." *Motive . . . motive . . . motive*, she thought.

Caitlyn raised her head and smiled. "There are evidently no secrets about tenure on this campus. In any case, Professor Andrews was emphatic that if he doesn't get tenure now, he is leaving to return to private industry. His comments were not off the record and should be part of our official report. In any event, according to Carla, it is all over campus. Professor Andrews said, and I quote: 'I won't waste my time at this second-rate university anymore. I am sick of its silly, Stutts-inbred bureaucratic machine and all the political crap here.'" She lowered her voice. "It might be politically incorrect for the chair to admit, but I'm sorry that Coronado University stands to lose yet another talented young scholar."

Murmurs spread around the room, many with not-so-veiled references to the Stutts Foundation.

Caitlyn dropped her papers to the table, raised her hands, and announced over the committee buzz, "The next candidate is that *same* Maryann Mathews from Education." She decided that discussion about university politics would consume too much time for this particular meeting. "It's important for the committee to remember that Professor Mathews came up for an early tenure review a year ago. We supported her candidacy, but Provost Moisescu did not. She is going through the normal process now. We need to review her last report and all the Provost's nasty comments, since the same issues will come up this time."

"Doctor Death outdid himself." Carlisle nodded in sad agreement.

Caitlyn didn't hide her disgust. She had heard privately that Provost Moisescu had made crass, highly inappropriate comments about Maryann Mathews to some unsuspecting male faculty. Everyone in the room also knew about those comments, but she felt a need to remind them. "As we all are aware, our Provost said something like 'Mathews is an example of an obnoxious liberated lesbian.' Can you *believe* that?"

Carlisle spread his hands open in agreement. "Of course. That misogynistic creep would say anything about women. He doesn't like women—or men, either, anymore, I hear."

Moisescu's supposedly off-the-record remarks had spread throughout the faculty like a forest fire after the UPC had given written notice of her prospective re-evaluation. Caitlyn knew Mathews was an outstanding candidate, so despite Moisescu's opinion—or because of it—Caitlyn had encouraged her to reapply for tenure review, in spite of the Provost's displeasure.

Also, she was a woman and a good friend, and Caitlyn chaired the committee.

Maybe she shouldn't have pushed a reluctant candidate to reapply for tenure. But because of the time she'd invested in the process, Caitlyn felt responsible for Mathews. She was determined to do the right thing and make amends to a fine scholar, and she could not believe that Moisescu, the supposedly disinterested Provost, would block Mathews again.

Caitlyn countered, "Mathews was the best thing that ever happened to the Education department. She energized a dead department and single-handedly rewrote the teaching curriculum. If anyone deserves tenure at CU, it's Maryann. She is also published. She wrote three major textbooks on disability inclusion in children's education, which were controversial and topical."

"She's at the cutting edge on disability politics," Carlisle added, "just like you are, Caitlyn."

Caitlyn nodded at him and began the brief introduction needed for committee review. "Education for all children with disabilities is undergoing proposed instructional reforms in US public schools. So-called inclusionists say children with disabilities should be educated *inside*, not outside, regular general education classrooms. They oppose a parallel special education system and separating children for any reason. Many teachers and parents are vehemently opposed to the 'all children' concept because they say 'all' children with disabilities apparently cannot benefit from the Gen Ed setting." She shook her head in irritation.

"She's stealing your thunder, Caitlyn," Ash interposed, smiling and goading at the same time, seeking to inspire some provocative woman-to-woman conflict.

Caitlyn stood, glared at Ash, and crossed her arms over her chest. "You're wrong, Ash. Maryann Mathews did more. She challenged the trend. She wrote about disability inclusion as a managed-care approach to education." Caitlyn's tone darkened. "Mathews argued the less-is-more approach for children with disabilities was dangerous."

"Gutsy woman, arguing against the Special Ed Mafia," Ash remarked.

Caitlyn looked down at him and lowered her voice again. "Right, Ash. And Maryann Mathews has been quoted in local and national newspapers and appeared on local talk shows. She has spoken to state legislators about educational policies and is now the most publicly recognized professor at CU. So ask yourself, why wasn't she granted early tenure?"

"Right, so why not, and what happened?"

The room went quiet. The committee members took in Caitlyn's anger-contorted face. She combed her fingers through her hair, arched her back self-consciously, and stretched her arms out to the side, wiggling her hands to relieve the pressure.

Ash reached up, patted her arm affectionately, and smiled at her. "Caitlyn, you might as well tell them the rest," he said. "Get it off your chest. Tell them about Provost Timur Moisescu's letter. Remind them of his message on Mathews's last tenure report. It's been eating at you for the longest time."

Caitlyn nodded. She spoke softly, carefully directing her words to each committee member in turn and reminding them of their prior evaluation of Mathews. "Last time, Mathews was unanimously supported by her colleagues, her students, and this personnel committee, but *not* by Provost Moisescu." She was gratified by unanimous nods of recollection. "When Provost Moisescu wrote his final report, not only did he deny Mathews tenure, but he also had to verbally attack her. He called Mathews's writings 'narrow, faddish, not scientific, and not basic research, therefore not significant or comparable to true academic intellectual inquiry.' His comments belittled her scholarship, and his ignorant put-down of her work with children was appalling." Caitlyn shook her head and then tossed her mussed hair back again, barely able to control her anger. *Motive ... motive ... motive,* she thought angrily. "Then Moisescu viciously added that any high school teacher could have written Mathews's textbooks. And the worst was still to come. Our cowardly, and now late, President refused Mathews even an explanation. It was all arbitrary and capricious—and quite personal."

Ash began to gesture and interrupt, but Caitlyn held up a hand and continued, "If Mathews isn't good enough, then *no one's* getting tenure at Coronado—that's my fear. That's what's eating me, my dear colleagues."

Ash filled the sudden silence. "The question is, what does Maryann do now?"

Caitlyn began again. "Professor Mathews told me she felt she'd invested so much of herself and her life in the university that she didn't have the energy to go somewhere else. After all this time, how could she go to the University of Oregon or Georgia State and start all over again? It took all her resources to move out here. Besides, what would they offer her as an Assistant Professor at Oregon or Georgia? No, Mathews is going to dig in her heels and fight this one out. She's angry and disillusioned. Thank God she hasn't had access to Uzinski's and Moisescu's annual review reports. She'd be crushed."

The silence that followed reeked of shared frustration, resignation, and anger.

Ash finally spoke. "You have done everything humanly possible to support her. No one will stand up to the Administration like you do. We all know you, Caitlyn, so bring it on."

On cue, the rest of the committee nodded agreement.

Caitlyn shook her head, too distraught to speak, and kept her eyes down for several seconds. She sipped her coffee, exhaled, and looked around the table. "I appreciate your support. As you may have guessed, I have decided to fight for Professor Maryann Mathews now because, for the first time in many years, we have no President to refuse her. For the first time, our committee will be operating on the level of a single, onetime review and appeal. This is our big chance."

Caitlyn looked at each member in turn for nods of positive fellowship. "All of you must be aware that, until Coronado University has a new President, we will be operating in a new, more difficult universe, dealing only with our infamous Provost. He is certainly a difficult obstacle. But this unique collision of dire events is an enormous opportunity—yes, full of unpleasantness and risk, but one that conjures up an equally painful administrative conundrum from the recent past, that of Professor Neil Braxton."

"Let's take a break first, Chairwoman Morrys," Conklin suggested.

10

CONFIDENTIAL PARANOIA

We have debts that must be paid. If we have not paid out these debts, then we must take them into another life. — Brian Weiss

Most UPC members had served on other university committees. They knew how tenure cases bloated the campus rumor mill, even though only they had access to actual specifics and were sworn to secrecy. This only made tenure matters worse for each committee member, because paranoia was life's breath to an academic respiratory system, and tenure research overflowed with the closely held achievements, failures, and past secrets of candidates. Everyone knew Neil Braxton was a Stutts appointment.

As usual, Professor Connor was first to speak, and free with an opinion. "There are three kinds of academic pigs who dig for expensive academic truffles in all the dark places: ass-kissers, ass-lickers, and ass-suckers. Moisescu is all the above with those Stutts professors."

Caitlyn nodded to no one in particular. "We can't have a repeat of what happened with this committee and the Stutts Foundation! Remember the letters about the need to eliminate the entire unfair, illegal tenure process from American universities?" She looked around the table as each member nodded. "Moisescu publicized his opinions and our responses all over campus about the secret vagaries of the tenure process. Remember the newspaper articles and TV shows about an antiquated system stifling creative and expressive people at universities? He said a cumbersome bureaucracy grants lifetime jobs to the walking dead in higher education. We didn't support Braxton for tenure, and so he used this committee's denial to dismantle the whole system.

"Now we are left with an uncontrollable, vituperative professor who's actually supposed to be leaving but won't. Since he was supposedly Uzinski's pet, I have no idea what central administration will do with this case, particularly with the President gone."

She surveyed the table. Silence.

"Few faculty were willing to risk their professional careers against a university's bureaucratic machine that could bring trumped-up charges to deny or eliminate their tenure. Arbitration cases are time-consuming and expensive."

"It is safer to watch and wait," Conklin commented. Others nodded.

"On another note," Ash said, "I want to remind everyone that our discussions and reports must remain confidential—specifically, there were all kinds of difficulties last year because of rumors and leaks of confidential information. In addition, you all know something about the sexual harassment litigation matter last year in which Uzinski subpoenaed one of our files. We sought to quash the subpoena and release of confidential faculty documents to the Administration."

"No more today." Caitlyn looked at Ash and shook her head. Ash nodded, and she continued, "Today the important issue for this committee is protecting the confidentiality of our personnel files. We have professional careers to protect. When the school received the Mathews subpoena, Moisescu called me and directed I turn over the files to Uzinski. I refused. I reminded him the file was still confidential and the UPC would not now—or *ever*—turn over a faculty file to the Administration." She tossed her hair back and glared around the table. "At that point, colleagues, as you can imagine, the Provost reverted to his inveterate and characteristic abusive threats. He informed me if I did not turn over the personnel file by two p.m. that day, he'd instruct the university's attorneys to sue me and every member of our committee."

Caitlyn looked around and smiled sweetly at each face around the conference table. "Of course, I did *not* turn it over. A lawyer I know said he'd represent the committee pro bono. So *their* attorney met with *our* attorney to discuss the file. The meeting was quite interesting from a legalistic point of view, given the issue of academic confidentiality and that several such cases have reached the Supreme Court. But I stopped Doctor Death. As usual, Moisescu transformed civil discussion into threats and gripes about the 'lazy' faculty."

"So, Caitlyn, you played Doctor Shrink to Doctor Death?" teased Ash.

"Really couldn't help but do anything else." Caitlyn sighed. "He is so patently hostile, I could barely restrain myself. In any case, we submitted our confidential file to the court with relevant names redacted. The judge decided that the file's contents weren't relevant to the harassment case. The Administration didn't get to see it."

"To my way of thinking, that was a close call. Too close," Ash said, scanning faces. "Even though it happened in the context of a lawsuit, it might have established a dangerous precedent, or at least emboldened the Administration to expand the circumstances under which it might try to grab confidential faculty files. If administrators got access to them, it would threaten our entire review process. They simply aren't entitled to that information. Can you imagine what Moisescu could do with all the personal data? As President of the union, I can say coercion and blackmail would be the absolute least of it all."

Caitlyn nodded and raised a fist. "*Veni, vidi, vici,* said conqueror Ashford Connor."

"Admit it, Caitlyn, as a psychologist, you know we're justified in being paranoid about Moisescu."

"How else could we all have survived these last years?" she said with a nod.

Carlisle raised his hand and turned to Ash. "Where's this going?"

"It's not just this case, Carlisle," Ash replied. "The administrative manipulation has been going on for years. Think about all the junior faculty we've lost—the talent, the energy, and the creativity that have died here. This university is like a withered old tree. Think about all the faculty denied tenure.

"Police investigating Uzinski's murder will wonder who has a motive. With Uzinski, who doesn't have a motive? Who isn't a suspect? The list of pissed-off faculty is so long that nosy Inspector Robertson will be months interviewing faculty and going through files. Remember the warning from *Catch-22*: Just because you're paranoid doesn't mean someone's not after you." Ash's laugh sounded hollow.

"Who is the paranoid one here, Professor Connor?" Caitlyn said, recalling text in the DSM-5:

> The essential feature of paranoid personality disorder is a pattern of pervasive distrust such that

their motives are interpreted as malevolent. Individuals with this disorder assume other people will exploit, harm, or deceive them even if no evidence exists to support this expectation.

"Was Uzinski paranoid?" she asked. "Maybe he should have been."

Ash gave her a thumbs-up. "Was he, Caitlyn? You got to know him, didn't you?"

"Not really." Caitlyn shook her head. "Mathews's case was difficult and complicated. Believe it or not, Maryann was recruited by Uzinski from some federal agency, probably the Department of Education. I think she was set up for failure as her tenure case unfolded. She was evidently handpicked by Provost Moisescu to set an example and undermine tenure in general."

"The union, Caitlyn, the union," Ash interjected. "There's no faculty without a union, all of you seem to miss the point here."

He pushed his chair back abruptly, stood, and walked across the room to the coffeepot. "Not that I want to shift the conversation, but where are the chocolate chip cookies?" Ashford Connor, the "chocoholic," made sure his reputation followed him everywhere.

Caitlyn recalled that Ash had once told her how important chocolate was. "It's somewhere between sex and breathing," he'd said, and laughed at her surprise. "Caitlyn you're too serious, all that thinking will make you constipated."

Surprise had turned to amusement, and she laughed so hard she thought she would wet her pants. Only Ash made her laugh like that.

"You know, Caitlyn, when you laugh, you radiate. I love to make you laugh," he said, and then he'd kissed her neck and shoulders while enfolding her in his strong arms.

"Damn it, Caitlyn, where the hell are you today? Haven't you heard a single thing I've said?" Ash said impatiently.

"Oh, shut up, Ashford, can't you see she's tired and upset? You really can be an insensitive jerk sometimes," Carlisle snapped.

"I'm upset, too, going through withdrawal, Carlisle. I need my chocolate chip cookies," Ash shot back, continuing to grumble under his breath.

"Caitlyn, you look ghastly. I'll finish up this Greek tragedy," Carlisle said, ignoring Ash's last remark. "To begin all this, our Education department went through a search process and recommended three possible candidates, all men. They didn't want someone like Maryann Mathews shoved down their throats but wanted to choose their own candidate. At first, Provost Moisescu rejected them and told the department to accept whomever they were sent, or they would get nobody—Ash, what are you doing, man?"

"I'm tasting all the cookies and they all suck. You can continue, Carlisle. I'm busy," Ash said, picking the nuts out of a very large cookie.

"Well, you're distracting us, do you mind?"

"Do you mind? Do you mind?" Ash mimicked. "Yes, I mind. Chocolate chip cookies are more important than rehashing this story again. I'm tired of going over this stuff. I want my chocolate chip cookies fresh. These have been sitting around for days."

Caitlyn slammed her coffee mug down. It shattered and coffee spilled over the table and dripped onto the floor. There was silence. "Stop it, Ash, please. I've now got a throbbing headache, and I don't give a damn about your cookies." Caitlyn reached for her briefcase.

Ash poured her a glass of water, not fazed by her at all. "Lucky the cup wasn't full, Caitlyn." He grabbed some napkins and wiped up the mess. "Okay, you've gotten our attention. Now what?"

She looked at his sheepish grin and then into his large, soulful eyes. *Does anything get under his skin? I've certainly tried.* She shook her head, took a deep breath, and then sighed as he conspicuously stared at her.

"Carlisle, please get on with it," Conklin said.

"Provost Moisescu picked Mathews *then* because he knew the Education department would never accept her. Believe me, Doctor Death is no supporter of women, and—"

"That, my dear Conklin," Ash said, still picking at the cookies, "is an understatement. I'd venture to say, Moisescu never had a mother and was hatched in a dead tree by a hermaphrodite heron." Everyone laughed, bringing on a noticeable release of tension in the room. Even Caitlyn cracked a smile.

"Very good, Ash," Carlisle continued. "I'll have to remember that one. In any case, the Education department was wrong, and we all knew it. Moisescu picked Mathews because he knew we would support her. We knew she was a star. It was a way to split the faculty. The whole thing was disgusting. And then at the very end, Doctor Death denied her tenure anyway. What an unholy mess. This was just what he wanted, faculty fighting faculty." Carlisle shrugged. "Do you all understand how diabolical the whole thing was? We didn't see it coming."

"Mathews didn't see it either. She was young and idealistic," Caitlyn said. "She for sure didn't have a clue she was being used by the Provost as a test case."

"We need to get back to the union," Ash said. "The current events on campus only make the Mathews case more painful. Caitlyn, you've lived and breathed these cases to the point of fanaticism and—"

"Someone else used that word about me today, Ash," Caitlyn said in a near whisper.

"Who are you talking about, dear?"

"Inspector Robertson. Remember, he's coming here to see us today."

"Oh, right, to treat us as suspects," Conklin blurted, his glasses slipping down his face.

"No, no, the Inspector only has questions about the peer review process," Caitlyn said calmly, rubbing her forehead.

They all started talking at once, questions, comments, voices all around getting louder and louder. Caitlyn waited for everyone to quiet down. The group never decided anything simply. Each eccentric in their own way, they discussed and dissected ad nauseam. Often they got into discussions about why they were discussing what they were discussing, without even realizing that was what they were doing.

She realized she loved being a university professor.

"Caitlyn, what specifically is the Inspector going to ask us?" Conklin said nervously, pulling at a button on his shirt like a kindergartener afraid the teacher might call on him. "Our committee meetings are confidential."

She shook her head at Conklin. "But the governor authorized this investigation, and Inspector Robertson is his direct representative."

Caitlyn focused on Ash. "Am I right, Ash?"

He smiled at her. "Right you are, Professor Morrys."

She smiled back, telling him with her eyes how much she loved him. It was sometimes hard keeping their personal relationship separate from their professional one.

"The Inspector wants to ask some questions about tenure. He can ask anything he wants to, but he's only getting answers about our procedures, not our people," she said emphatically.

"Hey," Ash added, "let's focus on what's important. These cookies suck. Really, Caitlyn, can't they send better stuff to our meetings? You'd think Provost Death would appreciate all the work we do for the university and send us better chocolate chip cookies." Taking a rejected cookie, he aimed for the wastebasket, arching his arm for a curving long shot. "In! Okay!"

Caitlyn tuned him out and returned her attention to how the personal connection between Maryann Mathews and President Uzinski had become obvious—good *or* bad. She sensed something in the chaos. She needed to see whether there was any evidence to support Robertson's suspicions about tenure as a motive for murder. *Is there something in the tenure application files, tucked away in the Records room, that would give someone away?*

"Oh, my dear colleagues," Caitlyn proclaimed, "this academic haven of ours has been compromised."

"Listen, we're all stressing out here. I think we need a break," Carlisle said, adjusting his papers, standing up and stretching.

"Okay, that's a good idea. The Inspector's not scheduled to arrive at an exact time."

"Yes, I need to wake up a little," Ash stated emphatically, and also stood up.

"We need more coffee," Caitlyn said, remaining seated. "I need it desperately. I'm going to brew up a fresh pot and do some more file research." No one was listening to her. They had disassembled into a bunch of sidebars.

A polite knock interrupted everyone. All turned toward the bald man with the bowtie standing in the door. He had arrived early. Caitlyn smiled to herself. It was a strategy she'd have employed herself.

11

DEADLY FOCUS

How do you feel about experiencing multiple religions, genders, and races across lifetimes? — Ellenmorris Tiegerman

"Why, this must be our guest," Ash said, motioning the Inspector into the conference room with a dramatic wave of his hand and offering him a seat near the head of the table.

"How nice," Robertson remarked, sitting in the chair and looking around at everyone. "Hope I'm not interfering too much, Professor Morrys."

Caitlyn glared at the Inspector's smiling face. "Please just ask your questions, we are very busy with tenure reviews."

"Okay, Professor, I see you're very stressed by these events."

"No, I'm not," she said abruptly and angrily.

Ash tapped his pen on the table, and Caitlyn looked into his bottomless eyes. "You're tired, Professor Caitlyn," he said. "Do let the Inspector proceed so we can get on with all this."

There was a long pause while Inspector Robertson took off his glasses and cleaned the lenses with a large blue handkerchief that matched his pressed shirt. He took his time, put on the glasses, looked slowly around at every name card, and began. "Listen, I'm not going to ask any questions about the tenure candidates because I know Professor Morrys and Coronado University set the ground rules long before I got here. Isn't that right, Professor?" He smiled at her all the way down the table, and his eyes twinkled.

Caitlyn pursed her lips tightly and rolled her eyes.

"What can any of you tell me about President Uzinski?" he said, ignoring at the top the agreed-upon scope of his interrogation. "You know, background or any peculiarities." The Inspector smiled. "This was a very odd murder. I mean, his pants were pulled down, a knife in his back, a flower—interesting, very interesting." Robertson looked around the table slowly, from face to face, but no one spoke. He turned to Caitlyn. "Professor Morrys, why not take the lead to get this group talking to me?"

She took a deep breath. "Uzinski was brought in years ago to raise money, transform the appearance of a somewhat neglected university, and invigorate a besieged faculty."

"Isn't that a little overly dramatic, Professor?" Robertson said.

"No," Ash interjected, "she's right. The grant from the Stutts Foundation allowed Uzinski to create ten endowed chairs. The Stutts advisors apparently saw themselves as an elite group of academicians with a mission distinctively different from the rest of the faculty. They were obnoxious, condescending assholes. Does that give you a better sense of things, Inspector?"

"Nice, very nice, Professor Ashford Connor. Is there anyone else?" Robertson raised his eyebrows. "Why don't we just go around the table and give everyone a chance?" He turned first to Professor Carlisle and nodded expectantly.

"Ash is correct, the Stutts people didn't work with us as colleagues," Carlisle began. "They didn't live in or come from the surrounding community, state, or country, even. They didn't want to have anything to do with us. They were certainly paid undisclosed off-budget salaries, probably more than full professors who'd been at Coronado for years. Uzinski justified their extraordinary salaries, as well as his own, by arguing that Coronado was a sleepy little hollow. To attract extraordinary people and maintain them at a second-rate institution, such as we evidently were, their salaries *had* to be extraordinary. He was persuasive but insulting. At meetings, he constantly asked us—his faculty—how 'distinguished scholars' could be recruited to Coronado University." Carlisle shook his head in fake disbelief and adjusted his ridiculously small glasses. "Uzinski, the visionary image maker, wanted to create what he called 'an island of distinction' in our little intellectual caste system. But he apparently based everything on class and money. Our academic society of so-called equal thinkers became a twisted culture divided by a hierarchy of distinctive classes—the haves and have nots. The Board of Trustees at Stutts evidently agreed with this elitist line of thinking, but the average faculty member around here felt it was an intentional slap in their face."

It was beginning to sound like a group therapy session. Carlisle had already said more than he normally did. Caitlyn needed to maintain control of the meeting, keep the members from saying too much. She raised her hand.

The Inspector noticed but ignored her. "Hmm, I see what you mean," he said. "Let's get back to Uzinski and his rather unseemly murder—"

"Inspector, there are appointment procedures here at Coronado University, and President Uzinski violated all of them," Caitlyn said calmly, trying to redirect the discussion.

"To pick up on Caitlyn's point"—Ash's voice was loud and strained—"Uzinski appointed Stutts professors, faculty procedures be damned! He intentionally violated the rules and challenged the union, and he wanted to rub our faces in it. This was about breaking the union, Inspector, I'm convinced of it. There was something going on with those Stutts professors. Where the hell did they come from and why were they here? Here, of all places, in the middle of nowhere."

"Goodness, Professor Connor, you sound as fanatical as Professor Morrys," Inspector Robertson remarked in a half-muttered aside while looking directly at Caitlyn.

"Don't answer him, Ash, he's trying to goad you," Caitlyn said.

"So? Maybe he is, but I've had my fill of Uzinski and his henchmen. Can you imagine how we felt when we read the insulting crap he leaked to the press? 'President Uzinski has recruited an outstanding group of scholars by means of a worldwide search!'" Ash smoothed his hands down the legs of his pants, leaned his head back on his chair, closed his eyes, and breathed deeply.

Caitlyn was amazed. She'd never seen Ash so upset— ever. She looked at him lovingly, wanting to comfort him.

Robertson was staring at her. He presumably knew all about Ash. How could the Inspector know what she was thinking? *That's impossible. Yet, he's familiar. I know him in my flashbacks. The blood. The wars. The battles.*

Ash opened his eyes and continued speaking through clenched teeth. "I'm president of the Faculty Union. To make matters worse, the Board of Trustees did *not* follow established procedures when they hired President Uzinski. They didn't form a search committee. The board supposedly looked long and hard to find their visionary, their reactionary leader who would transform their little Coronado University into a grand old Ivy League liberal arts college."

Caitlyn raised her hand in caution. "Curricula are not at issue here, Professor—"

"But they failed, didn't they?" Ash interrupted, making a sweeping gesture around the table and shaking his head in disgust. "And to think, Coronado University's social and clinical programs were once nationally known." He shook his head again. "But Uzinski did not believe in clinical programs. Over the years he carefully dismantled many of the doctoral and graduate programs in the professional schools to build up undergraduate enrollment with an elite group of students. Uzinski was an exceptionally good fundraiser, and, to his credit, he got the Stutts Foundation to extend the school a twenty-million-dollar development grant for campus improvements and scholarships to recruit foreign students. Now this university, which used to accept students primarily from the state and local areas, has a thirty-five percent foreign undergraduate enrollment, particularly from the Middle East. Saudi Arabia. Qatar. Bahrain. Lebanon. Egypt. Jordan. Have you seen the student groups and signs on campus?"

"Why is your peer review document—your Blue Book— so important?" asked Robertson, refocusing the discussion.

Conklin cleared his throat loudly. "Inspector, I'm Professor Conklin. The Blue Book delineates the procedures that apply here from the time a professor is hired on a tenure track until and through the tenure review process. The tenure process is sacred to us and has historically adhered to strict guidelines for professional review by colleagues. Caitlyn would say we are obsessed with our procedures, process, and protocol. Let's say we cherish the teaching experience in our classrooms. Simply put, if administrators and bureaucrats control *who* teaches, then they also control *what* is being taught. Look at our campus. Have you noticed the banners? FREE PALESTINE NOW. The antisemitism and Jewish-free zones are notorious here. The Administration has allowed the anti-Israel, anti-Zionist rhetoric to flourish here, like it has on campuses across the country. Consider what's happening at Columbia University, UC Berkeley, NYU, and the University of Southern California. There is a nexus between the Stutts Foundation and Mical Bazyli, the ultraliberal multibillionaire."

"From my limited understanding," Robertson said, shaking his head slowly, "it appears that a committee like yours functions similarly to a medieval secret society like the Masons. I don't want to appear presumptuous, but most people are in the dark about your procedures. I never realized how complicated it was to receive tenure. I certainly never imagined there was such a concern about confidentiality."

"Inspector," Caitlyn said emphatically, "this isn't a romance novel! This committee protects the rights of the university's faculty to govern themselves. Decisions about tenure, membership, and course content are sacred to professors."

"That's your problem, Professor Morrys, you're too serious." Ash laughed sarcastically. "Why, I think this would make a great murder mystery novel. Inspector, perhaps we all could collaborate. On second thought, I think we should leave Professor Morrys out of this. I don't think she sees the humor in the murder scene—that's how I'd start the book. There's nothing that would capture the imagination of the general public more effectively than a cartoon of the President with his pants pulled down and"—he paused, leaning toward Caitlyn—"a white lily up his butt." His scornful laugh triggered a round of snickers around the table.

But Caitlyn just clenched her teeth and shook her head. "No, Ash—"

"Okay, okay, Professor Morrys, I'll stop." Ash caught his breath and regained control. He began again to describe the tenure review process.

Robertson shook his head. "It seems a rather long and complex process, Professor Connor."

"Inspector," Carlisle said, "this lengthy evaluation process is necessary because tenure is a commitment. It's like a lifetime appointment to the federal bench. It ensures that faculty, like members of the federal judiciary, will enjoy perpetual protection from external political forces or consequences. The Stutts professors are all Middle Eastern radicals who will control what our next generation of students and teachers will learn politically on campus: hate Israel, hate Jews. This is a master plan to take over campuses all over the country. The Stutts Foundation is doing an exploratory experiment here at Coronado University. If it succeeds, it will replicate and spread across American campuses faster than it's spreading now."

Caitlyn was uncomfortable with this. "And Inspector, you are giving our tenure process a very negative spin. I don't see it as long and complex. I see it as thorough."

"Now, now, Professor Morrys, I'm only here to gather information." Inspector Robertson raised both hands in mock surrender. "As I understand it, your interviews delve into the personal as well as professional lives of each candidate. The committee never divulges information discussed during its meetings. Still, it's curious that your personnel records remain locked away in secure files. They are closed forever to everyone, candidates included, save a handful of faculty members. You are thorough—if that makes you feel better—but you are notoriously secretive as well.

"Now, give me some history about the university," Robertson said, changing topics abruptly.

"I'll take this question," Conklin said. "The school was established in 1875 by missionaries who were traveling west but got no farther. Financial difficulties in the last four decades resulted in the Board of Trustees searching for a charismatic President who would develop a strong vision to reinvigorate the university. The board wanted a leader with a cause to advance educational reform and develop an image." Conklin's tone became sarcastic. "In searching high and low among all the leaders in higher education, this Board of Trustees chose a philanderer named Cartwright, and then a union breaker named Uzinski." Conklin nodded at Carlisle, an apparent baton pass.

"Inspector, I'm Professor Carlisle from Mathematics. I liked Uzinski initially. I remember the first time I saw him at a faculty meeting. He was well-dressed and charming. As I got to know him better, I saw that while he was paternalistically polite—what you'd call an officer and a gentleman—he was also stiff and emotionally distant. His words expressed concern, but his voice was cold as ice. He used to wear a Paris designer suit with his initials, RIU, on the cuffs. No one ever figured out his middle name." Carlisle smiled and shook his head. "He never bothered to say, and no one dared call him anything but 'President.' The fact is, Inspector, he never—"

"Inspector, like I said before—" Ash spoke over Carlisle.

"—fit in with our Midwestern collection of university scholars—" Carlisle struggled to overcome Ash's interruption.

"—Uzinski was an autocrat," Ash continued, commandeering the floor, "a ruler, a prince, as it were, and he let us know how he felt about us and our little provincial world. There was a nearly physical clash between the old-line philosophical beliefs of our faculty—a modern, free-thinking group—and the fake conservative pragmatism of this self-gentrified President."

"Do you know anything about his past?" Robertson said, directing the question to Ash.

Ash leaned forward. "Consistent rumors put him in government service in the Middle East, maybe Qatar. He managed to avert a complete unredacted records check, of itself significant." He exhaled and raised his palms in exasperation. "Nobody knew if Uzinski was married or had any children. He never discussed his past or spoke about family.

"As faculty who struggled to survive his regime, we didn't embrace his avowed image as a brilliant visionary. His administrative changes were slow and subtle at the beginning. He first targeted particular individuals and, second, certain departments. He later threatened to cut teaching lines, secretaries, budgets, and general resources within departments. Eventually he attacked our governance documents—the heart, soul, and mission of a school faculty—which are encased in what we call peer review documents. Then he lowered the boom, making it harder and harder to get tenure." He clenched his right fist and shook it in the air. "Over the months and years, fewer and fewer faculty were granted tenure. That's why I'm so pissed."

"Okay." Robertson said, "I see why Uzinski's policies played out like a political chess game."

"That's what's interesting, Inspector," Conklin said, nodding his almost bald head and nearly dislodging the forgotten black-framed reading glasses perched on top. "At faculty meetings, Uzinski harangued us to death—uh, sorry, everyone, no pun intended here—about increasing research standards to some national level. He ranted about attracting worldwide talent. According to him, we had no talent among the faculty," he said, laughing nervously. No one smiled, much less laughed.

"Here we go," Ash said with a sigh and shake of the head. "Caitlyn's dysfunctional theory. I can't hear this again." He pushed his chair back and closed his eyes.

Robertson looked at Caitlyn over the rim of his glasses. "Well, this should be good." He chuckled. "Please, Professor Morrys."

"Professor Connor," Caitlyn responded, "I've never seen you act like this. I just won't bother saying anything."

"No, don't play with my head, I won't play guilty for you. This is not a psychological game, Caitlyn, it's a political one," Ash said, his eyes still closed.

"Why, Professor Connor, I don't agree at all," Inspector Robertson glanced at Caitlyn with a comforting smile. "The political game on this campus has been psychological warfare. That's why you're all feeling victimized—you've been emotionally manipulated." Then he turned to face Caitlyn. "I think you've got it right. Understanding psychological motivations will lead us to a murderer."

"You are correct," Caitlyn started slowly. "Follow pathology from character to character, beginning with Uzinski's dysfunctional relationship with his faculty. He was a disapproving parental type, often abusive. He didn't respect his faculty. The CU faculty represented the unloved child. They could never do enough to satisfy him or prove themselves worthy. The Stutts professors were like the perfect sibling, the loved child."

Caitlyn stood and took a deep breath, gathering impromptu arguments in her head. "Being caught in the middle of this dysfunctional situation inflicted emotional damage on faculty struggling for tenure approval," she continued, glancing around and meeting eyes. "Unattainable approval, but they didn't know it until it was too late. Actually, his relationship with us reflected an underlying emotional conflict. The faculty worked harder and harder as he kept raising the bar, an incessant moving target. The standards were, in raw reality, Uzinski's emotional demands, his way to impose control over us. And now . . . now they are all suspects in his murder," she whispered.

"Yes, it's interesting," Carlisle said.

"Carlisle, you're a cynic." Caitlyn shook her head. "You think like a mathematician and really think psychology is mumbo jumbo. Well, let me tell you about psychology: Someone wanted payback. They wanted to belittle the President, to destroy the image of an icon of power," she ended abruptly.

Robertson gestured. "Well, Professor Carlisle, what do you think of that analysis?"

"Inspector, I think I'd like to know which came first, the backstabbing or the pulling down of the pants," Ash suddenly interjected, breaking the tension in the room.

Caitlyn sat back down, exasperated.

"Hey, Inspector," Ash continued sarcastically, "see, now that is a great opener for my idea for a new murder mystery. Thank you, Carlisle, I'll give you an acknowledgment in the book."

"You're both hopeless," Caitlyn said. "This isn't funny. We each felt the desperation and frustration. The quality of life on this campus deteriorated until it became unbearable. When Uzinski eliminated tenure, he procured his final solution. Look at the student life and political activism! Mical Bazyli is alive and well on this campus, as he is across other American universities. We had a wonderful Hillel program for years, but now there are anti-Israeli protests and political rallies—it's anything but academic."

Caitlyn stopped, crunching her face up in confusion … or memory loss. She struggled.

Robertson and the others peered carefully at her. She'd gone off somewhere.

Analytical diarrhea, Ash called it. He leaned over and carefully closed her folder. "Caitlyn, when you lose sight of the importance of chocolate chip cookies, you lose everything. Instead of that *Diagnostic and Statistical Manual* of yours, I think you should find a nice recipe for chocolate chip cookies. It would improve your perspective on life." He leaned forward to shake hands with the Inspector. "We need some levity here, right, Inspector?"

"Just as an aside, Professor Connor"—Robertson chuckled—"the tenure process *would* provide a terrific story line for a mystery novel. I told Professor Morrys the very same thing just the other day. Most people have no idea how difficult it is for a professor to get tenure at a university. The general impression is you're overpaid for the nine months you work because you teach maybe four or five classes each semester. You have some great, but unrealized, human dramas in the lives of all these young professors."

"All in all, a good mystery novel, Inspector." Ash leaned against the table with a bemused expression. "We're not exactly *CSI*, *NYPD Blue*, or *Law and Order* here."

"There is political intrigue and drama here, Professor Connor," Robertson said. "I think there's a lot of material to work with. The idyllic setting of a university could well be a hotbed of sex and duplicity."

"Sex and duplicity at a university!" Ash burst out laughing. "Inspector, most people start yawning when they hear we teach at a university. They don't see anything sexy or exciting going on here—and certainly no high drama!"

"That's my point." Robertson chuckled. "This is a fertile field for a creative partnership. You and Professor Morrys could introduce a new genre in murder mystery literature."

"It's just amazing you're suggesting a mystery novel," Ash said, tapping Caitlyn on the shoulder. "As I said, I made that suggestion to Caitlyn. I thought of using Uzinski's murder scene as an opener, college president stabbed in the back, pants pulled down—"

"Ash," Caitlyn said sharply, "instead of *Murder on the Orient Express*, it's 'Murder at the University.' Of all the stupid nonsense. Oh please . . . and who would care?" Caitlyn said, tossing her hair back and rubbing her forehead and eyes with both hands.

Robertson and Ash both turned to observe her.

"Stupid?" Ash said. "Stupid is good, Caitlyn, you don't get the point. I like stupid just like I like chocolate chip cookies. If you're going to be stupid, be good at it!

"Inspector, I assume the meeting is over. Professor Morrys must return to her office and finish diagramming Uzinski's sentences." Ash stood up. "You should have her show them to you sometime. In–ter–est–ing, most interesting. Puts me to sleep, of course, but that's why I need chocolate chip cookies at these meetings ..." Ash trailed off as Caitlyn's green cougar-eyes seared into him, cutting off his attempts at humor.

Ash flinched. "Levity, Caitlyn—you're too intense. Get your nose out of the DSM and Poe and into Thackeray or Austen. Speak to you soon." He walked out of the conference room.

Everyone began talking at once, and in seconds the room was abuzz with chitchat. And then, in a flash, they had scrambled out. The meeting room door closed quietly, leaving an exhausted Caitlyn and an eager Robertson.

"I'm off to interview Provost Moisescu. Suggestions?" Robertson said as he stood to leave.

"Hmm." She chuckled at his words. "How much time do you have, Inspector?"

"Enough. Actually, I have an eternity, Professor Morrys, and ... so do you."

12

FLASHBACK MEDITATIONS

Life is a school that provides you with an opportunity to learn about yourself and other "students." Each relationship that you have will teach you something important about love because each relationship provides a lesson. —Ellenmorris Tiegerman

They sat across the table studying each other again, but more warily this time.

Although Caitlyn had only recently met Robertson, she continued to think there was something acutely familiar about him. *How can that be? In my flashbacks?*

"Sentence diagrams, Caitlyn? What is Connor needling you about?"

Caitlyn resumed where she had left off. "Uzinski could talk endlessly. He was boring, and the faculty always walked away from meetings wondering what he'd said. After a while I'd stop listening and doodle my impressions of his abstruse clauses and sentences. My training in linguistics gave me an understanding of sentence structure. I'd write down three or four of his long and complicated utterances just to dissect them, reduce them to simple base forms. I thought I might also find in his speech a clue into his thinking and his personality." She stopped abruptly and bowed her head in thought, then shook it as if to clear her mind. "I kept the diagrams in my desk. That's what Ash was babbling about."

She raised her eyes and frowned. "You know, Uzinski had a thought disorder."

Robertson removed his glasses and stared into her eyes. "How would you know that?"

"I had a short introduction *to* him, but a deep conversation *with* him."

"Do you remember asking me if you were a suspect?"

"No, I don't, actually. Well, I *am*, aren't I?" she carped, sharply emphasizing *am* as if it were a weapon.

"No, Caitlyn, you're the solution."

"What're you talking about, Inspector?"

"This is a past-life experience—we've been through this situation before. You know that, Caitlyn, don't you? You need to go home and put on a Brian Weiss CD and regress yourself to your earlier lives. You were at Dr. Weiss's training course at the Omega Institute a few years ago. I saw you. I was there. You participated in classes all week. Dr. Weiss offered to hypnotize you in class, which anyone would have jumped at—but not you!"

"You *saw* me?" She moved about in her seat. Her rational side screamed that the past-life theory was laughable. It was unscientific, to say the least, a mere popular New Age fad. Yet the Inspector seemed reasonable, logical, and sane. Could he be serious?

"You think I'm crazy," he said, reading her expression. "Put aside what you're thinking and what you learned in school. Close your eyes and tell me if it feels like the truth."

"I can't do this now, Inspector. I have a class and have to run."

"Can't, or won't? You were always single-minded and difficult—that's why we're here again. If you'd accept who you are and why you're here this time, we could both move on."

"Inspector, I don't want to be rude, but what you're suggesting is absurd." She gathered her papers and stood up to leave.

"Caitlyn, dear, you're not being rude, you're being you. You need to listen to me now because I don't want to do this script again with you in another life. Don't you want to know who I *really* am?"

"Not really!" she snapped.

Suddenly the phone rang. Caitlyn dropped her papers, and she watched them scatter all over the table and floor as if in slow motion. The phone kept ringing. She moved to the desk and reached for it. But then the room spun, and she fell into blackness.

Caitlyn could hear Robertson from a distance, calling her name. A strange name she could not quite make out—was it Jean? Her mind flooded with images.

She is in the chaos of a battlefield, a shield marked with a fleur-de-lys in one hand and a battle axe dripping blood in the other. Her pale white armor is splashed in blood and her open-faced bascinet helmet is pushed back aslant on her forehead so soldiers will know her. She hardly notices her own blood leaking from an arrow wound in her shield arm. Moans and screams fill the air all around, the field littered with the dead and dying, men piled on one another, writhing, crying for their women. The smoke of death and frost rises from the hellish black earth on that godforsaken, king-cursed Orleans morning. She leans on her shield, exhausted, finally feeling all the pain in the heady celebration of victory, in the joy of merely being alive.

The siege of Orleans has been broken. Evil has been vanquished for now, but at great cost.

Someone who looks like a dead ringer for Robertson—big, bald, and wild as warfare—is standing nearby, waving a spear. His craggy, scarred face looks a little different, but his eyes: They are the same piercing blue. A short line of blood runs from his neck down inside the armor at his chest. He calls out "Victory," calls out for the Dauphin over and over, jabbing his spear as though striking demons in the air.

She looks closer. Nearby, almost at her feet, she sees someone vaguely resembling Braxton on his back in the mud. Someone is straddling his body, jabbing a spear into his unarmored belly, over and over. No screams, but he isn't dead. Madness fills him, deadening his pain as he shouts defiance at the world he is leaving. His eyes meet Caitlyn's. He screams something at her. She watches as the twisted face of the other figure shoves down on bloody iron to silence the screaming madman. Who is it? She leans closer.

She heard Robertson yell at her. Seconds later, the image was gone; so, too, the blood, the bodies. All gone. The stench was overwhelming. Everything went black again.

Caitlyn opened her eyes to see Robertson leaning over her, his eyes twinkling. She was back in her chair. He was saying something, but she could not make it out. She was floating, still far away. *What a strange sensation. The image of Robertson with a bushy black beard in all that armor was absurd; it was strange, very strange.*

"Neil Braxton was there, spear-gutted in the mud at Orleans," she said quietly. "Battle scenes are all similar everywhere, aren't they?"

"Death is common in life, Caitlyn, and war is eternal." He smoothed her forehead where the helmet had left a red line. "You had one of your flashbacks? What did you see?"

"I saw you, I think, Inspector, with a dark beard and plate armor. You were thinner. Actually, you were quite sloppy looking, and damned noisy, waving your big spear."

"Nice. You should've seen yourself. You were no vision of feminine charm." He laughed.

"Wh-what do you mean?" she stuttered. "How do you know what I looked like?" She shook her head. "No, I'm not sure I really want to know . . ." Her voice trailed off.

"The same way you know I was with you on a battlefield during the Hundred Years' War. Yes, you were quite a sight to behold. You were called the Maid of Orleans—of the Dauphin. Everyone feared you and your influence with the king-to-be . . . except Ashford and me."

"Ash . . . Ash?" she exclaimed. "Was he there too? No, no, this can't be real." She groaned. "What was Ash doing? Who was he?" she asked desperately.

"Well, I don't want to overwhelm you all at once, Caitlyn. In your flashback, where did you see me?"

She closed her eyes and tried to retrieve the fragments. She scanned her memory picture—the field of dead and dying. "I saw you standing on a battlefield."

"What was I doing?"

"You were calling 'Victory' for the Dauphin . . . waving a weapon . . . a sword."

"Good, what am I saying to you? I'm also doing something. What?"

"You're waving your sword in the air," she said tentatively.

"No, no—look more closely."

"Oh, you're pointing the sword . . . I can't hear you. I can't hear what you're saying." Caitlyn's body stiffened. Her eyes fixed in thought. "I hear sounds like 'Charles, Charles.'"

She raised her arm as if to deflect a blow, teeth clenched in a time-frozen scream. "Someone killed someone who tried to kill me," she gasped. She put her head down and covered her face with her hands. "I saw the face before he died . . . speared in the stomach . . . blood washed out of him, spurted all over. He cursed me as he died. Oh, oh my God, how horrible." Her voice broke.

"Who killed whom? Look around again, you're almost finished," he encouraged.

"No, I can't," she moaned.

"Yes, yes, you can, damn it. Do it!" His voice was commanding and harsh.

She closed her eyes and again scanned the battlefield.

"Look carefully," he insisted.

"I see a white horse lying on the ground . . . it's dying. Someone's standing over it. He has a sword . . . Oh, horrible, he's killed his horse . . . He's tall . . . his face . . . Ash, it's Ash. What is he doing there?" Her eyes flew wide open.

"Caitlyn, don't get hysterical. Listen to me. You've had a major breakthrough here—you, Braxton, Ashford, and me on the battlefield during the Hundred Years' War in Orleans, France. Who was killing Braxton?" he insisted, leaning over the table and putting his hand on her shoulder.

"Braxton was with the invader. I was a leader in the army fighting against them, with Ash as my companion." Her voice quivered.

Robertson stood and walked to the door. "That's enough for today. You understand now you have the inner sight. Stop running away from yourself. Continual disbelief makes this life's lesson ten times harder to resolve into so-called reality."

As he opened the door to leave, she called to him, "Wait, Inspector. Since President Uzinski was murdered, will there be more deaths at Coronado University? Who could be next?"

"The way things are going, maybe you or Ash."

The finality in his tone jolted her. He turned and left, closing the door behind him without so much as a glance.

Days later, in the morning before her undergraduate Developmental Psychology class, Caitlyn sat in her office all alone. No one had arrived in the Psychology offices yet. Quiet dominated in anticipation of the normal hubbub. She loved this time of day.

She had been in the gym, running on the treadmill like a hamster and then pushing herself to another limit on the elliptical machine for what seemed an endless hour. Now the tightness in her chest and the mental stress had worked itself out, and she was sufficiently exhausted—or was it ennui, she wondered?—to start the day. She pushed her office chair away from the desk and swiveled around to peek out the corner windows to the mountains glowering over the world in the timeless prairie distance. She wanted to see behind them into the distance, behind the miles and hours, behind all the mind-shadows, to some reality, somewhere.

She'd ruminated for days about her blackout in the UPC conference room and Robertson's directive to meditate on her nightmares. Seeing? Could she really do that? Did that even make sense?

She had never successfully meditated into a past life, let alone used regression therapy to solve a problem or heal some physical or emotional malady. Caitlyn did understand the principle of healing in the present by going back to a point of genesis in a past life. After all, traditional therapy focused intensively on the relationship between adult problems and childhood events. So, if that relationship made sense, then going back further in time to a past life could also make sense—conceptually, of course. But to solve a murder? That was a stretch, even for New Age theory. Maybe she needed to refashion it through a religious perspective.

Caitlyn recalled something Wayne Dyer had written in *Change Your Thoughts, Change Your Life: Living the Wisdom of the Tao*: "If you change the way you look at things, the things you look at change." It fit the present situation perfectly.

Caitlyn had read virtually every self-help book on the shelves of Barnes & Noble. Bring up a New Age issue and she had the perfect book on the topic. She had the best reading lists for students on campus. She often told them, "The scientific, the mainstream, and the alternative." Reincarnation challenged most Western religions. Caitlyn understood that. Interestingly enough, reincarnation fit in nicely with

Chasidism, the Kabbalah, and Jewish mysticism—which she didn't know much about, but with Inspector Robertson in her face, she would have to learn. Add to the mix the strange coincidences that made her feel her life had *no* coincidences, but instead a pattern that subtly prodded her toward determinism.

Caitlyn's clinical training had helped her deal with unresolved issues from her toxic relationship with her mother. She knew, too, that the Morrys family had secrets. There had never been any family gatherings with relatives, and Caitlyn's questions about her grandparents were routinely met with angry silence or curt dismissal. After her mother died, things had gotten even more complicated and curious.

A cosmic revelation occurred when Caitlyn began sorting through her mother's things and found naturalization forms for her great-grandparents, who were named Isaac Abravanel and Rachel Levy, showing they had entered the United States in 1931. Listed under family members was an Esther born in 1910 in Milan, Italy. More revealing, their religion was identified as what she'd somehow sensed but could never prove: Judaic. So, there it was in black and white. Her response was a frenetic search on Ancestry.com for the skeleton of a family tree of relatives named Abravanel. Caitlyn poured herself into the family research, finding social security applications, ship manifests, census records, and death certificates, even buying a DNA kit to identify her many cousins. She delved in at a feverish pitch, tamping down her anticipation, until the results affirmed this truth: Caitlyn was Jewish.

She had no idea what being a Sephardic Jew meant. She found a website, Chabad.org, that helped her search a broad range of Jewish topics: Most Jews shared the same basic beliefs but differed in culture and geography. Sephardic Jews were from Spain, Portugal, and North Africa. *Sephardic* is derived from the Hebrew, meaning "south." The other major Jewish cultural group were the Ashkenazic Jews from France, Germany, and Eastern Europe. Most early Jewish settlers of North America were Sephardic, but most American Jews today were Ashkenazim who had migrated from Germany and Eastern Europe to escape the tortures of the Holy Roman Empire and National Socialism.

Caitlyn entered the name of her great-grandfather, Isaac Abravanel, and found a possible connection to a famous historical Jewish statesman and scholar born in 1437. The Inquisition, the papal-driven expulsion and persecution of Jews as heretics against the beliefs of the Roman Catholic Church, had begun in Spain in 1492. The Abravanels escaped with thousands of Jewish families to neighboring France and Italy. Isaac Abravanel finally settled in Venice, where he became a member of the Council of State and died in 1508 at the age of seventy-one. Caitlyn knew little about the Inquisition, which had raged in Spain and France for three hundred fifty years. But she was learning how kings and popes had mingled missions and vocations, persecuting and burning, holding secret religious trials with political motives. A king killing for his God.

She knows balefire burnings by English soldiers—pain, anguish, screams. An awful memory: tied to a wooden post, burning on a wooden pyre for someone's beliefs—for a king called Charles. Was the auto-da-fé she is cursed to recall a real horror, or only a fractured, unholy dream?

Apparently not all Abravanels had avoided the Inquisition. Had she *really* been in France with the fleur-de-lys of Charles VII? She recalled battle and blood and Joan of Arc.

They called her only *Joan* in history. Apparently, no one knew her family or surname.

> Jehanne knows it. Caitlyn sees the visions, the lights ... and hears Jehanne's young voice. "I was in my thirteenth year when I heard a voice from God to help me govern my conduct. And the first time I was very much afraid. I am not afraid now ... I was born to do this," Jehanne says to the mob—and the hungry flames.

The hundreds of years of ancestry connections—direct, clear, and factual—awed and overwhelmed Caitlyn. Here was direct descent from a community, a culture, and a religion that had lasted thousands of years. But all her family connections had been erased as though they had never happened. The train had veered off the tracks with her mother. What had really happened with her mentally complicated parent?

Caitlyn was angry. She felt cheated of a rich and vibrant history, as though she had been living her mother's lie, her mother's made-up history. Caitlyn now understood her mother's hysterical zeal and commitment to church services. Turns out her mother, and even a scandalized English cardinal, had tried to "erase" the Jewishness of her past, the generations of her religious culture. But what was *real*?

Had something happened between Caitlyn's grandmother and mother to cause a dramatic reaction over the several decades? The more Caitlyn thought about it, the more her confusing dreams made sense—finally. They had always been filled with mixed messages and symbols, representing the break between Caitlyn's present life and her past. A Christian life had masked a Jewish life. But why?

Now, to understand her past lives, Caitlyn had to uncover another complete life that had been buried under her mother's fabrications.

13

THE WARRIOR WITHIN

A single soul can be reincarnated a number of times in different bodies and in this manner it can rectify damage done in previous lives.
— Moshe Chaim Luzzatto

During her first meeting with Uzinski as chair of the UPC, Caitlyn had run into some confusion about procedural issues. Provost Moisescu's secretary called her to appear in Moisescu's office suite that same afternoon. Caitlyn begged off because of her schedule and asked what the meeting was about. The secretary ducked the question, saying only that the Provost would contact her directly.

When he called, he'd wasted no time laying into Caitlyn. In a guttural shout, he asserted that she had "violated" a peer review rule. "Our personnel committee does *not* speak to members of an Outside Review Committee until they are on campus; only *I* have the authority to speak to the ORC!" Provost Moisescu had rasped almost unintelligibly.

Feeling her blood rise, she'd responded in kind. "I suggest you lower your voice when you speak to me. It's offensive, and I'm sure you would *not* want to be perceived as abusive, particularly by the female faculty," she'd said quietly and precisely, before she quietly and precisely hung up.

He had called back much later in the day, and she agreed to meet him.

Caitlyn had a secret. She had developed mastery over voice pitch and body language over her many years as a psychologist—and as a self-aware, attractive woman. Pitching her voice down an octave worked on most men, even *these* men, those holier-than-thou types in higher education. She'd agreed to show up at four p.m., not at two p.m. as he'd demanded. This was another tactic she used: agree with some proposals, but only on her terms, at a time or place of her choosing.

As soon as she hung up, Caitlyn called several UPC colleagues and invited them to also attend the meeting. This, too, was an effective technique: appearing with uninvited colleagues. She wanted an audience—witnesses, as it were—not a private meeting between Provost Moisescu and Professor Morrys. It would be Professor Morrys with her backup team. She even plotted where she would sit, directly opposite the Provost and in the middle of her support team.

Provost Moisescu was, to say the least, annoyed when this group entered his office. He got even more irked when others responded to his questions to Caitlyn. She enjoyed listening to the others and watching him cringe and squirm in his chair. He hated psychological games and thrived on manipulation and control, micromanaging everything within his orbit, and this spectacle was turning everything on its head.

Eventually he lost all control and began choking and spitting and yelling. "Only one subject at a time," he gasped. "And only Professor Morrys, if you please!"

Caitlyn remained impassive. She crossed her legs, tossed her hair over her shoulder, arched her back to puff out her front, and put her right hand underneath her chin—familiar posturing. Then she pitched her first words to him, an octave lower than his growling. "Provost Moisescu, would you mind lowering your voice—and by the way, please repeat your last question so *all* of us can hear?" Caitlyn had marveled at her modulation and wondered how she'd gotten her voice so low-down and earthy.

"Get out!" the Provost ordered. "Get out, all you . . . people!" Timur Moisescu's hatred of Professor Caitlyn Morrys was obvious to her and everyone around her.

Caitlyn plainly saw the irrationality, and so could everybody else. "Of course, Your Honor," she said sarcastically. They all stood up like a chorus line and left.

The phone rang in her office. Caitlyn snapped back to reality and grabbed it. It was Ash, calling from the gym. He, too, was a gym rat. He'd raced in the New York and Boston marathons, and Caitlyn often traveled to cheer him on from the sidelines. She'd loved watching him, a great runner and wonderfully graceful. Ash had encouraged her to run with him so that they could train together, but Caitlyn was always reluctant. She was not the street-happy athlete he was, not for public exhibition. She advised Ash she was an indoor "hamster," not an outdoorsy animal. The elliptical was her machine of choice, and a gym functioning as a spa was her "preferred cup of tea," she often declared with a smile as they exercised in the gym.

"Caitlyn, you didn't sleep well last night. What are you doing and how are you feeling? And what were you obsessing about all night?" Ash could have an entire conversation running on a treadmill and not break a decent sweat or write a tortured paragraph.

"Actually, I was just getting ready for my class," Caitlyn fibbed.

"No, you weren't," Ash snapped. "Your phone rang ten times before you picked it up. What were you thinking about just now? Certainly it wasn't about sex, and definitely not about chocolate chip cookies. So, what has been absorbing your time and attention lately?"

"I was remembering our conversation about how administrative types hate me so intensely," she answered. "I was thinking about Provost Moisescu and the candidates who've been denied tenure who are now suspected of murder—that group is getting larger. Who is the most likely murderer? Who had the clearest motive and opportunity?"

"Yes, that's a consideration. But don't forget, Caitlyn, Moisescu hates women and would positively detest all that wacko stuff you're into, all the past lives and regression therapy. He has always seen you as a powerful voice and, lately, a threat, with what's happening with tenure at the UPC."

"Maybe he thinks *I* killed Uzinski," she ventured into his thought stream.

"Possibly, but Inspector Robertson's the only one who counts in this murder investigation. Has he accused you of the President's murder yet?" Caitlyn remained silent and Ash continued, "I think there's something else underlying these tenure cases and the murder. This is not just about hatred and ego, it's about ideology. There's a great battle brewing here for mission and ideas—and money. It all relates to the Stutts Foundation. Why are they *here*, of all places? Coronado doesn't rate that kind of time and money. Is Mical Bazyli running an experiment with us and this campus? Is this a setup for something bigger? Look at what's happening on campuses across the country—the political activism and the Marxist ideology.

"If I had your dreams and your powers, I would take Robertson's advice. See if anything in your flashbacks can give you a clue. I still have difficulties with your past-life theory, but that's for another discussion. Right now, you need to focus on a possible murderer."

Something hardened in Caitlyn's mind. She knew Ash was right.

It was a beautiful spring day. Tulips were speckled throughout the entire campus. Caitlyn sat in her office at her worktable, elbow-deep in papers but constantly distracted by past-life regressions. Memories of the past had increasingly intruded into her daily life—not just night dreams now, but incessant flashbacks during the day that interfered at inopportune moments.

She was yanked from her last daydream by heavy footsteps, which she recognized as belonging to Inspector Robertson. She disliked their conversations. He often made her feel like a little girl, and not in a good way. Robertson masqueraded as a part of her past. Now he was following up on earlier conversations about recent press releases. She stood to greet him.

He shook her hand and spoke without any greeting or preamble. "Professor Morrys, did you know President Uzinski recently advised the press he was about to change the whole tenure system?"

"No, I did not," Caitlyn said, contracting her eyebrows.

"Well, did you know he described CU faculty to press reporters as 'fat-cat teachers and abusers of the system who prove the need for tenure reform in education'?"

"So?" Caitlyn said. She was not shocked. She sat back down at the table.

Robertson plopped into a red-leather chair, opened a briefcase, pulled out papers, crossed his legs, and settled in comfortably. "Your President hated tenure because it robbed him of control and mitigated his overall mission to downsize a tenured faculty."

"He felt that tenure reform was the way to increase educational standards at institutions of higher learning," Caitlyn said. "That opinion, Inspector, is widespread among administrators."

"He certainly liked to embarrass his faculty," Robertson continued, shifting gears.

What did Uzinski expect the faculty to do, other than disagree? It was so hostile and abusive. He wanted his faculty to hate him. Why else would he set them up like that?

"Professor Morrys—Caitlyn—are you listening to me?"

"You know Uzinski had a borderline personality, don't you?"

"He had a what?" Robertson asked.

"A borderline personality, as in my DSM-5, my *Diagnostic and Statistical Manual*," she said searching for the book on her long worktable. "Here it is, and the—"

"Stop," he said, his voice raised. "My background information is important, but I'll keep it short so you can go back to your daydreaming."

"I'm going to allow you to annoy me today, Inspector. I surrender. What do you want?"

"The more I learn about the tenure process, the more amazed I am about the strict requirements." Inspector Robertson paused to adjust his glasses and then changed the subject. "Hmm, you really should consider writing a book about the process with Professor Connor." He chuckled.

"Inspector, what do you want?" she said, trying to steer him away from her private life.

Robertson ignored her. "As I see it, you'd need to write something to jazz up the dry details. How about a professor of psychology as the main character? You could even use all your diagnostic manual stuff. Frankly, I prefer a psychoanalytic twist to murder stories, and I *could* suggest other more creative possibilities for a mystery."

Caitlyn was in no mood for fiction ideas. "Get to the point, Inspector. I'm busy," she said, turning back to the reference book and some new paperwork.

Robertson complied. "Why do you professors think tenure is so important? There are employment safeguards in statute and law, so it isn't necessary. Why do so many faculty resist renewable contracts, which give the school more flexibility in hiring?"

His change in tone surprised her, as did the pointed sequence of questions. She had to collect her thoughts. *Where is he coming from? What is he looking for?*

She spoke slowly and deliberately. "You need to ask Professor Connor as president of the union, but I'll give you my opinion. Whenever Uzinski talked about tenure, it was always from a financial and business perspective. The university was a business to him, not a place for learning. The Administration became corporate management and the faculty were employees. Uzinski argued tenure was a lifetime job contract. He used to say, and I quote, 'Why should the vitality of any institution be confined and constrained by an aging, burned-out professional staff?'" She imitated the former President's thick speech and awkward inflections perfectly. "'My distinguished colleagues, the future is in attracting more young, distinguished theoretical researchers.'"

"Very good." Robertson chuckled. "I'm sure the caricature would've impressed him. Did he have a sense of humor?"

"None whatsoever, Inspector," she replied. "Uzinski was meticulous and controlling. Getting back to the question at hand, universities are *not* entrepreneurial businesses, and corporate rules, principles, and political expectations generally should *not* be applied to educational institutions. That's why Uzinski was so dangerous. He looked at faculty as expendable employees and students as consumer products—educational reductionism to satisfy a business plan. It was a so-called master plan designed by a diabolical manipulator. The only thing standing in his way was the union."

"You mean Professor Connor?"

"Yes, Ash has been courageous. We all saw President Uzinski as a union buster."

Robertson held up a slim magazine, *Frontiers in Higher Education*, opened to a folded-over page, and said, "That sounds like your article right here, if I may: 'Tenure has a long history and serves to protect freedom of expression and democratic ideology in American universities. The ability of a professor to discuss openly theoretical ideas, unpopular ideas, far-reaching ideas, new ideas—ideas for the mere sake of ideas—and without fear of administrative sabotage, without fear of administrative reprisals, was and is the foundation of democratic growth. Tenure has little to do with lifetime employment or meritorious scholarship and everything to do with academic freedom. Tenure is the only way to insure a free dialogue without the risk of punitive political reaction and termination. Tenure is a commitment to a professor—as a free thinker . . .'"

He stopped reading and commented, "An amazing historical stereotype, here and now. You're a rebel, Caitlyn. True to form, you always were—and still are—a heretical rebel." Robertson's voice settled into a low growl. "Don't you hear me? Tenure makes it difficult to fire people for ideological or administrative heresies!

"Don't you listen," he rushed on, "when they preach about the future? They'll burn you here, as they did in the past." His last words were said in a whisper.

"What *are* you talking about?" She knew he was probably right but didn't want to hear it.

"There isn't much time." Robertson was sharp and direct. "Go home. Lock your doors, regress yourself. It's the only way to solve this murder before someone tries to kill you." He stood, gathered his briefcase and papers, and left her office before she could reply.

Caitlyn felt panicky. There was something all too familiar here. Recent events had led to strange dreams and a constant tightening in her chest. In her dreams—vivid, violent scenes of wars, death, carnage, and burning—she always watched herself. Fighting with Uzinski or any of his henchmen agitated her. Perhaps that was the logical explanation for the reawakened nightmare flashbacks. Well, at least the turmoil was expressed—and not repressed.

The Inspector had asked a pivotal question. Did tenure supply the core motive for murder? Where was the article? She retrieved the magazine from her desk and reread. Halfway through, she stopped. Robertson was right. She sounded like a fanatic, a rabid political activist and warrior, fighting for justice, going against the grain.

Why did Mical Bazyli choose this particular college administration? She began with a broad brush. She reasoned that Uzinski opposed tenure because he didn't want to be fettered with any long-term personal relationships. But that was trite and too subjective. A bigger battle loomed here, something both personal and administrative. Was there something in Uzinski's past that might explain his behavior toward the faculty? *Get them young, use them, and then discard them* was typical of his type. No, that was too scandalous. What about money and budgets? Tenure cost the university a lot of money through promotions and professorial longevity. What about ideological motives?

What was someone like Richard Uzinski even doing at CU? Was the motive for his murder caught up in university strategy and purpose, or was it more personal?

14

THE PAST

Struggling to focus on her never-ending academic chores, Caitlyn mindlessly placed the student papers she was grading on the couch seat next to her. In seconds, she fell into a needed and well-deserved afternoon slumber. Forty-five minutes later, her impromptu nap free of recallable dreams for the first time in memory, she was abruptly jolted awake by an authoritative knock on the front door. She rose in a stupor, shuffled in the direction of the disruption, and opened the door to find a somber-looking Inspector Roberston.

"Inspector?" she slurred.

"Sorry to wake you."

"Wake me?"

"Yes, from that nap you've been taking for the better part of an hour."

Caitlyn stared at him incredulously. *This is getting way too damn weird.*

"We need to take the next step—and now. Time is fast becoming a critical factor. Lives are in the balance, most probably yours. I can't allow this to get done on your terms."

"What in God's name are you talking about?"

"I need to put you under. I need for you to revisit that part of your past directly relevant to the murder. The time for fiddling with past lives that are tangentially related, while good fodder for dinner rabble, is over. We need to accelerate the investigation into your past lives. We need some answers—and we need them now."

The charming and sometimes impish Inspector had transformed into a no-nonsense imperial law enforcement investigator. Not waiting for an invitation, Roberston pushed past Caitlyn into the house and commandeered a seat on her favorite reading chair, leaving a still-stunned Caitlyn frozen at the front door. Comfortably wedged in the chair, Robertson peered at her and nodded once toward the couch, an unmistakable directive that she take a seat there. She complied without a word, the school papers lounging in abeyance next to her.

Roberson discharged a chest full of air. "Do you trust me?" he began.

"Um, I think so."

"You *think* so? I need you to trust me unequivocally. I need you all in." He'd never spoken to her like this before. He was in control.

"Okay, okay. I *trust* you," she responded, annoyed but offering no resistance.

Robertson exhaled again, this time out of slight exasperation. "Okay, then, please follow my instructions ... close your eyes and roll them up under your eyelids."

Caitlyn adjusted her posture on the couch and obeyed.

"Do you believe in past-life regression?"

A slight pause. "I do."

"Do you feel safe with me?"

"Yes."

"Feel free at any time to open your eyes and end the session."

"Okay."

"Are you comfortable?"

Caitlyn leaned back on the couch, nestling her body against the cushion. "Yes, I am."

"Keep your eyes closed and stay comfortable. Focus your mind on one spot in the room you know well. Become aware of how it looks in each of its details—its look, color, shape, dimensions."

Caitlyn let out a breath and relaxed more deeply.

Inspector Robertson waited several seconds, allowing her to concentrate, before resuming. "Now, silently to yourself, count backwards from ten to zero. As you do, think about Uzinski's murder and tell yourself that this session can and will produce clues to help solve that crime. Know that this can happen. Know that you are in control of the process."

Caitlyn nodded softly, reassuring herself.

"In a moment, I'm going to count down from five to one, and when we reach one, I want you to relax into your mind as deeply as you can, letting all your energy fall outside of you and becoming a vessel to receive and store information."

He studied her face to make sure she was ready. "Nod if you are ready."

Caitlyn nodded slowly, her body as still as a sphinx.

"*Five* . . . Feel your eyes blinking slightly, coming to rest, continuing to focus on that spot in the room . . . *four* . . . Notice how your focus is changing . . . *three* . . . Your eyelids are growing heavier . . . *two* . . . Your eyes are almost impossible to keep open, they are heavier and heavier . . . *one* . . . Close your eyes, drop further and further into peacefulness . . .

deeper and deeper into calm relaxation ... Become aware of your breathing."

Robertson paused to feel the warm energy coming from Caitlyn. It was almost visible. He nodded twice to himself. "Now, feel the serenity inside of you ... deeper and deeper down and deeper down still."

He watched Caitlyn intently. Her breathing became quiet, imperceptible. Her shoulders gave way. Her chin dropped slightly. Her head was light and tilted.

"Exhale into a deeper feeling of relaxation."

She did, effortlessly.

"Go deeper ... and deeper. Feel the peaceful transformation. You are free to go wherever you want to go ... Feel all the stress ooze out of your body ... Feel the lightness of your being."

Caitlyn remained entirely still.

"You are deeply relaxed ... If you feel safe and secure, nod your head."

Caitlyn nodded once, ever so gently.

"You are becoming lighter and lighter as your spiritual being lets go. You are ready to see, experience, and learn ... and be awakened."

Caitlyn nodded unconsciously.

"Your memories are flooding back. They are beckoning your soul." Robertson paused again and leaned back in his seat. "I will soon count down again from five."

He took a deep breath and continued, "*Five* ... Feel the call of the past ... *four* ... Soar down and down into your younger existence ... *three* ... Drop into a particular country ... *two* ... Begin to see the contours of your past lives ... *one* ... You are on the ground ... safely ... breathing and conscious within your past life … see yourself … Where are you?"

"I am in Palestine."

"What is the year?"

"Summer of 1917."

"Are you a woman or a man?"

"A woman."

"Who are you."

"My name is Yael Yadin."

"Why are you in Palestine?"

"I am a spy for NILI—Netzah Yisrael Lo Yeshaker, a Jewish espionage network. We are helping Britain in its fight against the Ottoman Empire and its Imperial German allies."

"Do you have a spy name?"

"Yes, Ajda Yehudah."

"Are there others with you?"

"Yes."

"Who?"

"Three Turkish men."

"Tell me more about them."

"They are important military leaders in the Yildirim Army Group of the Ottoman Empire: General Yilmaz, Colonel Oszcan, and Captain Kucuk."

"Who are you to them?"

"I am personal secretary to General Yilmaz. I always attend his meetings so I can prepare his command reports."

"Describe what is happening."

Caitlyn began to recount the scene.

"Gentlemen, do you think the British will have the nerve to launch another campaign against Gaza?" says General Yilmaz.

"Won't happen," the impetuous Captain Kucuk chimes in, out of turn.

"Why not, Captain?" the General asks, noticing the annoyance on the face of his trusted advisor, Oszcan, at the irrepressible Kucuk's interjection.

"The British are emboldened by what happened in the Sinai Desert campaign. They might try to push their luck—"

"Meaning no disrespect, sir," Colonel Oszcan interrupts, flashing a disdainful look at the lower ranking officer, "but our intelligence is that the British army is in disarray and badly organized, and troop morale is poor after the second battle of Gaza. They've learned their lesson. They will be looking elsewhere. My suggestion is, we move some of our defenses protecting Gaza to other more sensitive spots and likely targets."

"Thank you both. Captain, if you don't mind, please leave me and Colonel Oszcan alone for a little while."

Captain Kucuk leaves as requested.

"Colonel, Kucuk has a point, don't you think?"

"For Christ's sake, sir"—his face flushes with blood—"he has always been a little light upstairs. You know I don't believe he is reliable. He is better following orders than providing insightful leadership. He has consistently overestimated the Brits and the Allied forces. Sure, they've been pushed back of late. But the British are done. They won't reorganize and come at us again in Gaza—not a third time. They can't afford to. It would be a crushing defeat, with ripples throughout the entire war effort. We are strong in Gaza, especially in Beersheba. We need to deploy elsewhere. We have those lily-whites on the run. We are in control."

"Okay, Colonel. Thank you. Give me some time to think things over."

Colonel Oszcan departs, leaving the General alone with his assistant.

"What do you think, Yael, about all this craziness?"

"Sir, I agree with the Colonel. I wouldn't worry about Gaza. The British are likely to mount a campaign elsewhere. Let's not forget, the British relieved their commands after what we did to them the second time in Gaza. They are not coming to Beersheba and Gaza again. The Colonel is correct that they can ill afford another defeat. We have them where we want them."

"Caitlyn, listen to me carefully. This is important. I want you to fix your sights on the three men. Do any resemble anyone in your life at Coronado University?"

Caitlyn hesitated. Robertson could see in her stillness a rewinding and concentration. He was eager for an answer.

"Yes, yes, Inspector. The General is a clone of President Uzinski. The others, I can't be sure. They *seem* familiar but I can't pinpoint them."

Robertson processed the information quietly, head down. It was not nearly enough, but it was an important step in the right direction. He could see a tiredness coming over Caitlyn's face, an impending exhaustion from the trip into the past. He decided not to push for more, fearing that doing so would jeopardize the clarity and accuracy of information. They needed at least one more session. But they were getting close.

"Caitlyn, if you want to return from the past, take a deep breath, and while I count down from five, let your mind relax. When it does, open your eyes.

"Five . . . four . . . three . . . two . . . one."

Caitlyn raised her shoulders and exhaled. She sat still for a few seconds and then opened her eyes to see a contented Inspector Robertson smiling approvingly at her.

"You did good, Professor, real good."

15

PROFESSOR BRAXTON

The study of reincarnation as past lives can help us to see patterns beyond the immediate. We must begin to see our physical lifetime is but a fraction in the life of the soul. — Ted Andrews

Caitlyn needed a distraction from the session with Robertson, so she buried herself in reviewing tenure files in the committee room—the work of institutions of higher learning must go on, homicides or otherwise.

She finally finished her "homework" and went downstairs to the Student Union, where everyone was busily munching on snacks and, of course, talking about the murder. Her presence was largely unnoticed, and she sat at a table to sip coffee and listen for a while. The particulars—including the fingerprints of a faculty member at the murder scene—engendered all kinds of speculation from students with little knowledge. Sketchy details fueled campus gossip. The juicy central fact that the President of the university had died half naked with a knife in his back was titillating, but the strategically centered flower was either not common knowledge or considered inappropriate lunch conversation. Caitlyn found it odd that almost every student recalled some incident in history or a movie or TV show that related to the campus murder. She mused that American TV dramas, saturated with thrills, invited everyone to spice up their mundane lives by investigating similar bloody journeys. Such vast communal hindsight could make everyone psychics or even vicarious murderers.

Caitlyn returned to her comfortable desk chair in her own office after spending what seemed like interminable hours looking through the personnel committee's computer files in the little anteroom behind the UPC conference room, looking through recent tenure cases for any obviously odd occurrences or connections. Since she had the clearance, she'd finally set aside the necessary time to search the locked hard-copy personnel files in the Records room—old, noncomputerized file cabinets locked in the basement of the Admin building. Not everything got stored on a computer.

She examined the tenure cases with a law enforcement eye, the eye of a cop-psychologist who would find a rogue professor at best and a psychopathic criminal at worst. Caitlyn was out to discover a *real* evil, rather than read about a computerized cloudy past.

For instance, background and locations: Uzinski's murderer could have been a lover but not a friend. Maybe a sexual fling where Uzinski had "picked on" the wrong person? People who engaged in risky behavior got murdered, by bad people. No, the word "bad" didn't ring true; there was something intimate about the murder. The nudity made the victim even more vulnerable. Stabbing Uzinski in the back was not particularly an act of passion, but more a consciously planned revenge. What for, and where did it all begin?

And there was something else here, something even more abnormal, more off the rails. The flower scenario did not fit, a mismatch that seemed deliberate. The flower itself was poisonous and impossible to ignore. The murderer had obviously used it to redirect attention to someone else, or maybe *away* from someone too obvious—a double fake, psychologically speaking. A chemist. Someone from the Chemistry or even Biology department. "Motive, means, and psychological character," she mumbled to herself.

Then she remembered Professor Katherine Toscana, an up-and-coming star in the Chemistry department, whose tenure application during Uzinski's first year, first few months actually, the Administration had rejected in the face of full, enthusiastic UPC support. Professor Toscana was a brilliant scientist who had done a remarkable thesis on the history of poisons and apothecaries. She checked off all the boxes to qualify for tenure—she was, to Caitlyn and her colleagues, a no-brainer. In fact, in an uncharacteristic slip, Caitlyn told Toscana so.

Her rejection had stunned everyone, coming as it did before the intrigue with the Stutts Foundation and Uzinski and Moisescu's political agenda reared their collective ugly heads. The proffered reasons for denying her tenure seemed pretextual, something to do with "her temperament." In fairness, Toscana had a short fuse and was known as someone you did not want to cross, as a few students had learned the hard way. But in the collective experiences of the UPC members, a mercurial personality never jeopardized tenure; in fact, it seemed almost a job requirement for a college professor. After the rejection, Toscana had fled the state, utterly distraught and feeling betrayed. Someone said she felt "personally misled by the Administration," but whatever that meant never got clarified.

The word at the time was that she had relocated to Washington, DC, to work for a pharmaceutical company. What were the odds that after all these years she might return to do such a dirty deed? And how could she have pulled it off without a trace? No one had said she'd been seen on campus recently. Nor was there, to Caitlyn's knowledge, any evidence she'd been in contact with Uzinski or Moisescu. If any of that were the case, surely Carla would have known, and surely Carla would have told Caitlyn? It was possible, she speculated, Toscana could have hired someone to off Uzinski. But really?

Back to Braxton, then. His computer history detailed only constant conflict in eloquent detail, without any consistent background or references. Braxton was another double life, with a name that reminded her of past horror, a centuries-old torturer.

Caitlyn could not stop thinking about Braxton's tenure case. Given its outcome, it was the most intriguing. For the past several years, Braxton had created a great deal of controversy in his department and among the UPC and the Administration. The UPC had voted unanimously against his tenure, following several interviews with him and members of his department. Separating his interpersonal problems from the merits of his teaching and scholarship had been difficult. Boyishly attractive, slim, and athletic, Braxton was an Ivy Leaguer with an academic pedigree who dressed meticulously and was studied in his movements. But he was also a nasty, elitist snob who smiled at you and then made demeaning remarks about you behind your back. Theatrical, flamboyant, and condescending, he let everyone know about his classical training and sophisticated interests. Caitlyn had observed that no matter where Braxton was, when he got agitated he would eventually clear his throat, cross his legs, and impatiently tap his fingers on surfaces, a routine born of many years of practice.

The tenure report brought everything to a head. Braxton had been challenged for doing something considered highly inappropriate by some and downright unethical by others. One semester, Braxton had removed all the student evaluation surveys collected at the end of every class from his department office and summarized them in a report he'd submitted to the Provost. After receiving complaints, the UPC confronted him, and Braxton had explained he was "trying to help Moisescu's office."

That was *not* his job.

Questions exploded everywhere. Why had he gone to Moisescu? What was their connection? This end-runaround protocol had triggered debate and further confused UPC members. The UPC had delayed its final vote for several weeks to allow animosity to settle. Adversarial discussions among Braxton's colleagues and the Administration had left a pall over the committee.

The acrimony over Neil Braxton had focused everyone's attention on Uzinski's and Moisescu's negative application of the tenure process, and particularly on their constant fights with the UPC. Braxton had been the weakest tenure candidate in memory. Yet Moisescu had supported Braxton resoundingly in annual evaluations and reports—although not for tenure.

"Professor Braxton's commitment and service to the university and his distinguished research are emblematic of Coronado University's new vision for the twenty-first century." Was that comment, typical of the man called Doctor Death, due to his wan appearance? Those annual reports from the Provost had left everyone on the UPC speechless.

More, the Provost had named Braxton part of some "New Order." What was entailed in the "New Order"?

Braxton had touted himself as a friend of the Administration for years. By his own narrative, he had been recruited by Doctor Death at a European conference in Geneva.

What was the name of the conference? Who was there? Find out!

Certainly, everyone had been convinced that if anyone was going to get tenure, it would be Braxton. The jealousy in his department was disturbing and confounding, eliciting bitter peer rivalry. Moisescu seemed to use Braxton to foster divisive conflicts among faculty. And Braxton allowed himself to be used. He wrote letters complaining about colleagues, and Moisescu earned his nickname, Doctor Death, by placing the Braxton hit letters in their personnel files with no due process or written notification.

What connects Moisescu and Braxton so closely? Find out!

Caitlyn recalled that the brutal administrative libel had made Ash furious. It was common knowledge that *anyone* could put a letter in your personnel file, and it was *your* responsibility to check your file. An administrator was not required to send you a copy of a negative letter that went into your file. If you weren't paying attention, too bad. The Braxton letters had been the source of more union complaints and faculty misery than Ash could ever have imagined. And, of course, nothing could be done to Braxton for using someone's personnel file as a means of settling a score. Ash had railed that the situation was insane, to no avail. He knew it didn't matter, as did everyone else with an opinion. Braxton was in.

But then, to everyone's perplexity and consternation, Braxton did *not* get tenure.

Something changed in Administration. What? Find out!

Provost Moisescu had announced Braxton's setback at a faculty meeting. Tenure wasn't everything at CU, but denial of tenure was most certainly a slap in the collective and individual curriculum vitae. Braxton's lack of a professional future at the university meant that his potential last semester on campus was drawing nearer each month. And then, as the weeks went by, it seemed that somehow the mighty-flighty Braxton had transformed himself into a frantic little moth around the Coronado Administration flame.

Caitlyn allowed the whole story to percolate in her head. *Does Braxton have a past connection to President Uzinski in this life? Find out!*

Stabbing someone in the back would be—metaphorically, at least—his style. There was, however, a difference between verbally confronting and physically stabbing someone. He was a weak and whiny germaphobe who abhorred the sight of blood. Caitlyn couldn't see Braxton getting his hands and clothes dirty. He was much too obsessive about his appearance.

But pulling down Uzinski's pants? Now *that* was an interesting and bizarre, twisted piece of the puzzle. All the failed tenure candidates had a motive, but could a professional insult ignite uncontrolled outrage?

"Tierney, my bet's on Tierney. Strong, determined, and aggressive," she blurted out to no one. And his Outside Review Committee was scheduled for next week.

Does Tierney have a history of uncontrolled rage or assault? Find out!

She was particularly intrigued by the contrast between the public image of President Uzinski lying across his desk and her own memory of that same grand office only hours before he died. And it *was* a power desk, a black granite oval, with even blacker blood from his slashed wrist puddled neatly on the shiny surface.

Caitlyn thought about other tenure candidates besides Tierney and Toscana. Many of their names and faces were familiar, and she was involved with minute details of their lives: Brown, Mathews, and many more. She couldn't believe an academic had committed the murder. Pulling Uzinski's pants down to shame and humiliate him with a flower was more grotesque than picaresque. What torn psyche had stabbed and stood close to its semi-naked victim, whispered sibilant hatred, and then celebrated an intimate death with a witch flower? The scene was exquisite in its near-feminine delicacy.

Examine your past lives, Robertson had insisted. *Examine your long-past terror-dreams and see if anyone looks familiar!*

Inspector Robertson had told her forensics found a muscle relaxant in Uzinski's blood, which had apparently immobilized him. A friendly drink before a bloody murder? Could the relaxant have left Uzinski awake, to watch Brutus gloat as Caesar bled to death, both internally and externally, from the deep wound?

How macabre. How grotesque. Just like an Edgar Allan Poe plot.

The murderer had evidently wanted Uzinski immobilized but alert, knowing what was going to happen. This would allow the murderer to talk to him and whisper hatred as he died a slow death. To Uzinski, this would be the ultimate torture. To the murderer, the ultimate control—and revenge. And perhaps Uzinski's pants were pulled down *before* he was stabbed. Perhaps other acts took place. The relationship between Uzinski and his murderer would establish the sequence of events before the actual stabbing. Or maybe the murder scene was arranged to suggest it was committed during a sexual encounter. If that was the case, then it could have been any one of the tenure candidates.

16

LOYALTY ASUNDER

The cure for separation anxiety is to recognize its root in a past-life event. The trauma has already happened. It is from another time, and it is not something to fear in the present life.

— Brian and Amy Weiss

Inspector Robertson announced his presence at Caitlyn's home with a knock noticeably gentler than the last time. It was that soft rat-a-tat-tat drumbeat that familiar friends often use to happily announce their presence. Expecting her visitor at precisely that time, Caitlyn was in lockstep. She tossed her reading material next to her, bounced off the couch, waltzed to the door, and flung it open without screening the knocker.

"Good afternoon, Professor," Robertson said as soon as the door opened, upbeat and smiling.

"Inspector," Caitlyn said, emphasizing the truncated greeting with a pinched smile. She pulled her hair back, stepped aside, and ushered him in with a short wave of the arm. Without comment, they beelined to the same seats as if scripted.

"Are you ready?" Robertson said without skipping a beat.

"Very much so. But before we begin, I need to share a dream I had the night we had our session. It's been on my mind ever since. It's not much, but I think you'll find it interesting."

"Please."

"That night I kept revisiting what I saw when I was under, but each time I unpacked it, I felt incomplete. It was like I'd arrived at a crossroads with unfinished business, staring into a black screen. As if the story I told you had only reached an intermission."

"Okay."

"At the time, I was sure I had told you everything I had called up. But as I started to doze, I slipped into a dream that revealed something new."

Robertson flipped his right arm outward as if to say "Out with it."

"About two hours after the meeting I reported to you, after both men left the General's quarters and the General returned to his office and I to mine, out of nowhere, the Colonel returned, asking—no, demanding—to see him. He didn't have an appointment and so I stammered something about the General being busy. The Colonel wasn't having any of that and insisted I tell the General he was here to see him. I stopped what I was doing and checked with the General. He grimaced disapprovingly, clearly not wanting to be bothered and not pleased about the impromptu visit. But after several seconds of introspective silence, he relented and told me to show him in."

"What happened next?"

"After the Colonel entered, I gazed at the General to ascertain what I should do, and he rocked his head back and forth almost imperceptibly, conveying that I should leave and close the door."

"That's it?"

"That's all I remember from the dream."

"That's fine, it's helpful. Let's see if we can return to that moment and plunge deeper. I know it's not typical to recall conversational details to any degree, but the trauma is fresh in your memory, so we may be able to do so now."

Cailyn nodded in agreement.

As he had before, Robertson put her through the hypnotic paces, using soft commands, making the requisite countdowns, and facilitating the nurtured breathing. He noticed how seamless it seemed this time, how Caitlyn's body language signaled complete surrender to the process, how amazingly relaxed she seemed from head to toe. She was now deep in.

"Where are you now, Professor Morrys?"

"I am in Palestine, standing outside an office."

"Who are you?"

"I am Yael Yadin."

"Why are you there?"

"I am a spy for Netzah Yisrael Lo Yeshaker against the Ottoman Empire."

"Is your spy name Ajda Yilmaz?"

"Yes, it is."

"What is your non-spy position?"

"I am the personal assistant to General Emir Yilmaz."

"Is the eavesdropping related to your spying?"

"It is."

"Who is talking on the other side of the door?"

"General Yilmaz and Colonel Oszcan."

"Tell me what they are saying."

"What brings you here, Colonel, without invitation?" the General says, not bothering to hide his annoyance.

"I keep coming back to our meeting with Captain Kucuk. I think you should seriously consider transferring the Captain to Istanbul. Put him behind a desk where he can do little harm. His judgment is unsound."

The General doesn't respond for a long time. He's been unhappy with the Captain, although why, I can't tell. In terms of military intelligence, the Captain seems smarter than the two of them. But there's something else going on that has made the General leery of the Captain. He's been having his own second thoughts about the Captain. Not because he is a mad killer, something else. But for some reason, he doesn't want to reveal it.

The long silence forces the Colonel to speak again. "No disrespect, sir, but sometimes it appears you are too fond of him, give him too much leeway. Sir, again meaning no impertinence, country comes first—before all else. We have a war to win. Besides, you and I are all we need on this front. We are a great team. Together we can conquer the British and lead our country to take total control over Palestine. We can't let anything stand in the way. This is our time. This is our opportunity for greatness."

General Yilmaz nods in evident agreement. He lets the Colonel finish.

"Kucuk is a fly in the ointment. He is best used serving his country in a different way."

"You confuse me though, Colonel. You've always favored Kucuk. You supported his elevation to Captain. Is this because he disagreed with you in the meeting? Can it be that petty?"

"No, of course not. It's not personal, I assure you."

"Sure sounds like it is, Colonel. Is there something I don't know that perhaps you want to share with me?"

Colonel Oszcan shakes his head and exhales forcibly. "No, General, of course not, not at all," he responds, less than convincingly. "Look, let's not forgot how he ascended up the chain of command. A brutal killer, renowned for executing helpless women and children. The man has no moral compass. None. We protected—"

"Moral compass? Is there such a thing in times of war?"

"You know what I mean. We shielded his war crimes from the light of day because of the urgency of war. But he's no brilliant military leader. He's a butcher who will eventually be a stain on your career, and mine, if we don't control him—and worse! If the British ever discovered what he did in Gaza, we'd be tried and executed as war criminals. It'd be our heads—and I don't mind saying, the greater good will be forever lost."

"Yes, Colonel. And you? What about you? You are so innocent and pure? You have no blood on your hands, do you?"

"General, that is unfair. We are talking about the soundness of his judgment. You know how it can be for some. The strain of what we do can inflict so much damage, it creeps up on us before we know it, and then it is too late—we snap and go mad. He and I have served together a long time. I know his every thought before he has it. I think Captain Kucuk is on the verge of a complete collapse. There is no telling what he will do. Call it a hunch if you like. But I've done this a long time and, as I said, I know him better than anyone. I've seen the signs before. He is beyond dangerous."

"Thank you, Colonel. I'll consider your perspective. Is that all?"

"Yes, sir, that is all—for now."

I rush to my desk, quickly adjust my seat, and bury my head in paper. The next second, the Colonel bounds out of the office and by me without even acknowledging I exist. Come to think of it, he has never acknowledged that I exist. I suspect he resents me, a woman who regularly has the ear of the battalion commander. Frustration oozes from his pounding feet as he plods out and closes my office door hard.

"Stay where you are Cait—uh, Yael. Don't leave. Tell me more. What happens next?" Robertson said.

About an hour later, Captain Kucuk arrives at my desk. "The General wants to see me."

"Yes, yes, sir, he told me. You may go in."

Kucuk enters the office, closing the door behind him. I quietly get up to see what I can hear through the door. The voices are initially hushed and hard to make out.

Then Kucuk raises his voice. "This is insane. You will fail here without me. You and that arrogant, know-it-all Colonel. You listen to him way too much. You need to trust me on this."

"Look, Ahmet"—wow, that's the first time I've heard the General address the Captain by his given name—"this will be better for you. You've been in this mess too long as it is, serving your country with distinction. Istanbul will be a welcome change of pace. Trust me. Please understand, I am doing this for your own good. Can you try to see that? I also put you in for Major. You deserve it."

There is a long silence. Through the door, I can feel Captain Kucuk processing. I can feel internal rage seeping through his entire system, demanding release. I can hear his breathing, first heavy and then declining. Processing, processing. I can feel him settling down.

"Am I the only one going back?"

"Actually, no. I am sending two Lieutenants under your command, Kaplan and Demir, to headquarters."

"Why them too?"

"That's not for you to worry about."

"That won't go over well."

"Many things in war don't go over well. Besides, one thing you've never learned is that soldiers are fungible. There will always be more to step right into their shoes. The military in time of war is an assembly line of human parts, each to be sacrificed for the greater good. The greater good, Captain, is what matters more than anything."

"But what about us, Emir?" Again, a first, both on a first-name basis. "Don't we matter anymore?"

"Ahmet, there is no 'we.'"

An excruciatingly long silence.

I move back to my desk, several feet away. Now it is my turn to process. What is going down in there?

As if a strong wind thrusts him from behind, Kucuk blows into my office space. When he gets to my desk, he abruptly stops for a moment, eyes still looking ahead, and finally turns in my direction.

He glares at me menacingly. "You fucking backstabbing witch. I know all about you. You are responsible for this. You will fucking pay, you whore."

Kucuk storms out. I'm not sure what he meant, although I don't think he is on to me. He thinks I am to blame for whatever just happened between the General and him. At least, that is what I hope it is.

I go see the General. "I thought I heard yelling, sir. Is everything okay?"

"Yes, of course. It was time to make a break."

"What do you mean?"

"I had to relieve the Captain of his command. He will not lead the battalion in Gaza as originally planned. I reassigned him to admin work. I dispatched him to Istanbul with some others. He will be leaving in two days. It's for the better."

"I don't understand. Why?"

"I've lost trust in him. He can't see the big picture."

"What about the military plans themselves? Have you reconsidered?"

"No. They won't change. We are redeploying as the Colonel recommended. The British would be suicidal to come to Beersheba. We will bury them."

"I understand, sir."

The General takes a long look at me, which sends a shiver up my spine. "Ajda, you should join me in my quarters for dinner tonight."

"Um—"

"Seven p.m. sharp," he says authoritatively, and then, with a smile, "Please."

I bow my head. "Yes, sir."

Robertson studied Caitlyn. Trepidation wrinkled her brow and exhaustion sagged her body. He did not want to push it. He was not entirely clear what to make of what she'd shared, except his gut was telling him it was chock-full of clues. He needed to ponder and figure this out. He had more refined theories now, each plausible in varying degrees, each taking him down different paths. For now, he would keep his thoughts to himself.

"Caitlyn, are you ready to return to us?"

She nodded gently, her body slumping, air releasing from her chest.

"Take a deep breath, and when I count from five, let your mind relax, and when it does, open your eyes. Five . . . four . . . three . . . two . . . one."

Caitlyn opened her eyes and shook her head like she was trying to dislodge loose hairs. She took in a deep breath and released it. She tilted her head and rocked her body, reconfiguring her mind.

Then, nodding in the Inspector's direction, she smiled faintly. "How'd we do, Inspector?"

"We are close, Professor, we are close."

17

THE ANCESTRY JOURNEY

Over lifetimes you will experience many different types of relationships that will enrich your soul experience and teach you about oneness with God. — Ellenmorris Tiegerman

Caitlyn couldn't sleep that Friday night. Ash had insisted she put everything aside for a couple of hours for dinner, a bath, and sex, and not in that order. But Caitlyn was too agitated to even consider his offer, let alone joke about the present situation. She had already had three cups of flat white and felt so wired that she couldn't sit still. She was bothered to the point of distraction, not only by what she'd unearthed about her past and the investigation, but by how close she was getting to the truth about her parents, particularly her elusive father, "Jack." So far, she hadn't found an element of truth in anything her mother had told her. It was one lie on top of another. Layers of fabrication, of confused, fictionalized bits of information.

"How will you know when you've found him?" Ash probed while making Caitlyn her favorite pesto sauce for the penne pasta she so loved to eat on Saturday nights. He was a fabulous cook, creative and adventurous with spices and ingredients. And best of all, he loved to cook for her. "Did you know Abravanel means 'priest of God' in Hebrew?" he said.

"Ash, I know his name was Yakov or Jacob, or Jack when it's anglicized," she said, attacking her chopped tomato and cucumber salad. "So far, I've been able to piece together birth certificates, passports, news clippings, photographs, letters of transit, and other documented evidence. I found a reference to his burial plot at Mount Hebron Cemetery in Queens, New York. There's a photograph of his headstone: YAKOV 'JACK' LEVY, BELOVED HUSBAND AND FATHER. The rest of the headstone is in Hebrew, which I can't read. Maybe you can translate that for me."

Caitlyn put her fork down and pushed her salad bowl aside. She picked up her glass of pinot grigio and walked back to the living room sofa, which was covered with piles and stacks of sorted documents. Caitlyn sat, folded her legs into lotus position, and let her head fall back on a pillow.

"Tired again, my love?" he said quietly.

"I can't sleep, Ash. I need to finish this mystery. I need to find out about my parents. My mother has lied to me over the years about everything. I need to know once and for all what the truth is and who I really am. Do you understand, Ash? I need you to understand," she pleaded.

Ash smiled at his beloved warrior and worrier. "Yes, Caitlyn, I understand completely. But I'm more concerned about a murder on campus and the real possibility that you're next. That's why I keep asking you about what you've seen—or should I say, whom you've seen—in your nightmares, and in your past lives." Ash shuffled from the kitchen doorway to stand next to Caitlyn on the sofa. He picked up the little striped shirt with the yellow Star of David and ran his finger along the edges of the star.

"You need to do this, Caitlyn. Take this journey by yourself. I can't go with you into the past world, my love." His words comforted her—she felt justified now in her decision not to tell him yet about her sessions with Robertson and the eye-opening revelations about her work in Palestine in World War I. He kissed the top of her head and retreated into the kitchen to clean up the dinner mess he had created.

Caitlyn felt addicted to her memory boxes of newspaper clippings, handwritten journals, documents, and hundreds of letters. She had been starving for information and family connections for years. And now that she had both, she could not get enough of either. Caitlyn sorted everything in the boxes into major piles: second-hand hints, historical references, and quotations about the Abravanels fleeing the flames of the Inquisition in Spain and France; then the paper trails of Jews fleeing to Auschwitz, Italy, Israel, and lastly to the family in America. How rigidly organized her whole life was, a backlash to a nightmarish and chaotic childhood. And now? What about *now*, with all this new information on her past lives combined with the campus murder? That mysterious voice in her head that was vaguely familiar. Who was it? That voice was after her in this life, that much she knew. Caitlyn needed to get back to those boxes. She could not suffer distraction at this point. She had a specific goal— her parents—and she needed to stay focused. She opened a packet of letters and a notebook written by her mother.

Her mother . . .

Now that Caitlyn could understand *how* the family breakdown with her mother occurred, she wanted to know more about *why* it happened. She was also anxious to understand how the American Abravanels had managed to make their way from Italy through Ellis Island and into mainstream society. Why America and not Israel? Caitlyn understood her mother was part of this group, the Abravanels in America. Whatever reasons her mother had given her were fabrications. She wanted desperately to sort out the facts, once and for all. She wanted to know who she was and who her relatives were. She wanted to talk to them and see them and connect.

She began reading her mother's notebook. The baby boomers or post–World War II (1946–64) children saw themselves as a special population and generation. They grew up during a time of relative prosperity and dramatic social, racial, and gender change: the Beatles, the hippies, the Civil Rights Movement, LSD, and significant innovations that enhanced everyone's quality of life. The cultural changes created a rift between parents and children, from religious observance, to drugs, to social mores, to homosexuality, to abortion, and on to politics. The Abravanels were no different from the millions of children raised under the auspices of Dr. Spock. Caitlyn's parents rejected their Orthodox Jewish faith, seeing traditional roles and the separate "seating" of men and women as stifling to women's rights and choices. They rejected everything conservative and experimented with drugs, sex, and the counterculture of the '60s and '70s. They changed their names to Rita and Jack, joined the hippie generation, and headed out to Woodstock in 1969 with thousands of other teenagers and young adults.

In leafing through her materials, Caitlyn found a yellowed article titled "The Israeli Radical Right: History, Culture and Politics," by Ehud Sprinzak. It discussed the rise of religious fundamentalism in the 1980s in Israel, including the work of a terrorist group named Gush Emunim—the Bloc of the Faithful—who used violent means to create Jewish settlements in the West Bank. It mentioned how the oppressive British had been expelled from Palestine because they had betrayed the Jews by violating the 1917 Balfour Declaration, an announcement of British support for the creation of a national Jewish home in Palestine. The Balfour Declaration had resulted from the British military victory in the Battle of Beersheba on October 31, 1917, its third attempt to wrest Gaza away from the Ottoman Empire. *Captain Kucuk was correct. The British did try again—and won!* Was there a connection between her work as a World War I spy in Palestine and this modern radical activity? Even more disconcerting, what about a connection with one or both of her parents? Or was this idle intellectual curiosity?

The notebook confirmed that Rita and Jack were gone for weeks at a time. They'd been attending City College, but once they left for Woodstock, they never returned to school or home. The generation gap was alive and well in these immigrant families—no one understood the lack of commitment to family, school, or jobs. Rita and Jack had given up everything that was socially acceptable and recognizable to their families. How could the children reject the Jewish religion after all their elders had seen and been through in the European concentration camps? How could the two of them just go off like that? How selfish! How crazy could they be? The families were not prepared for any of this. They couldn't fathom the roots of this anti-establishment cultural occurrence. And drugs? And communes in California? *Were they involved in radical Israeli groups, with everything else as a cover?*

According to letters, the families on both sides were at a total loss. At first, frantic with worry and shame, they sent cousins to look for the children, but the children did not want to be found. America was a big country with vast expanses of land and population.

The perceptual divide between these families and Rita and Jack's countercultural family was a deep generational chasm. Any possibility of reconciliation was fractured when Rita found Jesus and became an evangelical Christian. The psychedelic clothing, long hair, and tie-dyed peace signs could all be accepted as passing fads, but not the conversion. That was more permanent. The same for marijuana, cocaine, and LSD, all tolerable—but not the rejection of Judaism, not after Auschwitz. *Another cover? Or extreme cause and effect, from radical politics to a radical social life?*

Caitlyn reached the bottom of the boxes after working through the centuries with the Abravanel family in Europe, Israel, and America. She loved and admired their exploits and challenges. She now understood her past history as if it were a movie script. The letters, messages, notes, and newspaper articles all served to introduce her grandparents, aunts, uncles, and cousins.

The enormity of the family saga amazed Caitlyn, but she struggled to accept the aberration in the family line: her parents. The break with the family and its history was perplexing, shocking, and beyond her understanding. How could her parents reject everyone and everything and go off to a life of counterculture, of drug and alcohol abuse? Despite the family's multiple attempts to rope them back to New York, her parents had dived deeper into the drug-soaked streets of Haight-Ashbury in San Francisco.

Caitlyn had suspected that her mother was mentally ill, and her drug usage aligned with a self-destructive depressive personality. But she'd never considered that there was a generational component to her mother's pattern of behavior.

Growing up in the Woodstock generation added another dimension to her parents' youthful rebellion and acceptance of exploratory drug use. As Caitlyn reread some of the family papers and did her own research into baby boomers, she began to realize that drug use, accepted and even glorified in that generation, had blurred into drug abuse as they aged. It became clear from the family letters that drug treatment programs had failed, and eventually her father succumbed to a drug overdose, leaving her mother with three small children.

The family tried desperately to bring Rita's shattered family back to New York, but she was embedded in a religious cult that eventually became the substitute for the drugs and alcohol that had been the centerpiece of their lives as teenagers and young adults. Now there was Jesus, and there was no turning back. Church was the foundation for Caitlyn's earliest memories.

The substance abuse of the teenage years had turned into opioid abuse in her mother's middle and senior years. The long history of drug and substance abuse increased Rita's health risks, and she died at a relatively young age, leaving Caitlyn to parent two younger siblings. It was here that the letters from the Abravanels stopped.

Caitlyn read the last letter, folded it back into its envelope, and returned it to the pile of documents on the glass living room table. She crossed her legs back into lotus position and put her head back on the black Keaton nailhead sofa. She closed her eyes and thought about her parents' tortured journey into adulthood, parenthood, and finally death.

As a child observing her mother's erratic behavior and often wildly explosive emotions, Caitlyn had thought that her mother was "crazy," but now she questioned that judgment. Yes, her parents had been tortured souls, but not crazy. They were drug addicts caught up in a lost generation of users and abusers, searching for answers to life's mysteries. Had they also been political activists at one time? Not in the grand tradition of the First Amendment, but something darker and brutally violent? Or were they simply struggling to understand this life's meaning and purpose, trying this and that, experimenting and questioning?

Caitlyn had tripped onto past-life regression. How was that not a cult? Where was the underlying scientific evidence? And that was the point: the faith to follow a mission and a dream. She was no different than her parents, searching for answers and choosing a path based on faith.

It all made sense, but what was she going to do with it? She wanted to connect with her long-lost relatives. *That* she was sure of. She wanted to connect with Brian Weiss and explore the role of past-life regression in solving not just health-based issues but other problems. She kept thinking about Ash's key question: If people share lives in soul groups, then could CU's murderer be present in these past lives, too? If that was the case, then Robertson and Ash were onto something, and she should be able to identify the murderer in this life. The "voice" Caitlyn heard in her head—who in this life had that voice? It was familiar. She could sense the connection.

Ash came thumping down the stairs. He called Caitlyn three times, but she was so intensely lost in thought that she didn't answer. So he walked right past her and turned the Jura coffee machine on. *That* sound, she heard!

"So, my buttercup, you heard the call of the coffee machine," he said, laughing at her. Then he asked in a serious tone, "What else calls to you from those boxes?"

Caitlyn shared how she wanted to contact her relatives. She wanted to learn about Judaism, and the concentration camps in Europe, and the history of Palestine. She had searched online and discovered that the Friends of the Israel Defense Forces sponsored a trip every year in the spring. They started in Warsaw, Poland, visited the camps, and then flew to visit the IDF soldiers in Israel.

Caitlyn wanted Ash to join her on the trip. "Ash, you were Jewish, too, in that past life. Would you come with me? Are you curious at all about being Jewish and discovering your roots in that lifetime?"

"Hmm, Caitlyn, I haven't had any of your physical and personal experiences with past-life regression. Remember, I'm getting this all from and through you. I'm a skeptic. You can't expect me to connect to all of this based on what you're telling me about you or me. I need to find my way through it all by myself. Do you understand me here, in all of this?"

Caitlyn leaned forward and grabbed his hands. "Yes, yes, I do. I get it. You need to discover all of this yourself. But would you be open to coming with me?" She was pleading with him. "I don't want to go on this journey alone. I want to share this, whatever it is, wherever it leads, with my dearest friend and lover."

Ash came around the white quartz kitchen counter and enveloped Caitlyn in his arms. "I will go with you anywhere you want to go, but there's a condition," he said emphatically as he held her tightly. "Caitlyn, you must—I repeat, *must*—figure out who that 'voice' is in this life first. You need to identify the murderer on this campus."

18

THE PLOT THICKENS

Understanding the reality of reincarnation allows our fear of dying to diminish, because we know that our consciousness survives physical death.   — Brian and Amy Weiss

"Inspector, it's Caitlyn Morrys, please call me back right away."

Less than a minute later, Robertson obliged. "What's up, Professor?"

"I had a disturbing dream last night. We have to talk. Can you meet me somewhere? Only not here or in my office. Somewhere private."

"Sure, meet me at my hotel, room 420. We'll have total privacy."

"When?"

"As soon you can get here."

Caitlyn had awoken that morning in a sweat to a snoring Ash. The dream had been vivid and its relationship to what she had told Robertson under hypnosis undeniable. She had no intention of sharing any of it with Ash, even after he awoke and insisted on knowing where she was "off to with such a head of steam" as she scurried about, gathering her things. She mumbled something about forgetting she'd booked a student meeting for the early morning, kissed his groggy head haphazardly, and bolted from the house, never allowing Ash an opening for his habitual barrage of queries.

Twenty minutes later, she shuffled into room 420 to an eager-looking Roberston.

"Please, have a seat. Can I get you something to drink? Coffee, tea, water?"

"Water is fine, thank you."

Robertson grabbed a bottled water from the nearby counter and handed it to her. She took a long pull.

"Do I need to put you under?"

"No, I don't think so. I think I have full recall, at least right now. But let's see how I do."

"You have the floor, Professor." Roberston leaned back on the couch and crossed his legs in anticipation of a command performance.

"The dream put me at the night the General asked me to dinner. Evidently, it wasn't the first time I'd eaten with him at his quarters. The place looked quite familiar. I couldn't help but wonder what had happened to me the other times I was there. But I digress. When I got there, he was three sheets to the wind, and before long began asking me about my romantic life and whether I'd ever been betrayed by a lover. I didn't know how to answer him, other than to play along as best I could, hoping to learn whatever I could for my superiors at NILI. So I told him that once a boyfriend cheated on me—a lie—and that it devastated me."

"Did he respond?"

"Sort of."

"What do you mean, 'sort of'?"

"He said people who do that to others are bad people and deserve severe retribution, that loyalty was paramount in all relationships and infidelity the absolute worst sin imaginable between two humans who supposedly care for each other. The comment took me aback. Who was this man, I thought. In all my work with him, he'd been steady and even, sometimes cold and calculating, as you'd expect from a military person of his standing. Now, however, he showed an emotional side, something I'd never seen. He was at once angry and passionate. He seemed human, even vulnerable."

"What did you do at that point?"

"I waited. I was all ears, eager for him to emote some more. But then he stopped and looked away, and crunched his forehead, as if he realized he had said too much."

"Okay. What happened next?"

"He asked me if I was religious, and I said, 'Yes, of course.' And then he asked me if I read the Bible, and I said, 'Of course, sir.' He asked me about my favorite Bible stories, and I think I said something lame about the loaves and fishes—I didn't know how otherwise to answer the question—and he asked whether I was familiar with the story of Sodom and Gomorrah and, flabbergasted, I mumbled, 'Um, somewhat.'"

"Did he pursue that?"

"No, he stared off into space and then said, 'We should eat,' and directed his servants to bring dinner."

"What happened during the dinner?"

"Nothing of note, only small talk about the military. It went by fast. He talked. I listened for the most part, making mental notes for my report and occasionally asking him questions. The next thing I remember is sitting near the fireplace with him after dinner. I said, 'I should be going,' and he said, 'Stay a little while longer and have tea with me.' He had his servants bring him his nightly tea, evidently a well-established routine, but I declined the offer to share. I couldn't get out of there fast enough. I worried what he might do. I tried to recall whether he had violated me in the past, but nothing came up, and all we did after was engage in more military banter, probably for about thirty minutes. And then, it happened." Caitlyn exhaled heavily.

"*It?*"

"He began to choke, as if his lungs had collapsed. He grabbed his throat and his eyes bulged out of their sockets and he rocked violently back and forth in his seat, gasping for air. The tea mug tumbled from his hand and crashed to the floor and his body followed. He struck the ground with such a thud that the room shook and I flung myself back in my seat with a loud gasp. I knew immediately he was dead."

"What did you do?"

"I checked his pulse. He was for sure gone. I grabbed the mug and took a long, slow whiff of the inside. I detected garlic."

"Okay, so the General liked garlic in his tea—unusual, I give you, but not earth-shattering."

"On the contrary. It had the odor of orpiment arsenic, a lethal and water-soluble poison."

"Well, now, that's interesting. What did you do?"

"I knew staying was not a good option. I'd be blamed for certain, or at least suspected, and who knew where that'd lead. I felt totally exposed and at risk. I got out of there immediately, trying to be calm. I had his unsuspecting driver take me to my quarters, which he'd planned to do anyway, so it wasn't unusual. As soon I arrived at my place, I got in touch with my contact, who in what seemed record time retrieved me before military authorities could descend upon me. Then I disappeared."

"Anything else?"

"Yes, one more thing. The person who came to get me, a fellow NILI comrade, the person who helped me get out of Palestine safely to France, was the spitting image of Ash."

19

THE MURDER ANALYSIS

The part of you that continues on after the death of the old body and that then reincarnates as a baby is often called the soul, or the spirit, or the eternal consciousness. — Brian and Amy Weiss

It was late, very late. Robertson had warned Caitlyn not to stay late on campus by herself, but she was determined to settle the issue of Braxton. She resolved to go to the personnel committee conference room to comb through his files. Although the walkway leading across campus to the Admin building was well lit, she was haunted by an eerie feeling.

Worse, the door of the personnel committee office was half open. Caitlyn flipped the switch and realized someone had ransacked the office. Personnel files were strewn over the floor and across the conference table. Her throat tightened. She froze, wondering what to do. Should she call the Inspector, or security, or one of her colleagues—or Ash?

Feeling a rising sense of urgency, Caitlyn decided to try to identify what documents had been removed before anyone else got into the office. Instinct screamed that someone else had searched for the Braxton file. Who? Why? Maybe the *who* would reveal the *why*.

She locked the door and began to search through the scattered documents.

Someone searching for a file in this office would have no real guide. As far as Caitlyn knew, no one had *ever* shuffled through all those file cabinets, not even officers of the personnel committee. There was something sacred about the confidentiality of professors' lives and careers—an unspoken rule.

Files had been tossed aside like trash. Fighting a sense of violation, Caitlyn bit her lip and fought back tears of anger. What a mess! *Carnage* was the word that flashed through her mind. She stepped on and over many files, looking quickly at labels to spot certain names: Braxton, Tierney—and hers.

After shifting most of the mess on the floor and pushing paper aside into heaps, further compounding the confusion, she crossed the office and searched the file cabinets' opened drawers for Braxton's name. His main file folder was open and almost empty. Names and information were gone—files, reports, correspondence missing. But interestingly enough, Braxton's résumé remained, obviously not important to the intruder.

She picked out the remaining pieces of paper, which described a professional timeline of conferences Braxton had attended. As she quickly scanned the conference list, something clicked in her head: San Antonio, Texas, a short course presentation in 2010. She recalled that San Antonio had appeared on someone else's résumé but couldn't remember whose.

She heard a noise below in the quadrangle. Instinct said look. Through the office window she glimpsed a shadow on the walk below, at the corner of the building. Then it disappeared. Caitlyn felt a swell of panic in her throat, a paralyzing tangle, a fear she knew could immobilize. *No! Keep control!*

Grabbing her hair and tucking it into a tight bun, she gritted her teeth and called campus security. By the time security reached the building, she had decided not to mention the shadowed figure and only report a break-in. She answered all their questions as best she could, then called for people to clean up and maintain file security.

Two hours later, after the work was finished and everyone had left, Caitlyn returned to her car. She needed her computer at home.

As she drove, she thought about the San Antonio conference and her attempts at past-life regressions. She saw them in her memory, and suddenly her focus was drawn to Provost Moisescu. Doctor Death had presented a paper at the same conference. The realization shocked her. Instinctively, she depressed the gas pedal to accelerate her return home. She squeezed the steering wheel so tightly that her fingers went numb. Was she imagining all of this? She was tired, frightened, and craved some coffee. She knew that her computer contained all the relevant papers, and she wanted to confirm an impossibility that horrified her.

Where was Robertson? Funny, now she wanted to talk to him. Well, why wasn't he reading her mind now? He was an eccentric man—no, that was not the appropriate adjective.

Trying to reach him on his cell phone, she got his voicemail and hung up. She frantically dialed Ash.

Ash answered. "Who the hell is calling so late? This better be a catastrophe—"

"Ash," she screamed, "I think I found something."

"Where are you, Caitlyn? You sound horrible. What is it?" he asked with his own sense of urgency.

"I think there's a connection between Braxton and Doctor Death—"

"You mean the Texas conference? Caitlyn, Conklin and I got that one right off. I told Inspector Robertson all about it. The jovial Inspector is a brilliant investigator. He said there had to be something going on between Braxton and Doctor Death. He had Conklin and me following every conceivable lead. I hope you've got something else, because although I love you, I'm exhausted," he said, finishing up with a noisy yawn.

Caitlyn was speechless. She felt defeated and tired and drove on autopilot.

"Caitlyn, talk to me," Ash insisted. "Don't go off into one of your reveries. What else do you think? You're the psychologist. We normal souls don't understand underlying motivations, that's *your* area of expertise." He raised his voice, sensing her reluctance. "Focus on what you know to help solve the murder. Any ideas about the murderer . . . or murderers?"

"This wasn't a simple murder," Caitlyn said slowly. "The person who murdered Uzinski was making a statement about sexual violation."

"The murderer's or Uzinski's violation?" Ash asked with palpable curiosity.

"What do you mean?"

"The murderer's violation of Uzinski, or Uzinski's violation of the murderer—which?"

"Ash, that's it! I don't know why I didn't think of that myself. I was coming at the murder from the wrong direction," she said excitedly.

"Caitlyn, my sweet, you're losing me."

"The murder was staged to be sexually explicit, embarrassing to Uzinski. The murderer wanted Uzinski to appear as a victim, that he was no longer in control. The murderer wanted Uzinski leaning over his desk with his pants down to be the final image of Coronado University's charismatic leader. The murderer had been betrayed in some way by Uzinski. They were ... were ..." Caitlyn stopped.

"Lovers? Is that what you're trying to say?" Ash insisted.

"Maybe ... it could be—I don't know ... Right now, let's say there was a failure to communicate."

"What is this, a Paul Newman movie?" Ash laughed. "This sure doesn't sound much like the science of psychology."

"Ash, I'm not sure what kind of a relationship they had, but they were intimately close. This was a crime of passion. I said there was emotional betrayal, so there had to be violated expectations."

"How do you know it wasn't an intellectual or philosophical difference?" he asked sarcastically.

"If this were a crime of ideology, Uzinski would have been murdered methodically. This was up close and personal; that's why the signature is sexual." Caitlyn was elated. The whole disgusting mess finally made sense to her, albeit in a rather murky way.

"A signature," Ash repeated, confused. "Whose signature?"

"The murderer's signature," she announced proudly. "The construction of the murder reflects the murderer's thoughts and feelings like a medieval painting. I don't want to talk about this anymore. Ash, I miss you."

"I miss you too. A painting? Your analogy is that a murderer plays out his feelings like a painter with a canvas?" he said, as if talking to himself.

"Yes, doesn't that make sense? Can you come over now? I'm almost home and I don't want to be alone tonight," Caitlyn said anxiously.

"I'll leave now and be there in fifteen minutes. I don't know, Caitlyn, I keep thinking this murder has a feminine signature. I don't mean to sound sexist, but doesn't this seem to be a crime staged by a woman?"

"When we figure out how Braxton fits into all of this, we'll have the answer to a number of questions. I can't talk anymore, I'm pulling into my driveway."

"Caitlyn, I am duly impressed. I have a renewed, but still distant, respect for psychological analysis. Leave the door open, buttercup!" he said, laughing.

She loved his deep, resonant laugh.

There must be something in those personnel files, some terribly important detail she had missed. Her computer might have the answers.

20

THE STUTTS FOUNDATION

We do not need to carry the fears and the symptoms that we have been shouldering for thousands of years. Discovering and understanding their root causes releases us from these ancient burdens.

— Brian and Amy Weiss

Caitlyn's house was dark. As she approached the door, she noticed the lock was broken and the window cracked. *Another break-in?* She crept around to the driveway-side window to peek in. There was a light in her study. Her computer light was on.

Whoever had been there was obviously gone. She cautiously entered and explored. As she moved from room to room, she didn't detect anything taken or moved, but there was a handwritten note taped to her computer.

"YOU WILL DIE IN THIS LIFETIME TOO," was scrawled carelessly in pencil.

This, Caitlyn knew implicitly, was not a mere threat. It revealed more than anyone could possibly know about her. She was lucky there was a chair right behind her, or she would have collapsed to the floor. She eased into it. *I can't lose it at this point.*

She reached for the telephone and called the Inspector. He didn't pick up, and the recorded message left the number for his beeper. She left a message, hearing the strain in her voice and feeling her throat closing as she pushed to speak. Then she dialed the beeper and frantically entered her number.

The house alarm had never been used in all the years she'd lived off campus. She'd installed it when she first moved here from the big city, but after a while, even she slept with her second floor windows open. The code for the alarm was her birthday. Now it was useless.

Caitlyn was frightened. She felt vulnerable and small. Anyone could get at her. All she could do now was wait for either Robertson or Ash to show up.

She sat back in her chair, closed her eyes, and let her mind wander, which took her to the note. On the back of the note was more scrawled lettering. The writing was odd—foreign, almost like hieroglyphics. She focused on it, turning it in different directions.

How much time is left? Where had that thought come from? Damn it, why did she feel all of this was familiar?

Suddenly, her cell phone rang. She was jolted back to the present. Ash? No, Robertson.

"So, Caitlyn, my dear, are we going to go through this again?"

"Stop saying that," she snapped.

"Okay, listen to me. Now, do you know how little time is left?"

"Yes, Inspector," she said meekly.

"Well, this is real progress," he growled. "At least your past-life memories are in working order. How many years did you train to be a psychologist?"

"Why are you being sarcastic at a time like this? Stop with the riddles and get over here. Let's focus on what's happening over here in my home."

"I'm not being sarcastic. I'm frustrated with you. I need you to put aside everything you learned in this life. What you *think* is real is not, and what you think is *not* real is. Look at the note."

"Oh my God, don't tell me you know about the note? I can't take much more of this. Who are you, really? I think I'm going to lose my mind." Her voice was strained.

"No, you're *finding* your mind. Caitlyn, listen to me. We only have a short time left to stop this, once and for all. I may not reach you in time—that happens repeatedly in each lifetime together. Go to your computer and find out about Braxton. Tell me what you are doing and why. The issue for you in this lifetime is not—I repeat, *not*—what is going to happen, but why. What's the motivation for murder here? You can figure out who is responsible, but what's most critical is the underlying reason this is all happening."

"I need to get into the files to look at Braxton's and Moisescu's résumés. No luck at personnel, but Ash said you know about the Texas conference," she said.

"Yes, and it's good he's on his way to your house. I've been trying to reach him all afternoon."

"Wait, Inspector, how did you know Ash is on his way here?" Caitlyn was always completely surprised by Inspector Roberston.

"He's always on his way to you when things get screwed up. Is it dawning on you yet?" Robertson pressed.

"No, no, and no," Caitlyn said, exasperated.

"Let's do this step by step. We are all connected in this life, Caitlyn. Souls travel together across lifetimes. You must recognize the repeating themes in order to change the death sequence at the end," he said, emphasizing every word.

"What death sequence?" she asked, confused.

"Yours, damn it! Caitlyn, your life is running out." He sounded anxious and exasperated. "If Ash gets to you in the next thirty minutes, we're okay. Otherwise, we're doomed again," he said, his voice controlled but tense.

Caitlyn sat at her computer, searched for and printed out Braxton's and the Provost's résumés. "Okay, I've got them here right now."

"Now, look carefully at the résumés. See anything peculiar?"

"Same times and places. They knew each other several years before Braxton got to CU."

"So-o-o?" he urged her loudly.

"They knew each other. That's why Uzinski is dead. He knew too much about Doctor Death's past." She paused. "Wait a minute." Caitlyn was having trouble breathing.

"Yes, keep talking, hurry up."

"Inspector, I found another connection on their résumés. It's Stutts. They were both involved with the Stutts Foundation. And so was Uzinski. So they all knew one another through the Foundation. Doctor Death brought Braxton to CU. Now I understand why Braxton's personnel files were stolen. Braxton was Doctor Death's protégé. But then, why didn't the Provost support him for tenure? Why? Why? Why can't you just tell me and save a lot of time?" she protested.

"Time, my dear, is the one thing that we do not have to save. That is the whole point. This is your lesson and if you do not resolve it, you will repeat it!"

"You're speaking in riddles, Inspector. Anyway, I always thought it was strange that an undistinguished Midwestern university located in the middle of nowhere would receive millions of dollars in grants. So the three men are connected to each other and to the Foundation." Caitlyn was frantically searching through documents.

"Caitlyn, I already know all about these characters. You're the one who doesn't see and who doesn't believe. You're not going to solve this problem on the internet. What you need to heal this problem is to accept your soul is timeless. Great title for a book, don't you think? *Healing Through Time*? Or should it be *Through Time into Healing*? Anyway, there *is* hope for the evolution of mankind's spiritual awareness."

"Inspector, I am not interested in New Age psychology at this point!"

"Oh yes, you are, my dear. I hear you clicking away. What did you find?"

"The Stutts Foundation came into existence in 1978."

"That's when you were born. Does that suggest anything to you?"

"Why should it? A lot of people were born in 1978. Besides, just because two events occur in the same year doesn't mean they're related in any way ... Berlin," she burst out. "The Foundation started in Berlin and then moved to Buenos Aires in 1985. The Stutts Foundation is one of the largest supporters of higher education in the United States. That's peculiar ... why would an international foundation located in Buenos Aires be interested in higher education in the US?"

"You're getting there, Caitlyn."

"Let's see … mission … committed to internationalizing higher education initiatives … globalizing universities to create a worldwide liberal focus to educate students for corporate conglomerates … applications dealing with political theories that aim at breaking down artificial barriers within business organizations … What does all that mean in terms of money?"

"Look, what can you find about money?" he said, trying to break into her monologue.

"Okay, here we go," she said, ignoring him. "Projects funded … management and labor, efficiency and labor, production and labor, mergers and labor, international markets and labor, employee training and labor … lots of labor issues and themes here … now this is interesting. Starting in the early 1990s, the funding shifted to supporting legal settlements involving unions at universities. Inspector, I don't get the connection to Coronado at all. Most of our funding went to support the Stutts faculty and their activities on campus."

"Yes, and what exactly were their activities? Think about Ash's complaints."

"The Stutts professors supported the President's policies." She paused to pull back her hair. "I don't think there was an original thought from anyone in that entire group. So what are they, some brainless, mindless group of professors?"

"And what was the personnel committee's relationship with this brainless, mindless group?"

"Nothing, because the Stutts professors were brought in by Uzinski. They were not part of the bargaining unit … and … not … part … of the union governance." Caitlyn stopped and grimaced. "Now I'm feeling sick ... nauseous, actually." She slumped back in her chair.

"Finally, Caitlyn, you're getting to the core of this. One small but significant suggestion—look at the number and type of universities that have Stutts professors."

Caitlyn forced herself to concentrate, ...ignoring her queasiness. She began again. "I don't have to, Inspector. I know the answer. I know now why Uzinski came to Coronado. He was part of a worldwide web of higher education administrators who were given high visibility by Stutts grants. This made Uzinski and the others very attractive to small and midsize local universities needing funding for large capital projects."

She sat up and pounded her desk with her fist. "Yes! Small universities like Coronado became incubators to nurture the Foundation's mission to globalize education through woke liberal policies that could filter down to K-through-twelve schools across America. Uzinski's specific task was to come with his cohort of appointed faculty and weaken our governance documents and eventually break the union ... first here at CU and then nationally. He tried to systematically demoralize and dehumanize the tenured faculty and manipulate the process so no one would be tenured. Uzinski thought we were weak. He thought his job would be easy."

"Yes, and then what?" Robertson urged her on.

"Eventually, the University Personnel Committee, the local chapter of the American Association of University Professors, and then the national union would challenge Uzinski's attempts to circumvent the union process and hire faculty on nontenure track lines or with easily renewable contracts. His attempt to break the tenure system would be fought out in the American courts . . . for years. How diabolical," she whispered.

"Fought out?" Robertson wanted her exact explanation. "Sounds a bit melodramatic, doesn't it?"

Caitlyn broke away from her reading to explain, "The union's resources are limited, Inspector. There is little public sympathy for eccentric, elbow-patched, absent-minded professors who only teach three or four courses a semester. We clearly have a public relations problem, as well as an image problem."

"Okay, Professor, continue."

"While the union was tied up in the courts for years, Uzinski would replace our junior faculty with the Stutts professors. They would be here teaching our students their woke philosophies while the union continued to battle in the courts. Uzinski would have won the battle while the war went on for years. The Stutts professors would indoctrinate the future business leaders and teachers of the twenty-first century. The new order of trained leaders would be placed in strategic positions in governments, corporations, and schools around the world. So, what happened here at CU would set a precedent for Stutts administrators and professors at other American universities to challenge unions—no more tenure."

Caitlyn stopped and thought a moment, then resumed. "What a political blow to labor unions if governance documents defining academic freedom and free speech could be weakened in the most powerful country in the world! How Machiavellian! Who would believe such a convoluted worldwide plot?"

"True," Robertson agreed. "They just didn't factor one thing into the equation."

"What is that, Inspector?"

"They didn't count on *you* showing up in this lifetime—like you've done in the past."

"Now it's *your* turn to explain. And enough with the suggestive references to past lives. Who are *they*?"

"First things first, as they say in addiction-recovery programs. We need to resolve this murder case, and you need to explain the motive for the multiple deaths. Go back and review the characters given your new understanding of the Stutts Foundation's role. Remember, the political intrigue became the backdrop for the murders.

"It's time for you to be a psychologist, Caitlyn. I knew it would serve *some* minor function sooner or later. Begin your class lecture, Professor, and let's see if you've figured out the motive for the murders. The whole plot fell apart because of the human factor. Human emotions are always the unanticipated variable, even with the best of political plans and plots."

"What does all this actually mean?" Caitlyn practically hissed the question. "You're certainly opinionated! Get to the point!"

"Now, now, this has nothing to do with opinion. It's all fact, and I was right about you through several lifetimes—you just won't admit it yet! Enough. Let's get down to the work of relationship analysis. Why did the plot fall apart? Think about why the Ottoman Empire was caught off guard by the Allied forces' third move on Gaza in the Battle of Beersheba. What mistake in judgment did the military leaders make and why? And think long and hard about who Colonel Oszcan and Captain Kucuk resemble in this life."

"A tangled personal web imperiling sound military judgment?"

"Keep going."

"Okay. How's this? Uzinski recruited the Provost because they were having an affair. The Provost recruited Braxton several years later because *they* were having an affair. Uzinski didn't know about Braxton's love affair with his Provost, and the Provost didn't know about Braxton's affair with Uzinski. The love triangle became complicated over time.

"I'm curious about two points: the disagreement between Uzinski and the Provost about Braxton's tenure case, and the peculiar way Uzinski was murdered, pants down and stiletto in his back. Uzinski must have suspected something first—that explains the only time he and Doctor Death disagreed on a tenure case. Doctor Death found out about Braxton's affair with Uzinski and they argued. It was at this point that both men discovered the mutual betrayals.

"Braxton, however, had his own plans. Uzinski knew his murderer—he was betrayed by his lover. That's why there was no forced entry. Braxton gave Uzinski a muscle relaxant in a glass of cognac. There was a great deal of scuttlebutt on campus about their taste for very expensive cognac. He stabbed Uzinski in the back and left his murder signature by pulling the President's pants down—physical humiliation for emotional betrayal. Doctor Death was left petrified and silent, given his own intimate involvement. It also explains Braxton's erratic behavior the last couple of weeks. Am I at least correct in my analysis of the underlying motivation for the murders?"

"Excellent, I couldn't add anything to your analysis."

"Inspector, I hear something or someone outside. What should I do?" Caitlyn stopped talking abruptly. "Maybe Ash is here," she whispered hopefully.

"No, it's not Ash. It's either one of my men or your murderer," he said sharply.

"Well, I'm glad you're so calm about all of this," Caitlyn whispered.

"One of us has to be calm. Where are you, exactly?"

"I'm still sitting in my study in the back of the house." Caitlyn kept turning around, looking from window to door.

"Okay, I know exactly where you are. Go downstairs to the basement and into the boiler room. Climb out the back window. You'll have to pile up some boxes to reach the window, but all that gym activity should help you. Lock all doors behind you."

"Wait a minute, how do you know the layout of my house? And that window hasn't been opened for years," Caitlyn hissed frantically into the phone.

"Not now, Caitlyn, we can discuss that later. I opened that window myself yesterday. Just give it a good push—you know, like you push the weights on the machines."

"You've been following me?" she almost yelled out loud.

"So has your murderer. Get the hell out of there, now! Run to the gas station around the corner, one of my men will be waiting for you. As biblical as this may sound, do not stop to look back. Remember Sodom and Gomorrah."

Caitlyn jumped up and ran toward the basement stairs.

Suddenly, gunshots exploded through her house. She froze at the stairs as confusion and noise chased all the quiet from the night. The house was actually shaking. She could hear footsteps running and guns blasting. She was sticky with sweat, her clothes clinging to her. And now the basement had a peculiar odor. Gas, she smelled gas. She raced down the stairs, jumping the last few steps, and shoved open the door to the boiler room. She had to get out of there. The fumes were killing her! She felt sick, head throbbing. She scrambled to pile boxes so she could climb to the window.

She could not make it up. Last thing she remembered was the sound of broken glass, the window shattering, and something or someone jumping down to her.

From a far distance, she heard the call of her name mixed in with other names she seemed to recognize: "Caitlyn … Cheng … Alianar … Ajda … Caitlyn." Her head throbbed. Everything went black. Then she was floating comfortably above her body, and she could see a long tunnel of light ahead. She wanted to approach the light, but a persistent voice got progressively louder, calling her back. She wanted it to go away. She did not want to go back. There was something warm, safe, and secure about the light. Why was she being bothered? Then she thought she heard a voice emanating from the light, telling her she had not finished her lesson.

She was drawn back toward the Inspector's demanding voice.

21

THE MYSTERY NOVEL

Our current bodies are the stage characters, our souls the enduring actors. While onstage during the play, the characters can experience terrible misfortune—even death. But the actors are never harmed.

— Brian and Amy Weiss

The first thing Caitlyn saw was Robertson's bespectacled face. She groaned; the pain was acute. "Oh God, am I dying?" She reached up and felt a pillow ... she was on a bed.

"That's a sorry way to greet your timeless hero," the Inspector joked. "I risked life and limb to rescue you. How are you feeling, Caitlyn?" He smiled at her evident confusion.

"Inspector, you are the last person I wanted to open my eyes and see. What happened?"

"If you hadn't opened your eyes and seen me, my dear, you would be dead—all over again." He laughed like it was a punchline to a joke.

Caitlyn couldn't share his humor. "Okay. Okay. Tell me what happened after I passed out, and then let's decipher all these cryptic references to past lives."

"Simply put, I got to you just as you were overcome by gas fumes. Several of my men and I got you out of the basement and to the hospital."

"I heard shooting. Was I just imagining it? Who was it, anyway? Did you get him?"

"You heard shooting, all right, and we got him—again," Robertson said emphatically. "Braxton is in custody and will soon be charged with murder."

"What about Moisescu?"

"Gone. We think he fled the country."

"Was he involved?"

"Hard to know right now. But he remains a suspect." He handed her a crumpled sheet of paper. "Now, look at the death threat. What does it say?"

Caitlyn tried to focus, but the lines on the paper seemed to move. She felt her eyes crossing and beginning to tear. "It says something about my being killed again."

"Yes, but that's only what you see on the paper. Look at the hieroglyphics carefully. Use your inner sight and see beyond this physical illusion. Focus, Caitlyn. Breathe . . . relax . . . focus . . . good."

"I can't see anything!"

"Yes, you can. Close your eyes and see the note in your mind. What does it say?"

Caitlyn struggled with the words. "I . . . It . . . It says . . . *Noy . . . ani . . . kobi. Noy ani kopi . . . carta pati manu.* It says *. . . I return to heal the unfinished and when I have learned it all I will not.*" Then she felt an overwhelming sense of internal peace that radiated energy from the inside out. There was an eternal truth here. She heard a voice in her head. Was it the Inspector's voice? She opened her eyes quickly and their eyes met.

"No, it's not my voice you hear, Caitlyn. It's the Eternal Teacher. It is time for you to decide. Are you finished returning, and are you ready to become a teacher yourself? Life is a school for learning, and you have been here in many different forms, many times, to learn a lesson over and over again."

"Who *are* you, Inspector? I mean who are you *really*?"

"Do you remember your dreams, Caitlyn?"

She nodded and clenched her eyes shut at those memories.

"Go back to the dreams," he urged. "When you accept the message in your dreams from the Eternal Teacher, you'll know who *you* are. I'm a Guide in this life. I was your father in another life, and of course you were difficult, single-minded." He shook his head. "But that's a story for another—"

Caitlyn held up her hand, raised herself up from the pillow, and tossed her hair back in irritation. "Okay, Inspector, please spare me!"

Robertson waved her objection away. "You and I have been related to one another, in many different ways, in many different lifetimes. You've been a reluctant student and learner, Caitlyn, refusing to move along the spiritual ladder. It's your choice. I agreed to keep an eye on you, so to speak, from life to life. You're an interesting soul, and you have certainly chosen some interesting lessons to learn."

Caitlyn sat up, gathered her hair in both hands, and tried to smooth it down. She saw the Inspector's eyes directed toward her chest, felt air on her skin, and realized her hospital gown was open in the front. She grabbed the gown and pulled it closed over her much-too-much-exposed skin.

But he had paid no real attention, had looked at her bra by habit only. He was thinking of Ashford Connor and of all he still had to tell her.

"Your Professor Connor loves you in this life, but he reads your past while looking at his own future. Notice how he studies the great moments of death in the human race— the Glacier Apex paving the way for the Neolithic age; the Great Death, the bubonic plague epidemic, bringing about industrial times; and the great Civil War ushering in modern times—all times of great death and overwhelmingly important, but subliminal, discovery."

She nodded. "Ash's professional life is about 'harvests of humanity,' as he calls them."

"Yes," he agreed. "You should know. You're always crusading against social evil and on the verge of being murdered or assassinated. It was my soul's choice to try to get you out of your predicaments and help you finally accept who you are so we both can move on."

"Is Ash a teacher too?" she asked.

"He could be," he answered. "Ash can't handle the real truth either. He is your soulmate." He smiled at her expression. "Guess I'll see you around in another lifetime." He patted her cheek, adjusted his glasses, smiled again, and turned to go.

"Inspector, can I ask you a personal question?" she asked in a low, husky voice.

"Yes?"

"Who really was that little girl who died ... on the bubonic plague cart?"

"Little girl?" Robertson repeated softly.

"You're a part of one of my dreams, Inspector. Who was she?"

"You," Robertson said sadly.

"Oh nooo," Caitlyn groaned.

The door flew open with a bang. Ash, out of breath, burst into the room. "Oh my God, Caitlyn, you gave me such a fright." He looked hard at Robertson, then back at the disheveled Caitlyn. "Are you alright, my love? I thought I lost you," he said, kissing her forehead, trying to sit next to her on the bed. "Move over so I can get in." He beamed at Roberston.

Robertson moved even closer to the bed. "You look like an overgrown five-year-old with that ridiculous grin on your face, Professor Connor." He laughed. "Caitlyn, shall we tell him?"

Caitlyn sat up even straighter, hugged the gown to her, and glared at the Inspector. She nodded her agreement.

"Don't get upset, it's not good for you, my buttercup!" Ash said. "Tell me what, dear?" He stroked Caitlyn's long, dark hair while the Inspector watched, amused.

Caitlyn and Robertson stared at each other intently, and suddenly they both started to laugh.

Ash looked back and forth between the two of them. "Hey, what's going on here?" he asked petulantly. "I feel left out."

"Far from it, Professor, you're right in the middle of it," Robertson teased. "You love her, don't you?"

"I've always loved her," Ash said, looking deeply into Caitlyn eyes.

She felt herself falling . . . again.

"You don't know how true that is, Professor Connor. Hopefully you'll learn—finally." Robertson turned to leave the lovers alone.

"Inspector, don't leave, please don't," she said. "You have to tell him about our lives—or about our deaths."

"Why *should* he know? Will he even listen to me?" the Inspector asked.

"What is it between the two of you?" Ash asked. The intensity in Robertson's voice surprised him.

"What's between us, you wonder?" Robertson said. "How about thousands of years of history? How about many lifetimes?" Robertson resumed walking to the door.

"Inspector Robertson, wait," Ash called. "Hey, I've been thinking about your offer to collaborate on writing a murder mystery about tenure."

Robertson paused and held up a hand. "That was supposed to be a secret between us. Caitlyn was not to know about that until we were well along."

Ash laughed and shrugged as Robertson walked out of the hospital room. He was so excited about being alone at last with Caitlyn, he could barely contain himself. He pulled out a file of papers from his old, beat-up leather briefcase and placed it carefully on the hospital bed. He snuggled up closer to Caitlyn and gave her one of his famously charming smiles.

"Well, my buttercup, I've been busy on our new book project. I've got an outline here!"

"You have?" she answered, absentmindedly twirling her hair.

"Yes, yes, yes. We are going to write a murder mystery with a past-life twist. The main character is going to be a professor of psychology at a small Midwestern college. There'll be a campus murder solved by means of past-life regressions." Ash paused and looked at Caitlyn from the corner of his eye. She was sitting with her arms folded over her chest, peering at him over the rims of her Gucci glasses. She didn't say a word and looked directly at him.

But she hadn't killed the idea, so he pushed on. "I think we could contact Dr. Brian Weiss and ask him to write the foreword to the book. We could email him or go see him at his clinic in Miami. In fact, I just happen to have—"

"Ash, you didn't!" Caitlyn nearly screamed. "Tell me you didn't contact him!"

"No, my buttercup, I didn't send the email!"

"Email? What email?" she pressed.

"Why, this one here," he pleaded. "See, I just wrote it. I explained who we are. I told him you're interested in past-life regression and have a book project you want to discuss with him. See? Look, it's perfectly harmless! Here, my love, you read it." He handed her the printed email.

Caitlyn scanned it quickly, then looked at him lovingly. She wanted to laugh, but her sides hurt terribly. She put down the memo and leaned over to kiss him.

Ash sighed with contentment, greatly relieved that Caitlyn hadn't stuffed the email down his throat. "Listen, my love, it's a fabulous idea for a New Age novel. It's timely and edgy. My only suggestion is that the backdrop on campus should be different in the book: George Soros and the liberal left, with its impact on upcoming national political elections. I particularly like the campus violence angle and the free speech ramifications.

"And I want you to know I have an editor interested in the book project. I purchased *Guide to Literary Agents* from Amazon and found agents all over the country who specialize in murder mysteries or New Age manuscripts. I emailed or faxed them our bios, a detailed synopsis of the book, and a table of contents. And guess what?" Ash paused barely long enough to swallow and take a breath. "I've gotten a lot of requests for the first six or seven chapters over the past few weeks. The most notable came from an agent in New York who told me he had closed his literary agency but would be willing to edit the manuscript when it was finished! His exact words were, and I quote, 'The book synopsis is a marvelous journey into places and situations most people have never experienced. The storyline is potentially entertaining, with interesting characters and plots presenting some academic details that, oddly enough, may lead to a well-conceived murder mystery.'

"Listen to me, Caitlyn. You and I, between the two of us, have written nine academic textbooks. Wonderful. Marvelous. Terrific. There has to be more we can do with all this knowledge and writing ability. I'm not saying writing a novel requires the same skills, but I *am* saying we can develop a nascent talent. We have a great story with a very intriguing plot." He paused and took a deep breath, looking at her over the rims of his small rectangular glasses. He didn't want a response and so held up his hand.

His voice deepened and filled with emotion. "And I've been thinking about our future together. This whole incident scared the hell out of me. Now, don't laugh at me, but I'm still young enough to make a career change. I'm thinking about going into business for myself. But what can I do with anthropology and history? Really, what am I good for in the real world of business enterprise and pragmatic entrepreneurship? I couldn't even get a job in a factory! Maybe I could get a job as a high school history teacher if I go back to school and pick up fifteen credits in education," he plowed on without pausing for breath.

"Listen, Caitlyn, I've thought this through. I know this sounds far-fetched, but one of us needs to have a secure position with a livable salary. You and I are dependent serfs at old CU, surviving off overload and summer courses—it's too stressful.

"I've decided this is a great chance for me to venture out into the real world. I want to be a literary agent and writer! I want to see if I can interest this New York agent in a collaborative business opportunity! What do you think, buttercup?"

He was so engrossed in his monologue that he hadn't noticed that Caitlyn had slid lower down into the bed. She had pulled the covers up to her chin and closed her eyes. She was smiling to herself as Ash, satisfied with his argument, snuggled closer to her.

Imagine, Ash at a Brian Weiss seminar! That would be priceless! That would be worth a conversation about his crazy idea of a campus murder mystery solved by means of past-life regression.

Caitlyn laid her head back on the pillow. She had kept a huge secret from Ash for months. How delicious. She was finally going to have the last word in a conversation with Ashford Connor.

Who would believe the past forty years have been merely the next chapter? Who would believe there was such a Past and such a so-called Future for us, with a child on the way?

Her mind insisted on asking, *Is this all true for everyone?*

Suddenly, she felt nauseous again. She couldn't wait to tell him about her secret.

READING RESOURCES

BOOKS

Alexander, Jim. *New Lives, Old Souls: Amazing Evidence from Past Life Regression Cases.* Self-published, 2019.

American Psychiatric Association. *Diagnostic and Statistical Manual of Mental Disorders.* 5th ed. Washington, DC: American Psychiatric Association, 2022.

Andrews, Ted. *How to Uncover Your Past Lives.* Woodbury, MN: Llewellyn, 2011.

Barak, Ehud. *My Country, My Life: Fighting for Israel, Searching for Peace.* New York, NY: St. Martin's Press, 2018.

Chadwick, Gloria. *Discovering Your Past Lives: The Ultimate Guide into and Through Your Past Life Memories.* Amazon Digital Services, 2018.

Charles River Editors. *Menachem Begin: The Life and Legacy of the Irgun Leader Who Became Israel's Prime Minister.* Charles River Editors, 2019.

Dyer, Wayne W. *Change Your Thoughts, Change Your Life: Living the Wisdom of the Tao.* New York, NY: Hay House, 2007.

Elsen, Pieter Jan. *When Souls Awaken: Real-Life Accounts of Past-Life and Life-Between-Lives Regressions.* Self-published, 2019.

Kelley, Mira. *Healing Through Past-Life Regression and Beyond.* New York, NY: Hay House, 2012.

Luzzatto, Moshe Chaim. *The Way of God: Derech Hashem.* Nanuet, NY: Philipp Feldheim, 2009.

McHugh, Greg and Natasha Pokos. *The New Regression Therapy: Healing the Wounds and Trauma of This Life and Past Lives with the Presence and Light of the Divine.* Scotts Valley, CA: Self-published, CreateSpace, 2017.

Murthy, Venu. *Why Me? Could Your Chronic Problems Be Rooted in Your Past Lives?* Self-published, 2018.

Newton, Michael. *Journey of Souls: Case Studies of Life Between Lives.* 5th ed. Woodbury, MN: Llewellyn Worldwide, 1994.

Oren, Michael. *Ally: My Journey Across the American-Israeli Divide.* New York, NY: Random House, 2016.

Ross, Dennis and David Makovsky. *Be Strong and of Good Courage.* New York, NY: PublicAffairs, 2019.

Weiss, Brian. *Many Lives, Many Masters.* New York, NY: Simon & Schuster, 1988.

Weiss, Brian. *Only Love Is Real: A Story of Soulmates Reunited.* New York, NY: Warner Books, 1997.

Weiss, Brian. *Same Soul, Many Bodies*. New York, NY: Free Press, 2005.

Weiss, Brian. *Messages from the Masters: Tapping into the Power of Love*. New York, NY: Grand Central, 2001.

Weiss, Brian. *Through Time into Healing: Discovering the Power of Regression Therapy to Erase Trauma and Transform Mind, Body, and Relationships*. New York, NY: Fireside, 1993.

Weiss, Brian and Amy Weiss. *Miracles Happen: The Transformational Healing Power of Past-Life Memories*. New York, NY: HarperCollins, 2013.

WEBSITES

1st Art Gallery. "Caravaggio: Judith Beheading Holofernes (detail 1) c. 1598." Accessed 2023. https://www.1st-art-gallery.com/Caravaggio/Judith-Beheading-Holofernes-Detail-1-C.-1598.html.

Anti-Defamation League. "Antisemitism: The Longest Hatred." Accessed 2023. https://www.adl.org/anti-semitism.

Carravaggio.org. "Judith Beheading Holofernes, 1599 by Caravaggio." Accessed 2023. https://www.caravaggio.org/judith-beheading-holofernes.jsp.

Chabad.org. "Don Isaac Abravanel—'The Abarbanel.'" Accessed 2023. https://www.chabad.org/article_cdo/aid/111855/jewish/Don-Isaac-Abravanel-The-Abarbanel.htm.

Chabad.org. "Kabbalah Online." Accessed 2023. https://www.chabad.org/kabbalah/default_cdo/jewish/KabbalaOnlineorg.htm.

Holocaust Encyclopedia. "Auschwitz." Accessed 2023. https://encyclopedia.ushmm.org/content/en/article/auschwitz.

Holocaust Encyclopedia. "Displaced Persons." Accessed 2023. https://encyclopedia.ushmm.org/content/en/article/displaced-persons.

Holocaust Encyclopedia. "Exodus 1947." Accessed 2023. https://encyclopedia.ushmm.org/content/en/article/exodus-1947.

In Body and Soul. Reincarnation through the Past Lives Therapy (PLT). Accessed 2023. https://animaweb.cat/en/author/animaweb/.

Inspirational Stories. "Joan of Arc Quotes: I was in my thirteenth year when . . . ." Accessed 2023. https://www.inspirationalstories.com/quotes/joan-of-arc-i-was-in-my-thirteenth-year-when/.

International Holocaust Remembrance Alliance. "What is antisemitism? The working definition of antisemitism." Accessed 2023. https://www.holocaustremembrance.com/working-definition-antisemitism.

Jewish Encyclopedia. "Abravanel, Abarbanel, or Abrabanel." Accessed 2023. http://www.jewishencyclopedia.com/articles/117-abarbanel.

Jewish Virtual Library. "Immigration to Israel: 'Exodus 1947' Illegal Immigration Ship." Accessed 2023. https://www.jewishvirtuallibrary.org/quot-exodus-1947-quot-illegal-immigration-ship.

Jewish Virtual Library. "Rabbi Don Isaac Abravanel (Abarbanel)." Accessed 2023. https://jewishvirtuallibrary.org/rabbi-don-isaac-abravanel-abarbanel.

Jewish Virtual Library. "World War II: Displaced Persons." Accessed 2023. https://www.jewishvirtuallibrary.org/displaced-persons.

Ligner, Isabelle. "France marks 70 years since 'Exodus' ship voyage to Israel." The Times of Israel. July 9, 2017. https://www.timesofisrael.com/france-marks-70-years-since-exodus-ship-voyage-to-israel/.

United States Holocaust Memorial Museum. "Antisemitism and Holocaust Denial." Accessed 2024. https://www.ushmm.org/.

ACKNOWLEDGMENTS

First, my husband, Joseph Farber, had the idea for this novel. We were on vacation on the island of St. John, and I was exhausted from an absolutely insane year teaching full time at a university and running a school for developmentally disabled children, when my dearest friend and life partner suggested I "needed a book project." I laughed because I was too tired to cry. I was, however, intrigued when he handed me an outline for a murder mystery. And so the novel was "born." As it was developed over time, I felt something was missing, and that's when I met Dr. Brian Weiss at a Past Life Regression seminar at the Omni Center in Rhinebeck, New York. The seminar changed my perspective on life and the underlying theme for this novel. The main character, Caitlyn, shares my actual experiences serving on a university personnel committee and teaching at a suburban university.

Second, to my colleagues and dearest friends at the Tiegerman Schools: Dr. Christine Radziewicz, Karen Katzman, Helena La Forgia, Dr. Helene Mermelstein, and my son Dr. Jeremy Tiegerman, thank you for your input, insights, and creative suggestions. My journey with PLR began when

Helene and I attended the Brian Weiss training course and Caitlyn came to life.

Finally, to my four sons, Jeremy, Jonathan, Douglas, and Andrew: Of all the things that I have done in my life, I am the proudest of all of you and your families. You are the "miracles" in my life . . . in this life!

ABOUT THE AUTHOR

Dr. Ellenmorris Tiegerman is the Executive Director of Tiegerman School and a Professor Emeritus at the Derner Institute for Advanced Psychology Studies at Adelphi University. As the founder of Tiegerman School, Dr. Tiegerman is responsible for the creation and the development of the preschool, school age, and integrated programs within the school.

In 1994, Dr. Tiegerman served on Governor Pataki's Transition Team for Education. She was appointed in 1995 by means of an Assembly appointment to the 21st Century Schools Committee. In 1996, Dr. Tiegerman was appointed by means of a gubernatorial recommendation to the New York State Early Intervention Coordinating Council. Most recently, Dr. Tiegerman served as Chairperson of the Parent Involvement Committee.

Dr. Tiegerman has served on the faculty of several universities in the New York Metropolitan area. She has functioned as the Director of the Adelphi University Speech and Hearing Center as well as being the Founding Director of the Adelphi University Preschool Language Stimulation Program.

Dr. Tiegerman holds a PhD from the City University of New York. She also has Masters degrees in: Speech Language Pathology (MS and MPhil), Special Education (MS) and Social Work (MSW). She has extensive experience in the areas of child language development and disorders. She has been involved in many research projects and is the author of textbooks in the areas of language disorders, early intervention, parent language training, and childhood autism. Dr. Tiegerman's area of clinical expertise is autism spectrum disorders.